God/Goddess

Exploring and Celebrating
The Two Sides of Wiccan Deity

By

A.J. Drew/Patricia Telesco

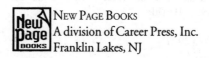

NEW PAGE BOOKS
A division of Career Press, Inc.
Franklin Lakes, NJ

GOD / GODDESS
EDITED AND TYPESET BY KRISTEN PARKES
Cover illustration and design: Jean William Naumann
Illustrations by Kate Paddock
Printed in the U.S.A. by Book-mart Press

To order this title, please call toll-free 1-800-CAREER-1 (NJ and Canada: 201-848-0310) to order using VISA or MasterCard, or for further information on books from Career Press.

The Career Press, Inc., 3 Tice Road, PO Box 687,
Franklin Lakes, NJ 07417
www.careerpress.com
www.newpagebooks.com

Library of Congress Cataloging-in-Publication Data

Drew, A. J.
   God/goddess : exploring and celebrating the two sides of wiccan deity / by AJ Drew & Patricia Telesco.
      p. cm.
   Includes bibliographical references.
   ISBN 1-56414-692-8 (pbk.)
      1. Witchcraft. 2. Gods--Miscellanea. 3. Goddesses--Miscellanea. I. Telesco, Patricia, 1960- II. Title.

BF1571.D73 2004
299'.94--dc22

2003059369

Dedication

For The Great Teacher Ki-lo-knee, who has been much more than my guide in the art of Ti Kwan Leep. Without the assistance of your great wisdom, my half of this book would not have been possible.

Hail Discordia
Hail Eris
Hail Hail
Hail Yes

—A.J. Drew

Dedication

With gratitude and respect, this book is for three Goddesses who have blessed my life: Kwan Yin, who protects my home; Bast, who gently oversees our beloved pets; and Sekhmet, the "fast friend" and helpmate of my heart.

—Patricia Telesco

Contents

Preface:
The Birth of God

—A.J. Drew

Lord of life and Lord of death
Let your name be on my breath

First they told us that God is a man. Then someone reminded us of when God was a woman. Now folk argue which came first as if they were there when the thing was invented. Yes, I did say "the thing." You see, these things that we call gods and goddesses are archetypes, they are constructs of understanding that we invented so that we can better understand the world in which we live and the Creator of that world. Yes, the gods and goddesses exist, but not in the finite form that can be found in this or any other book. Instead, our holy mother and father are found in the very soul of the person who has decided to look for them. We can neither know their true form, nor their true name. Interestingly enough, it is also the soul that demands the search begin.

So then, which did come first? God or Goddess? Well, I don't know about your soul, but mine is always more interested in survival than philosophy. Don't get me wrong, I adore philosophy. But I imagine that when modern man climbed down from that tree or up from the primordial bog, "Where did I come from?" was not at the top of the list of things with which he was concerned.

Instead, I imagine he encountered a strange and sometimes hostile world. Let's face it, compared to the relatively mild creatures of today's world, we do not run very fast, jump very high, or hide very well. Chances are that the very first human thought was, "Oh no, can that eat me?"

The second thought was probably, "Hey, can I eat that?" Voilá, the first concept of divinity was born. But born not out of encountering the wonders of the world, nor born out of the desire to explain the world in which folk lived, but instead out of one desire and one desire alone: the desire to remain alive.

Today, this early form of religion is called *animism*. Aha, a new word. Or maybe a word you think you know, but you probably don't. Now don't be shy, most folk either misunderstand the word or they confuse it with the word shamanism. So let's see what the *American Heritage Dictionary*[1] says about animism.

1. The belief in the existence of individual spirits that inhabit natural objects and phenomena.
2. The belief in the existence of spiritual beings that are separable or separate from bodies.
3. The hypothesis holding that an immaterial force animates the universe.

Interestingly enough, the three definitions given in the dictionary are in the very order that I believe humanity developed the idea of gods and goddesses.

1. Spirits exist in lightning, trees, animals, rocks, and all natural phenomena and objects.
2. Deity begins to emerge. Here we see individual gods and goddesses who exist separately from physical form, but who can take physical form.
3. The idea of the Creator (or Lord and Lady) is the total of all living things. That the love of the Creator (the fifth element) is the drive behind all unions and divisions.

The transition between point one and point two is where the application of gender probably came into play. It is certainly where most of the grief in my career as an author has come into play. You see, today some folk hold an insane belief that men and women are equal. If that were the case, then a man could sue for sexual discrimination after being denied a job as a wet nurse.

Men and women are not equal. They never have been, and they never will be. Equal under the law, yes. Of equal potential value, okay. Equally loved by our Lord and Lady, sure. But equal? No, not equal. For that matter, neither are any two human beings. We each have areas in which we excel, and we each have shortcomings.

As a gender, men have a few advantages over women. We tend to be larger, stronger, and we are equipped with genetic tools that women simply do not have. Did you know that as many as one in 12 men (8.3 percent) have a form of color blindness? Now compare that ratio to one in approximately 250 women (0.4 percent). Aha! Men are almost 21 times more likely to "suffer" from one or more forms of color blindness. Now that doesn't sound very equal to me.

There are many other examples, but let's just use these few. Men are more likely to be able to recognize animals despite their natural camouflage. Yes sir, that condition that men are 21 times more likely to "suffer" from is the very same reason the U.S. military is keenly interested in color-blind folk. While they might not be able to tell the color of one wire from the other, they can spot camouflaged troops and equipment much better than folk who see the full spectrum of color. In fact, they generally have much better night vision. Add this to the fact that women are much better at breast-feeding and you can probably guess who receives the role of hunter in this initial assignment of gender roles. Not because sexism started early, but because it is the way "Mother Nature" built us.[2]

As survival became more and more complex, so must have gender roles. Man became not only the hunter (provider), but the sentinel (protector). As men assumed these roles, so did the gods who men fashioned in their image. As with all stereotypes, there are exceptions. However, the overwhelming amount of anthropological and archeological evidence (along with common sense) tells us that when men went to hunt, they prayed to a male deity.

Now when I use the word hunt, I am not speaking about high-powered rifles with telescopic scopes being used to down animals from the safety of a tree stand at the local hunting club. Instead, we are speaking of a life-and-death struggle between man and beast that today we can barely imagine. Remember what I said about humans not being very good at running or jumping? Well, to even the odds, they had what amounts to pointy sticks and rocks. Even with the pointy sticks and rocks, I am sure it is not much of a stretch to figure that the number of men who returned from the hunt was not always as large as the number of men that left for the hunt.

As our Lord was associated with hunting because it was men that hunted, so was he associated with not only the animals that died during the hunt, but the men who died as well. He became Lord of Life through the sustenance that he provided, and Lord of Death through the ever-present eventuality of that end.

But it was not only in his conflict with other creatures that our Lord became associated with death. You may have noticed that humanity does not always play nice with others. As a result, the role of sentinel grew into the role of warrior. As that gender role grew for men, so too did the role of our Lord.

Then something happened that would change the view of the gods forever: we moved! Prior to this event, we all lived in Africa. We had approximately the same appearance, hunted approximately the same game, and lived under approximately the same weather and climate conditions. It was only natural that our view of the gods was approximately the same. But then we left the garden of our birth and set about the long journey, which would birth the many world religions along the way.

Looking at the number of wars fought over religious differences, it is hard to believe that the many seemingly different views of God all originated in a matter as simple as need. To illustrate the idea further, consider the religion that dominates our culture. Is not the savior of Christianity himself a sacrificial god? Does his story not speak of the god of the hunt being the animal that is hunted who lays down his life for the betterment of his people? Aha!

But what of God as Creator? Well, here we have yet another chicken and egg problem. We don't know when the concept of a Creator God came about because we weren't there to take notes. In fact, no one took notes. We know this because at the advent of history (written records), the idea that Creation involved both men and women was firmly in place in the Creation stories of some cultures, but ignored by others. Where the modern Pagan culture continues to perpetuate the idea that the original Creator was always female, a study of the most introductory level mythology shows many figures similar to the Egyptian god Re, who gave birth to the goddess Tefnut (moisture) and god Shu (air) through an act of masturbation. Tefnut and Shu then went on to conceive the god Seb (earth) and goddess Nut (sky) in the more conventional manner.

I choose to use Egyptian mythology to illustrate this point because if you have any familiarity whatsoever with the modern Pagan movement, you have heard reference to our Lord as Father Sky and our Lady as Mother Earth. And yet here they are, our Lord and Lady in Seb and Nut as Father Earth and Mother Sky. As you can see, things are not as cut-and-dry as they are sometimes presented. You see, the move from Africa that I spoke of earlier took place prior to written history. So, by the time humanity put pen to paper, or chisel to stone, humanity had already achieved such a diverse view of the gods that coming up with one unified view for that time is not next to impossible, it is impossible.

In order to solve this problem, when we speak about our Lord, we do so in the broadest of terms and then see which of those very broad terms fit our very narrow condition. Thus he becomes a role model for men and is himself that which men aspire to become.

Sure, it is sexist to say that men *are* the protectors and providers. But the other day when my young lady friend and I stopped to assist a female motorist with a flat tire, it was not until we were back in the car and on our way that she even thought to mention how sexist it was that she handed me the tire iron and jack. It just seemed like the natural thing to do. But before you feminists attack her for expecting it of me, let me tell you that after we drove away, I took a nap. Why? Well, because I was tired and because I could. You see, she was driving, and that was natural as well. I like the arrangement because I like to nap. She likes the arrangement because she does not like to change tires.

So then, with the knowledge that women give birth but men are necessary for conception to take place, when I envision the Creator I deviate from the Egyptian story of a man masturbating life into existence. I also deviate from the view of the Creator as a female who conceives immaculately. Instead, I choose to view the Creator in the way that we create. I choose to view our Creator as the union of our Lord and Lady in love, the same way I know humanity creates.

But God's story shouldn't stop there unless we choose to view him as a deadbeat dad or nothing more than a sperm donor. If that is the case, then what is the point? After all, one of the most important functions served by God is that he is a role model for men, young and old. As such, he is something to aspire to in all aspects of our life. He is child (master), adult (father), and senior (sage) just as we are child, adult, and senior.

You will note that in the preceding paragraph I said that God's story *shouldn't* stop at Creation. Unfortunately, that is exactly where it did stop. For reasons yet unknown, something revolutionary happened around the globe at approximately the same time. This was an event so large that some of today's more speculative authors have attributed it to the intervention of space aliens. Truth be known, the event was of such a scale that I have difficulty believing it was not the product of divine intervention.

I am speaking of the Paleolithic revolution. Current thinking is that humanity was born between 169,000 and 148,000 B.C.E., but it wasn't until about 78,000 B.C.E. that we successfully left the garden of our birth

(Africa). From that time until the Paleolithic revolution from about 6,500 to 7,000 B.C.E.[3], we migrated to the Four Corners of the world. Then, for reasons not yet fully understood, our migration stopped and the construction of large-scale communities, cities, and monuments began. Hunting and gathering did continue to some extent, but it was largely replaced by animal husbandry and agriculture. We changed from a people who lived off of nature to a people who negotiated with nature. We changed from a people who could just move to avoid conflict to a people that had something to defend.

With the change in the roles played by men came the change of the roles seen as played by the gods. With the building of cities came the need to protect those cities. But now the stakes were higher. Now there was something to loose and now there was something other than the wilds of the forest to protect it from. The Paleolithic revolution brought the invention of modern warfare. Because it fell to men to make war, it fell to the male half of divinity to become god of war. Yes, there were exceptions. There were a significant number of warrior goddesses, but for the most part it was men who stepped up to meet the new need.

Before long, the male half of the Divine, who was once predominantly seen as the protector and provider, was described as scornful and sometimes bloodthirsty, not because those were his predominant attributes, not because someone had seen God and decided to describe his nature, but because humans desperately needed to feel good about the things we found necessary to do for survival. When it was necessary for men to kill men in order to protect a city, God became the killer of men.

But survival did not always mean defending one's own city. When we look at the records kept by the ancient Pagan cultures, we see a deep understanding of the relationship between war and survival. In ancient Rome, a holiday named the Robigalia was celebrated on the 25th day of Aprilis.[4] This holiday honored a deity of rust. At this festival, folk prayed and conducted rituals in the hope that their devotion would bring about the rusting of weapons rather than the rusting of crops. Clearly, the ancient Roman Pagans understood that war was not always something that was conducted as a matter of defense, but as a matter of survival as well.

Although it may sound distasteful, the law of nature is that the fittest survive. Should one nation experience blight, it is in fact natural for that nation to attack another nation just as much as it is natural for any starving creature to steal food from another. While the Roman celebration of Robigalia does demonstrate that the ancients were not all that fond of war, it also demonstrates that they knew it was necessary pending certain conditions, and they took clear religious steps to ensure that it did not become necessary. So, then, the gods of war were born .

* Ah Cun Can (Mayan)
* Ah Chuy Kak (Mayan)
* Ahulane (Mayan)
* Ara (Armenian)
* Ares (Greek)
* Beg-tse (Tibetan)
* Belatucadros (Welsh)
* Burijas (Early Iranian)
* Bugid Y Aiba (Haitian)
* Buluc Chabtan (Mayan)
* Camulus (Celtic)
* Cariocienus (Spanish)
* Caswallawn (British Isles/Celtic)
* Chemosh (Moabian)
* Ek Chuah (Mayan)
* Futsu-Nushi-no-Kami (Japanese)
* Guan-di (Taoist)
* Gun (African)
* Huitzilopochtli (Aztec)
* Ictinike (Sioux)
* Indra (Hindu)
* Kartikeya (Hindu)
* Ku (Hawaiian)
* Laran (Etruscan)
* Mars (Roman)
* Maru (Maori)
* Mentu (Egyptian)
* Oro (Tahitian)
* Reshep (Syrian)
* Rugiviet (Slavonic)
* Samulayo (Fijian)
* Segomo (Gallic/Celtic)
* Septu (Egyptian)
* Set (Egyptian)
* Shamash (Babylonian)
* Si (Mochica)
* Svantetit (Slavonic)
* Triglawus (Slavonic)
* Tu Matauenga (Polynesian)
* Tyre (German)
* Wepwawet (Early Egyptian)
* Wurukatte (Early Hattic)
* Zababa (Akkadian)
* Zi-yu (Chinese)

Of course, there are thousands upon thousands of others, some which you will find easily in your further studies and some who have never been documented because the culture in which they were sculpted has come and gone without much record keeping.

It is here, in the wars of men, that we see the loss of our Lord just as plainly as we have seen the loss of our Lady. But the loss is not in the birth of monotheism, as the Pagan community seems to think. Nor is it in some undocumented need felt by men to make war, as some feminists seem to think. But it is in the needs of all and the willingness of men to accommodate that need because they are better suited for the task.

As cities and territories became larger, that which could be lost at war became more and more. As populations became larger, so, too, did the amount of food necessary to feed those people. As a result, a nation's ability to make war became more and more important. So, then, did the importance of the gods of war increase.

In an effort to prove the existence of a global matriarchy, some folk have pointed out the existence of Venus figures, which have been dated 35,000 to 10,000 B.C.E. But what they overlook is the dichotomy of a diverse pantheon. Using just as much speculation as is necessary to *prove* that a prehistoric find is a Goddess image, one can easily point to cave paintings of a much earlier date and *prove* the earlier existence of horned God images. Yes, if there is one God and that God is female, then it is likely that a matriarchy would exist. However, with a diverse pantheon of both male and female deities, a matriarchy just does not occur on a regular basis.

With an honest look at history, prehistoric finds, and a bit of common sense, we see that the modern Pagan party line that Christianity created the current patriarchy is centered more in fantasy than in fact. Neither the existence of goddess statuary nor the worship of any one or any collection of goddesses defines a matriarchy. Okay, so I just blasphemed the entire modern movement. What of it?

If we believe the fiction, then we are hard-pressed to understand why it is that a patriarchy exists in India where most folk follow the Hindu pantheon of both gods and goddesses. We would also be hard-pressed to understand how it was that in ancient Rome, men were in charge. So, too, were they in charge in ancient Greece and Egypt; and virtually every culture found in history was structured as a patriarchy. Even when nations had female leaders, men were in charge. Again, there are clear exceptions, but for the most part, the current patriarchy exists not because when God is a man, men are God, as so many seem to want to believe, but because when God is the most important force in a culture, then men are the most important gender in that culture. In short, Christianity did not invent the patriarchy. It was alive and well long before the birth of Christ and even before the invention of Judaism.

Although many would have men feel shame for its creation, men did not create the patriarchy. Our community determined a need (war) and, because men were best suited to the task, the overwhelming number of folk who met that need were men. As our community decided war was more and more important, the gods of war became more and more important. Not because men demanded so, but because society (both men and women) demanded so. Of course, one could argue the point, but if a

U.S. citizen were to do so, I would have to point out that during the Civil War (the one that is responsible for the death of more Americans than any other), many of the women could be found watching and cheering on the men from the hillsides. If that isn't enough, let me tell the story of Rosie the Riveter and the able-bodied men who were frowned upon during World War II for not volunteering for military service. Rosie the Riveter was the icon of a woman who took to the workplace to fill traditionally male occupied labor positions in order to help the war effort. Every night she danced for a dime at the USO, but never danced with a man who was not in uniform. However, if a man dons a military uniform and spent the night at a USO function, he was almost guaranteed companionship with Rosie or one of the many women living up to her legend. So then, what was that the feminists were saying about men being wholly responsible for war?

As a result of the war-like attributes of our Lord, many have claimed that we have lost touch with Goddess. To address that issue in this book, the Goddess half is being addressed by my friend Patricia. To address that issue in the modern Pagan movement, we have scores of books and authors.

As a result of that same shift toward the importance of war, many have overlooked that we have lost touch with God. To address that issue in this book, the God half is being addressed by me. But to address that in the larger Pagan community, we have very few books or authors. I doubt this is the result of either author or publisher. I have seen some very fine books on the subject come and go from the shelves of my bookstore due to lack of interest. I am willing to bet that that doesn't happen to this book, because although we desperately need both Lord and Lady to be complete, I have a feeling it will be the interest in the Goddess half of this book that will keep it on the shelf.

You see, while some of the world religions eventually did a very thorough job of taking the dominance of Pagan gods of war and turning them into the monotheistic gods seen and feared today, it has been those interested in rediscovering the ancient Pagan ways that have fallen far short of the mark in rediscovering the ancient pantheons. Where Goddess is gradually returning, many folk have ignored efforts to restore our God into our culture. If you doubt this, listen carefully after sneezing in a room full of Pagans and see how many folk say, "Goddess bless you." And yet, there I was changing that tire with neither the female motorist nor my young lady questioning why it was that I was the one doing so.

Could it be that the deeply felt connection to divinity that many Pagans profess is little more than rebellion against the God of the monotheists? I rather think so. Could it be that we do not need to allow those monotheists to continue to control that deeply felt connection to divinity? I rather think so. In fact, that is the very point of my half of this book.

Notes

1. Definitions from the *American Heritage Dictionary of the English Language, Fourth Edition.* Copyright ©2000 by Houghton Mifflin Company.

2. *That Mother Nature bit just cracks me up.*

3. *Some cite this period as early as 10,000 B.C.E., but such cites are in the minority.*

4. *Please see* A WiccanBible *for information on the Roman calendar and its dates.*

Preface:

Gimme That Old Time Religion

—Patricia Telesco

Queen and huntress, chaste and fair,
Now the sun is laid to sleep,
Seated in thy silver chair,
State in wonted manner keep:
Hesperus entreats thy light,
Goddess excellently bright.

—Ben Johnson

And the Goddess?
She stands
between the worlds.
She is ivory,
her breast bare, her bare arms
braceleted with gold snakes.

—Denise Levertov

The female figurines are the earliest examples of the 'graven
image' that we possess, and were ... the first objects of worship
of the species Homosapiens....
—Joseph Campbell, *Primitive Mythology*

Back at the dawn of human awareness, people naturally looked at
the world with awe. The understanding of wind and rain, dark and light,

17

predators and prey, and cause and effect was lost on this innocent and inexperienced mind. To early humankind, their environment was wholly new and filled with dangers or experiences they simply didn't understand. Thus animism developed—the belief that each thing (a tree, the lightning, a star) housed a spirit. And, of course, the best way to manage in a harsh environment was to appease those spirits!

It wasn't long, however, before humans became a little more complex. With every small step forward in caves or communities, the face of the Divine also became more refined. In areas where hunting (typically a man's job) was important, people often worshipped a male hunting god. Conversely, in areas where there was a lot of edible, gatherable vegetation, people often worshipped a female agrarian goddess.

While these two examples are obviously oversimplifications, it gives you an idea of how humankind created both God and Goddess in our image—the image of our times, our surroundings, our experiences, our awareness. Try for a moment to imagine the whole of the universe based on what we know from science. No matter how intelligent we may be, that's still pretty hard to conceptualize. Similarly, the ancient human mind, while growing rapidly in knowledge, could not begin to try and understand something timeless, infinitely vast, and all-powerful. Psychologically speaking, it was simply too big! So, we reached out and held tight to personified fragments, those that were needed to feel more in control of our fate, or have some sense that perhaps "something" out there could help us survive just one more day.

I'd say that in the scheme of things, we are not that different than our ancestors when it comes to trying to define those things that, by their very nature, fall into the realm of faith. Thus, the goddesses shared throughout the ages and these pages represent but a small fragment of divine potentials, personalities, and attributes. No one book (or even volumes of books) could begin to cover this topic completely. Please keep this in mind as you read, and be aware that if you find a goddess that resonates with your spirit, you may have a lot more research ahead of you before you get to know her fully.

That caveat aside, let's take a look at what written history reveals of this ancient Lady. Statues dating between 35,000 and 10,000 B.C.E. have been located that depict a pregnant woman, which many people hypothesize represents a fertility goddess. This image is called the "Venus figure" and exhibits exaggerated sexual parts. There are, however, some disagreements between historians and archaeologists as to whether statues such as this one are really goddesses or simply artistic renderings of the feminine form.

To help answer this conundrum (at least tentatively), we look to later statuary assigned specific feminine Divine names. To find these items in the same region as previously unnamed statuary sets a precedent to which we can ascribe a theory. In other words, we can use the later labeled pieces as a strong indicator that the earlier art was, indeed, a goddess. This is no different than when we utilize written history as a starting point, knowing that it's very likely there was an oral history on which the written account was based.

I cannot help but conclude that early people sometimes characterized Spirit as a woman because women gave birth, and it wasn't a huge leap to guess that a Sky-Woman could birth all of humanity. However, it's worthy to note that the Goddess was rarely alone. In effect, Deity was genderless, but characterized as both male and female, with both often being worshipped together.

Throughout the Goddess' history, as you'll soon discover, she proves herself to be a very flexible lady, with thousands of names and faces. We see her taking on the roles of creator, maiden, mother, crone, destroyer, warrior, huntress, hearth keeper, wife, lover, guardian of nature, queen of the skies, consort, artist, healer, magician, and herbalist, just to name a few! It's also interesting to note that her abilities and roles grew alongside the growth of the cultures in which she was worshipped.

Let's move forward to more specific illustrations of goddess worship in various civilizations. We'll begin in southern France with a bas-relief called the *Venus of Laussel*. From what we can tell, this rock shelter was a hunting shrine dating to about 19,000 B.C.E. The woman shown is painted red (perhaps symbolizing blood) and holds a bison horn in hand, probably representing a successful hunt. This would make for excellent sympathetic magick for hunters because the image already shows a victory! This type of imagery wasn't limited to just this region, but shows up in the Pyrenees as a naked goddess who oversaw the hunt, wild animals, and the hearth.

Other female depictions show up throughout various stages of the Neolithic era (from 9,000 B.C.E. until 3,500 B.C.E.). Some feature decorations that imply worship. One striking image, in particular, from Africa shows a black, horned woman that later became Isis. Nonetheless, this ancestor of Isis was bisexual and, therefore, self-fertilizing!

Speaking of Isis, predynastic Egypt had its own Goddess around 3110 B.C.E. This woman was known by the simple designation of "great one" (*Ta-Urt*). In art she is depicted as a pregnant hippopotamus standing erect on its hind legs. This connection with animals isn't unusual. If we look at the Tigris River region around 4000 B.C.E. we find similar goddesses associated with snakes, oxen, pigs, goats, bulls, and cows. In other words, things that people valued and with which they were familiar often became sacred symbols for the Goddess.

Humans were not simply associating natural things with the Great Lady. In Sumer (4000 B.C.E.), for example, the princess or queen of any city was thought to have a direct link to the Goddess. She became a living symbol! What greater honor could be bestowed upon someone in authority? Later writings give us a little more insight with prayers directed to Iananna around 2300 B.C.E., one of which from a cylinder scroll begins:

Queen of all the me, Radiant Light,

Life-giving Woman, beloved of An (and) Urash,

Hierodule of An, much bejeweled,

Who loves the life-giving tiara, fit for en-ship,

Who grasps in (her) hand, the seven me,

My Queen, you who are the Guardian of All the Great me,

You have lifted the me, have tied the me to Your hands,

Have gathered the me, pressed the me to Your breast.

The Hebrew religion increased in power around 1800 to 1500 B.C.E. This, combined with the Zoroastrian reform (583–660 C.E.) and the first sparks of Christianity, marked the beginning of the end of the Goddess's popularity throughout that part of the world. When combined with the inception of Christianity, the wholly male God ruled with an iron fist. All Pagan gods and goddesses were decried as evil in an effort to suppress all forms of such worship. The Goddess, however, was not about to be wholly undone, no matter what this new Deity's designs were. There was a whole world out there where the Goddess still danced— where she was remembered and celebrated among her followers in many different ways.

In Alaska, for example, the Eskimo people were now developing some type of established culture (during the old whaling period of 1800 B.C.E.). And, as is often the case, rudimentary religion developed alongside that culture. While the Inuit had very little time for a rigidly structured religion, the harsh environment inspired both awe and the hope that spirits in any form would be kind! In particular, the myth of the goddess Sedna became important, especially for fishing villages, which represented a mainstay for many communities.

The story goes that Sedna took a boat trip with her lover and father. It seems the lover was none too happy about this, and became both violent and jealous. He tried to attack Sedna with everything he could grab. Sedna was not a frightened child, so she boldly jumped into the freezing cold waters only to see both men dumbfounded by her actions.

Her father reacted even worse than the lover and took an ax to Sedna, whose fingers became seals and other sea creatures. She, realizing her place was now in the waters, went to live (and sulk) at the ocean's bottom. To this day, Sedna is regarded as the creatrix of all sea animals, and is a patroness for fishers.

Around the same time in Egypt, Bast (the cat-faced goddess) burst on the scene with great jubilation. This playful, agile, musical, and kindly goddess became the protectress of the Libyan Pharaohs. In fact, they went on to make Bubastis their capital, enriched her temple, and created a new shrine for her at Thebes.

Another region in which Goddess worship seemed to flourish amazingly well was ancient Crete. The word from which Crete derives, *crateia*, literally means "strong goddess." In the famous labyrinth she's called the "Lady of the Labyrinth" *(Laburinthos Potnia)*, or more simply "my Lady" among commoners and kings alike. Art throughout this region depicts the Goddess with animals including birds and snakes; with pillars and a tree; with poppies and lilies; with the sword and the labrys. This tells us much about her attributes including that this unnamed Power is a huntress; a warrior; the Lady of Dance (for ritual); the ruler of the earth, sky, and seas; a household guardian; and much more!

Goddess figurines found in this region dating between 1600 and 1000 B.C.E. (the late Minoan era) are made with clay and come complete with ritual equipment, houses with intact culinary tools, and an ancient pottery kiln. Of them, the most widely recognized is the Snake Goddess; an image of one of her priestesses was found at the Palace of Knossos. This servant of the Goddess wore the garb associated with the Earth Mother. She carries snakes (an emblem of both death and rebirth), and bears a crouching lion cub on her head (a symbol of leadership). Her crown bears poppy buds, a plant sacred to the Goddess (and probably used for communing and divination by her priestesses).

This reverence toward a Goddess figure seemed to be appearing everywhere in the Mediterranean at this time. We see the Great Goddess of the Aegeans, for example, dressed like a woman of Crete. She was fertile, skilled in war, and very protective of her own. Some feel it is from this persona that the image of Athene may have arisen, and she would be but one of many beautiful Goddess figures the Greeks left for all of history to enjoy and ponder. In fact, it's worthy to note (albeit a bit out of order in our timeline) that just 500 years later, historical art revealed a plethora of images of Athena. In some, such as the Parthenon frieze, she's shown alone in her glory. In others, such as the Acropolis relief, she's celebrated as the Patronness of Athens. In others we find her as a goddess of war (Temple of Zeus, east metope) or holding her owl of wisdom as is seen in so many carvings and brass reliefs.

Around 1000 B.C.E. writings regarding creation first appeared in Assyro-Babylonian mythology, having been likely committed to memory before that. These stories tell of the goddess Tiamat, the feminine personification of the sea who gave birth to the world. Tiamat's energy is chaotic, forcing more orderly beings to sort things out!

Then we come to the Romans. By this time, the ancient civilizations were very familiar with the Goddess in many forms. Romans simply borrowed what they liked of the Greek pantheon with suitable adaptations. So we find Juno, the principle of celestial light and goddess of childbirth; Vesta, a goddess of hearth and home as well as the temple fires; Minerva, who protects commerce and schools; and Flora, the goddess of spring (among many others).

As the Romans continued expanding their empire, they would come in contact with the Celtic people, some of whom shared their myths with the travelers and merchants they encountered. And while much of Celtic mythology wasn't recorded properly until the Middle Ages, historical evidence suggests that these beliefs date from pre-Christian times. Included in these beliefs is the now familiar threefold Goddess that many Wiccans follow, and Epona, a horse and water deity (which may have been equated with fertility).

Thousands of miles away, and farther forward in history, the Goddess was still going strong. During the time of the Buddha (approximately 500 B.C.E.) the worship of Shakti was commonplace. Shakti represents the ultimate feminine power, and the animate aspect of God. Shakti empowers God and offers fertility. She's also triune, with her other aspects being Lakshmi who nurtures, and Parvat or Kali as both consort and destroyer.

Her worship isn't the least surprising to students of history, considering that as much as 6,000 years previous to this the regional sacred stories of the Devi (goddesses) were already circulating in oral tradition.

We see similar reverence in Japan. At the advent of Shintoism in 660 B.C.E. the goddess Amaterasu is credited with starting the royal line. In addition, two of the most important sacred texts of Shintoism (Kojiki [Chronicles of Ancient Events] and the Nihongi [Chronicles of Japan]) speak of Creation, which begins with the kami (the gods). Two of these primeval kami were Izanagi (male-who-invites) and Izanami (female-who-invites). After giving birth to the land of Japan, they produced many other kami together.

Thus far we can see that there is plenty of documentation regarding Goddess worship around the globe prior to the Christian era. But it doesn't help us to know what happened to her afterward, does it? Did she simply bow politely and fade away? Absolutely NOT! In *On the Nature of Things*, the Epicurean poet Lucretius describes the cult of Cybele as thriving well into the Christian era. This began somewhere around 200 B.C.E. and continued with strength, thanks in part to Claudius's reign (41–54 C.E.). Prior to his reign, common citizens could not partake in her worship, but after it, worship of her and her lover Attis took its place in the state cult.

We also know that the Teutonic people certainly continued with their customs, particularly the veneration of Frigg (or Frija). The name Frigg means "beloved spouse," most likely alluding to this goddess's marriage to Woden (Odin). Among Scandinavians in particular, Frigg is depicted as a wise, insightful mate who often gave council to her husband. She also had the gift of foreknowledge.

If that didn't frustrate the emerging Christian clergy enough, there are documented accounts of people in Ephesus worshipping a Divine Mother well into the mid-400s C.E. I believe that it's possible for this to be the same female figure worshiped as the consort to YHWH (often bemoaned by clergy along with Sun worshippers). In this region she was called the Mother of Animals, and she was depicted with numerous breasts with which to feed all of Creation.

The importance of the Divine Mother became very obvious in 432 C.E. The bishops attending the Council at Ephesus were met by throngs demanding that her worship be allowed to continue. Thus the prime candidate for an alternative (adaptive) image, Mary, was found to calm the masses. The bishops were so desperate to assuage the masses that they decreed that Mary be called the Mother of God (*Theotokos*), but NOT Mother Goddess. They also stripped away the sexuality, and neatly gave her a wholly secondary role to the Divine. Pretty sneaky, smart, and pretty effective!

Among the Slavonic people, documentation coming forward in the sixth century c.e. indicated a strong reverence toward nature, the spirit of which they called Mati-Syra-Zemlya (Moist Mother Earth by the Russians). Every year in August the peasants would go to fields with hemp oil and bless the land while calling upon this being. The invocation went something like this:

(to the East) Moist Mother Earth, subdue every evil and unclean being so that he may not cast a spell on us or do us any harm.

(to the West) Moist Mother Earth, engulf the unclean power in your boiling pits, in your burning fires.

(to the South) Moist Mother Earth, calm the winds and all bad weather. Calm the moving sands and bad weather.

(to the North) Moist Mother Earth, calm the winds and clouds, subdue the snow and the cold.

In fact, so great were these people's esteem of the Earth Goddess that it was she who witnessed oaths and many other binding agreements. It would take quite awhile before Her power would be watered down when mingled into various Christianized stories, or the poetry of the region. Even then, Moist Mother Earth's importance shines throughout Slavonic mythology.

Turning our attention toward Finland proves rather revealing. We're now talking about the Middle Ages when the Norwegian kings forbade travel to Finland because of their magickal practices, which were mostly shamanic. As late as the 16th century we know the Swedish authorities were confiscating Laplander's drums, which were used for astral travel and communing with spirits. So it's really not surprising to discover the goddess Luonnotar (Daughter of Nature) giving birth to the celestial egg of Creation in the *Kalevala*. This epic tale also recounts other goddesses, including Mother of Metsola (the forest) and Mother of Mannu (the earth). The shamans sought out these beings and other spirits for insight and aid.

Another very interesting group that honors both aspects of the Divine are the Shakers. This unique Christian organization fled persecution in England, and arrived in America in the 18th century. They believed that

Ann Lee, the founder of the Shakers, was the prophesized second coming of Christ, that God had both male and female aspects, and that any act can be an act of worship. They were among the first individuals in the United States to practice and preach the equality of men and women, and to racially integrate their congregations with not only African-Americans, but also Native Americans.

So it seems we have an odd dichotomy. Some areas have forgotten the Goddess altogether or transformed her into a secondary story, with little (if any) divine power. Quite honestly, in such areas it didn't matter if it was an unnamed Goddess, God, or Spirit—if it threatened the security of the church, it was demonized. Now, in defense of the church, this certainly wasn't the first time such tactics were used. The Romans weren't much kinder to folks of other faiths either! The tradition of using the fears of mostly uneducated populous to control and inspire conversions is a very old (and effective) human strategy! So where this demonization occurred, the Goddess's image remained that of the dutiful mother of God. While such a designation represents no "small" task, it's certainly not the glory with which ancient civilizations held her in regard.

Thankfully, there's good news. Other peoples held tightly to the Goddess and maintained their traditions either unaware or unconcerned about the new God on the scene. She continues to be mentioned in the writings of the Far East, in documents regarding Native American beliefs, and in various tribal cultures. And, we've thus far overlooked the New Age, which has proven to be a huge shot in the arm for Goddess awareness.

It would be remiss in a book of this nature not to discuss the importance of what's been happening since right around 1970 (but with roots that reach back to the woman's suffrage movement). When women in the United States (and elsewhere) began to be thrust into unanticipated roles rather than that of the dutiful wife, daughter, or matron, something else happened. They wanted a role model—a source of inspiration. Guess what? The Goddess was ready, willing, and waiting to fill that need. The "New Age" (which is not new at all) effectively liberated her awareness in the minds and hearts of thousands of people. To verify this truth, just go to any bookstore and look at the sheer volume of books dedicated to Goddess worship, or look at the posters, paintings, and statuary that have again become commonplace.

Now, I'm very grateful for that shift in awareness, but it has not been without some cost, some ups and some downs. For awhile, the feminist overtones in the New Age movement turned the Goddess into a Power and image that seemed fairly restricted to women. Wicca, Neo-Paganism, and other related emerging faiths were considered "women's traditions" by the public. Even today, if you ask 10 random people on the street if men can be witches, you'll get some really interesting answers! Thankfully, that stereotype is being erased by dedicated, Goddess-worshipping men!

In addition, the flexibility and vision-driven nature of the Goddess movement has created a religion without specific, black-and-white constructs. There is no Goddess "Bible," no commandments from Zion to show people and say, "This is the Goddess—this is what she means." So, Goddess worshippers find themselves many times (even now) being thought of as part of a cult, or some fad that, if ignored, will simply fade away. Be that as it may, the Goddess is being proclaimed and celebrated in all sectors of modern society, and she shows no sign of retreating to her previous state of obscurity.

The Goddess movement of today is proving to be a popular attempt at offering new answers to age-old questions. This movement has somewhat blatantly, and with a bold face, tackled issues of sexuality and gender in an adult way to bring people, specifically women and Deity, back into equality and symmetry. And as we look around at Her evergrowing band of followers, the Goddess has found favor in every sector of society—among academics and philosophers, computer technicians and clerical workers! In truth, she seems as flexible and multi-tasking as she was in early history!

The Goddess has indeed emerged from the shadows. With her she brings a renewed awareness of the earth as sacred and our bodies as sacred. She reminds us that there is a natural order to the world, which we have a responsibility to honor and protect. And she gently nudges our spirits anew, whispering in the language of the soul, and saying, "Come to me!"

In closing this very brief historical review, I leave you with a poem credited to Doreen Valiente. Her words have become a treasure to Goddess worshippers, and a potent reflection of our beliefs. This is the "Charge of the Goddess":

> Listen to the words of the Great Mother, who of old was called
> Artemis, Astarte, Dione, Melusine, Aphrodite, Cerridwen, Diana,
> Arianrhod, Brigid, and by many other names.

Whenever you have need of anything, once in the month, and better it be when the moon is full, you shall assemble in some secret place and adore the spirit of Me who is Queen of all Witches.

There shall you assemble, who have not yet won my deepest secrets and are fain to learn all sorceries. To these shall I teach that which is yet unknown.

You shall be free from slavery, and as a sign that you be free you shall be naked in your rites.

Sing, feast, dance, make music and love, all in My presence, for Mine is the ecstasy of the spirit and Mine also is joy on earth.

For My law is love unto all beings.

Mine is the secret that opens upon the door of youth, and Mine is the cup of wine of life that is the Cauldron of Cerridwen that is the holy grail of immortality.

I am the Gracious Goddess who gives the gift of youth unto the heart of mankind.

I give the knowledge of the spirit eternal and beyond death I give peace and freedom and reunion with those that have gone before.

Nor do I demand aught of sacrifice, for behold, I am the Mother of all things and My love is poured upon the earth.

Hear the words of the Star Goddess, the dust of whose feet are the hosts of heaven, whose body encircles the universe.

I, who am the beauty of the green earth and the white moon among the stars and the mysteries of the waters,

I call upon your soul to arise and come unto Me. For I am the soul of nature that gives life to the universe. From Me all things proceed and unto Me they must return.

Let My worship be in the heart that rejoices, for behold—all acts of love and pleasure are My rituals. Let there be beauty and strength, power and compassion, honor and humility, mirth and reverence within you.

And you who seek to know Me, know that your seeking and yearning will avail you not, unless you know the Mystery: for if that which you seek, you find not within yourself, you will never find it without.

For behold, I have been with you from the beginning, and I am that which is attained at the end of desire.

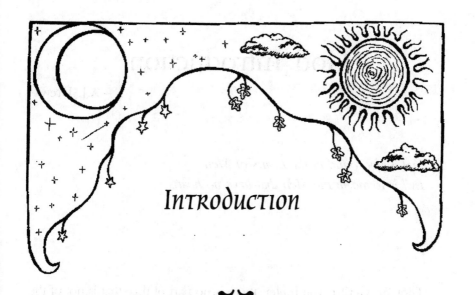

Introduction

God/Goddess

God Introduction

—A.J. Drew

Evil is not found in the hearts of Men
Evil is found in the Men that have no hearts

Thou art God! If you prefer, there is no part of thee that is not of the gods. But don't let that go to your head. You see, there is no part of me that is not of the gods as well. I am God. Sounds pompous, doesn't it?

You might not have heard this before because it does sound rather arrogant. It has been deliberately made to sound that way because if you are yourself part of God, then what need do you have for a mediator (priest)? And thus, you have no need for a service unto which you must pay alms or tribute. So then, with the rise in power of those who sought to capitalize on mediation between man and God, the true and incarnate nature of God was lost.

Then, right when we started to reawaken to the idea that each and every person is his or her own connection to the Divine, someone stepped in and reminded us of the atrocities that were committed in the name of God. Ah, but what of Goddess? Now that word doesn't have thousands of years of abuse attached to it. So the Feminist Witchcraft movement rushed forward and somewhere in that movement the idea of God, the male principle of the Divine, was lost.

But that does not mean he was lost forever. No, the idea of a masculine Divine may be down in some circles, but he is definitely not out. No matter how hard the far-right religious zealots tell us that God is a vengeful force that should be submitted to out of fear, no matter how much the far-left feminists tell us that God is really a woman, the truth rests where it most often does; right smack in the middle. Which, not coincidentally, is right where we find ourselves. Not above, not below, not in the future, not in the past; but right here and right now in the sensible middle where God is the word we use to describe the masculine principle of both our Creator and the created.

So why here and why now? Because he is needed. This New Age of interest in the metaphysical and the rekindling of old ways has failed. Sure, in the hands of the male-dominated monotheistic religions our world slipped into ruin. But even with the Goddess movement in full swing, our beloved Earth has continued to die, along with its flora and fauna. The Goddess alone has done nothing other than create a huge industry to feed our hungry minds. Surprise! We have thus far received little more than junk food, and so our spirits die due to malnutrition.

As is with most things in the universe, the recent interest in God consciousness has come because it is needed. Our world is dying and it will take a great deal more than feminine principle of our souls (Goddess) to save it.

Now before you begin to think that I am one of the greatest sexists to ever grace a bookshelf, let's get one thing clear: I am not speaking of the _male_ and _female_ principles of the soul. I am speaking instead of the _masculine_ and _feminine_ principles. Every male and every female is a composite of both the masculine and the feminine, just as the Creator is a composite of the masculine and the feminine. When I speak of God, I am referring to the Creator's masculine principles. When I speak of Goddess, I am referring to the Creator's feminine principles.

Let me also be clear that when I speak of God, I am not talking about the big guy in the sky. Nor when I speak of Goddess am I speaking of the big gal in the sky. These terms and the physical form of humanity that we assign to them are constructs for understanding. Do I believe they exist? Yes, but I do not believe humanity is able to fully understand, perceive, or explain that existence in its totality. So we use constructs to accomplish that understanding and perception so that we might explain our view of the Creator to others, which is what this book is all about.

Look at the folk involved in the rebirthing of the old ways. There you will find folk crying about the state of the world. For example, I recently met a man by the name of Damien Echols. Perhaps _met_ isn't the right word; you see, Damien is on death row and has been for about 10 years. He wrote to me asking for little more than spiritual guidance and the chance of friendship. After watching trial video and reading the transcripts of the case, I do know one thing: religious discrimination had a serious impact on the outcome of Damien Echols's trial. In fact, public library records were part of the evidence brought against him in his initial trial; he read books very similar to the one you are reading right now. Ah, if he reads books on alternative spirituality, he must be guilty of horrific murders.

As you can imagine, I felt compelled to begin a campaign of direct action to bring this religious discrimination to the attention of folk such as yourself—people who might find themselves on trial for little more than the books they read. Perhaps I should not have been surprised that the overwhelming response was that this was a horrible incident and people want to comfort him, but few wanted to stand and be counted as actively opposing the state's abuse of his constitutional right to freedom of religion. Few wanted to actively fight to prevent the loss of not only Damien's life, but also the loss of American liberty. Of course they weren't willing to take an active roll. You see, that which is *active* is a masculine principle and an overwhelmingly large part of the community has turned its back on those masculine principles. Someone else has already fought for our freedom, why should we bother? So then I ask, What healing will the Goddess be giving to Damien once he is dead?

The answer to this is that Goddess (passive/receptive) can do very little at this point. While some continue to demand that what is needed is healing in the arms of our beloved Goddess, if the wounds that need mending were not acquired in the holy battle to put right what has gone horribly wrong, then the one being healed is doing little more than littering her arms. You see, your freedom is not something that is given; it is something that is taken. The survival of our Earth is not something that will come with the tears of folk who will do nothing, it will come with the actions of those who stand and say *No* to the seemingly overwhelming forces that clearly seek to destroy it. At the risk of sounding like an alarmist, there is a war at hand and that war is a matter of both microcosm (one individual such as Damien) and macrocosm (the survival of our Earth). If something is not done soon, then none of this matters. Not the books, not the rituals, not the traditions, nothing will matter.

So, where do we begin? For so long we've been told that the nature of God is anything but Divine. Then someone told us that the Divine resides in the feminine. We begin to know the truth by knowing ourselves. Not by reading the *words* in some book, but by hearing the *call* in books such as this to search our own hearts and to discover those forces inside of us that compel us to recognize that there is right and wrong, and then to allow that inner voice to call us to arms.

From time to time you will note that Trish and I argue a few key points. That is intentional. Neither of us expects you to treat this book as fundamental truth. Instead, it is our hopes that having collaborated on this book, our readers will see that though we sometimes have vastly differing opinions, we can work together toward the same goal. You see, if that is not possible, then the war of which I spoke is already lost.

But I do not think it will be. I have faith in you. Why? Because "Thou art God."

Goddess Introduction

—Patricia Telesco

God may be in the details, but the goddess is in the questions.
Once we begin to ask them, there's no turning back.

—Gloria Steinem

Thou art Goddess! While you might not feel much like one first thing in the morning before a shower and coffee, this powerful aspect of Spirit resides within each person—men and women alike. Yes, that means you— thou art Goddess!

Wondering why you've never heard that before? Quite simply, because it's a realization to which we are only now reawakening. Throughout human history we have often lost sight of this aspect of the Divine. Various things caused our temporary blindness—a strong patriarchy, technological advances, human ego or apathy, and, of course, the rather fast-paced world in which we live that leaves little time for spiritual contemplation and reconnection. Nonetheless, no matter how far circumstances attempted to shove the Goddess into a societal, mental, or spiritual abyss, she never left our side or our awareness. Just look at the continued reverence for Mother Mary, the images of beautiful female fairies, and emerging Goddess art to verify this truth. Despite changing times and shifting cultural approval, the Goddess found a way to make her presence known.

So what exactly has brought this ancient and powerful Presence back to our attention today? It almost seems like a dichotomy. On one hand we have a highly scientific and technologically driven society, and on the other, the number of people following metaphysical systems is growing geometrically and creating a huge industry. In reality, it is the strong rational and masculine overtones to our computerized society that has coaxed the Goddess' stirring in our hearts again. We needed balance and symmetry. Where technology stresses the yang in us, the Goddess offers yin—the emotions, the intuitiveness, the nurturing, and the healing.

If one looks at our world, there is no question that we need these attributes from the Goddess. Many of our children have grown apathetic or given up altogether because they feel lost in a sea of humanity. Many of our great visionaries have gone to Summerland, leaving huge gaps in our arts where their voice once motivated others to greatness. And many, many people need healing—emotional, mental, physical, or spiritual. Our planet and our people as a whole are very ill at ease. The Goddess is here, offering hope and help. The time for renewal is NOW.

But where does one begin? For so long we've thought of the Divine in only male terms. Putting a skirt and breasts on a statue of Jesus just won't do here! That won't help us get to know the Goddess intimately, nor find a way to welcome her into our lives along with the God. That's where *God/ Goddess* comes in. Our entire goal in writing this book is to honor both sides of the Divine equation in the most common facets known to us (the ones to which we can all easily relate).

Specific to the Goddess, our exploration includes the youthful girl filled with zeal and charisma. Next, we consider the friend who offers a good ear and sound advice, the lover/wife who is a strong companion and helpmate, and the professional woman who makes her way in a wild world. There is also the mother and housewife who cares for the family, and the grandmother with the unique wit and wisdom of age to guide us. In simplest terms, the Goddess has specific names, faces, and characteristics that correlate to all the important moments in our lives, all the things that make us truly human.

Having said that, it's very important to stress balance in our exploration. What is the *she* without the *he* to balance her, empower her, honor her, celebrate her, motivate her, challenge her, and (of course) love her? This age-old symmetry is an intimate and inescapable part of being human, no matter your gender, sexual orientation, creed, or walk in life. Thus, while I explore the Goddess, it is not without a thought to the God. And as A.J. explores the God, it is not without thoughts of the Goddess. Somewhere between these two, magick dances. When we see that dance, and learn its steps, we will begin reconnecting with this ancient Power in new and intimate ways.

Thou art God and Goddess!

1

God as Master/Son
Goddess as Maiden/Daughter

God as Master/Son

−A.J. Drew

When I was a boy I dreamed of being a man
When I was a man I dreamed of being a boy
When I am neither I will dream of being both

Thou art God.

All things natural have a beginning, middle, and end. For this reason, nature-based religions view divinity in the same way. In the case of our Lady (Goddess), most readers will instantly recognize these roles as Maiden, Mother, and Crone. In respect to our Lord (God), these are the less known Master, Father, and Sage. In this chapter we will discuss the nature of the Wiccan view of God, and we will address him in his role as Master.

Before we start thinking of the term *master* in any other context than a state of youth, let me tell you that as a child I received many a letter from my grandfather addressed to Master Drew, as opposed to Mister Drew (my father). While it is not in as common use as it once was, the title *master* is similar to the title *mister,* but with a reflection of youth. As a child, I might have been called *Master Drew* while my father would have been called *Mister Drew.* Thus the term *master* as used here refers only to the first stage of a threefold look at one's lifetime—youth, mature, and senior.

The Son, or Master, state of our Lord lives in every man as the boy that we have never forgotten. He is the playful energy that nearly forces us to put the girls' pigtails in the inkwell. Though many of us have seemingly grown out of that state in life, he is forever present in our soul. He is the reason why, although I am 37 years old, I still drool whenever a fireworks catalog comes in the mail or when I decide that the best part of being an adult is being able to have ice cream for breakfast. Sure, the adult in me tells me that fireworks are dangerous and ice cream is not a healthy breakfast, but every now and then that adult in me is looking the other way.

He is also the innocent who lashes out because he does not always have the ability to express himself in another way. He is that portion of ourselves that we tend to forget with age and the one that we must make an extra special effort to embrace.

You see, of the three stages of life, it is the youthful stage that society does its damnedest to suppress in men. From day one we are told to "grow up" or to "act like a man." Over and over again, our playfulness is pushed down and set aside as if it were not part of our nature. "Take it like a man," we are told. Even when our youthfulness is recognized, we are told, "Boys don't cry." The hell we don't.

Youth is a time of wild emotions. It is a time of fire in both love and anger. It is when emotions fly, sometimes without control. It is also a time when the rest of the world tells us to control these emotions, to push them down and to listen to the more sensible (adult) portion of our being. It is a time when we want to point our sled down the hill and go as fast as we can, as well as a time when adults insist on pointing out the possibility that we will fall from that sled and tumble out of control.

Some of the better known masculine archetypes associated with youth include:

Hippomenes: The Greek youth who used wit and intelligence to overcome a physical challenge in the games of love. After falling hopelessly in love with Atalanta, he found that she had vowed never to marry a man who could not best her at sport. So the day came that they would compete in a footrace. If Hippomenes won, he would marry his love. If he lost, he would surrender his life. Ah, but Hippomenes had love on his side. Actually, he had Aphrodite who had given him three golden apples. During the race, Hippomenes dropped the apples one at a time, Atalanta slowed to pick each up, and Hippomenes won the race.

Kama: The Hindu god of love who is shown as a winged child with bow and arrows, similar to Cupid and Eros (Greek).

Laran: An Etruscan god of war who appears as a child clad only in a helmet. His lore points out the connection between the masculine youth and acts of violence. Although our modern feel-good books will often discount this connection, it is evidenced by the recruiting age of our military that the archetype of the young warrior is alive and well.

Maponos: Celtic god of youth.

Oengus Mac Oc: Irish god of love and youth. His name means "song of youth."

Sulpa'e: Sumerian god of fertility and, to a lesser degree, war, whose name means "shining look of youth."

As we can see, the ancients understood the connection between youth and emotions. They knew that both love and war were attached to the wilds of an untamed heart. They knew it, they warned of it, and yet like the society that tells us that boys do not cry, they embraced it and desperately sought to rekindle the youthful heart.

The Fountain and the Land of Youth

The ancients valued youth so much that lore concerning a fountain of youth or magickal process by which a person's years could be turned back can be found in many Pagan cultures. The belief was so strong that it could be found on the island of Bimini in the Bahamas, that there is an historical account of the explorer Ponce de León searching for it there.

In Japanese lore, there is said to be such a fountain found on the sacred mountain of Fujiyama where it is guarded by the blossom goddess Sengen.

In Russian folklore, it is not a fountain that gives eternal youth; it is the golden apples that the Firebirds (a mythical creature) eat. When consumed by humans, the gift of these apples is eternal life along with youth and health.

In Celtic mythology there is Tir na n-Og (Land of Youth), which is sometimes described as an island hidden from the rest of the world until the moment of death. In other lore, the island is obtainable by the living.

Special Gifts for Young Boys

You have certainly heard the lore that a unicorn will only befriend a maiden. What you have probably not heard is the Cherokee story of the Sint Holo. As with the unicorn that reveals itself only to a maiden, Sint Holo shows himself only to the master (male youth), and only upon the master's demonstration that he excels in intelligence. Sint Holo grants inspiration to him.

The Awakening of Sexuality

In using a term such as "youth" there is often a hesitation to discuss matters of sexuality. Today's news is filled with reports of the sexual abuse of children and most are afraid to even mention the fact that when it comes to youthful men, the time of sexual awakening is often in the early teens, if not younger. Ignoring this fact will not make it go away.

When interviewed for a book titled *A Witch Like Me*, I answered a question in a way that still embarrasses my mother:

Question: How did you first become involved in the Pagan movement?

Answer: I was trying to get laid.

The fact is that something happens to us as our testicles drop and our blood surges with testosterone for the first time. We move from being that young innocent boy to being the randy youth. Here we see our Lord as Pan, the boyish spirit of the wood, forever chasing the nymphs until they finally succumb to his youthful lust. Here, too, we see our Lord as Dionysus with his boyish ways, which are not far from what I experienced during my days in high school.

Pan (Greek): His name means "everything" or "all-inclusive." He is the son of Hermes. Perhaps the best known of the Satyrs (horned boyish companions to Dionysus). Although depicted with a wrinkled face, he is a randy god, skilled at rock climbing and chasing nymphs; his antics often annoyed the more mature gods and goddesses.

Dionysus (Greek): Also known as Dionysos. Although he is often equated to the Roman Bacchus, Dionysus is a boyish god whereas Bacchus is a more rounded adult. A better Roman translation would be Faunus. Little can be said about Dionysus with a period after the statement because his lore differs wildly from one classic reference to the next. One story tells us that he is the son of Zeus and Semele, but that he was raised by the nymphs that he would later chase. In another account, he is the son of Zeus and Persephone, who is tormented and tricked by Hera. In both stories, he becomes the god of wine, intoxication, and sexual pleasures. However, he is also god of the farm, nature, and the fertility necessary for both to prosper.

Faunus (Roman): In his role as protector of cattle, he is sometimes called or equated to Lupercus ("he who staves off the wolf"). By most accounts, he is the son of Picus.

Ah, but Pan and Faunus were not the only ones chasing young things through the wood with a jug of wine in one hand. Here are the rest of the boys:

Fauns (Roman): Led by Faunus, the Fauns are often depicted drinking, dancing, and chasing after young ladies.

Satyres (Greek): Led by Pan, the Satyres are often shown accompanying Dionysus. Their favorite pastimes are drinking, dancing, and chasing nymphs.

Rites of Passage

Youth is a confusing time, especially with all the mixed messages sent by the culture in which we live. On one hand, we are warned about impulsive actions and the broken hearts that come from allowing our emotions to rise. On the other hand, we are bombarded by commercial advertisements offering the fountain of youth in a bottle or a pill. Sure, there are legitimate medical needs for products such as Viagra, but have you seen their advertising? It certainly does not seem to be aimed at men who have a legitimate medical need. How about the many products to regrow a "youthful" head of hair?

Perhaps the most confusing matter to address when it comes to the youth state of the masculine Divine is just where the line between the master and father state is. This matter is difficult to both address and understand because the gods really are a part of our culture and in our culture we find equal confusion. Generally speaking, one must be 16 to drive a car, 18 to join the military or vote, 21 to purchase alcohol, and 25 to enter many clubs that serve alcohol. The age of sexual consent changes from state to state, as does the legal age at which one can wed without the permission of his or her parents. If this is not confusing enough, at age 18 you can join the military and be trusted with a machine gun, but you have to be 21 before you will be trusted with a hunting rifle. If you want a real challenge, try to figure out when it is that an accused person can be tried as an adult and when it is necessary that they be treated as a minor.

Now that you have all of these ages floating around in your mind, consider the age at which most religions mark the assent into manhood. If I remember correctly, I was 13 during my confirmation into Catholicism and my best friend at the time celebrated his Bar Mitzvah at about the same age. The average 13-year-old is in the 8th grade. Hardly an age at which we would call him a man and probably the reason I chose the name Luke for my confirmation—it is the only name that can be found in both the Catholic Bible and the movie *Star Wars*.

So when do we mark the transition from master to father? It is certainly not with the fathering of a child. The world is plenty crowded right now and there are already enough people with the mistaken belief that bringing life into this world is a universal merit badge. So then, when?

The answer is that the whole of one's youth is preparation for one's maturity. Our first word is a rite of passage as is our first step. We are perpetually young, moving forward into adulthood until the day that we die. Or at least this is what my mother constantly reminds me, the perpetual child. Is that not the stereotype for all men? Are we not always boys at heart?

Boys Will Be Boys, So Men Must Be Boys

Think back on your teen years and see if there wasn't a bit of Pan and Faunus in your past. If they were in your past, are they not a part of who you are now? Hopefully we have grown not only in age, but in maturity. Hopefully we have learned moderation and discovered the many rewards of conducting ourselves in more rational ways. But hopefully we have not learned those lessons so well that the boy that remains in every man is lost forever.

You see, aside from our own mental health, there is the relevance of the youthful masculine archetypes to our children. Think again how Pan and Faunus ripped at your soul when you were a youth, and know that their spirit is surging through the spirit of today's youth. Remember when you first discovered something stirring in your loins and know that your child will discover it right about the same age. Worse yet, what if your child's date discovers it first? What about alcohol and other intoxicants? I am sure you can see how Pan and Faunus were not always beloved by parents.

But it is in the embracing of these principles, in remembering what it was like when the world was new and our hormones raced to explore it, that can bring us a little bit closer to our own youth and to the youth of our children. You see, it is from that vantage point that we can further understand and shorten the gap between men and boys as well as fathers and sons.

In the glory of our Lord and Lady, so mote it be.

Goddess as Maiden/Daughter

—Patricia Telesco

"Atlanta"

Come with bows bent and with emptying of quivers,
Maiden most perfect, lady of light,
With a noise of winds and many rivers,
With a clamour of waters and with might,
Bind on thy sandals, O thou most fleet;
For the faint east quickens, the wan west shivers
Round the feet of the day and the feet of the night.

—Algernon Charles Swinburne

"Hindu Hymn to the Goddess of Dawn"

The radiant Dawns have risen up for glory, in their white splendor like the waves of waters. She makes paths all easy, fair to travel, and rich, She has shown herself benign and friendly.

We see that you are good: far shines your lustre; beams, splendors have flown up to heaven. Decking yourself, you make bare your bosom, shining in majesty, Goddess Morning.

Red are the kin and luminous those that bear her the Blessed One, who spreads through the distance. The foes she chases like a valiant archer, like a swift warrior she repels darkness.

Your ways are easy on the hills: you surpass Invincible! Self-luminous! So lofty Goddess with your ample pathway, Daughter of Heaven, bring wealth to give us comfort.

Dawn, bring me wealth: untroubled, with your oxen bearing riches at your will and pleasure; You who, a Goddess, Child of Heaven, hast shown yourself wholly lovely through bounty when we called you early.

As the birds fly forth from their resting places, so men with store of food rise at your dawning. Yea, to the liberal mortal who remains at home, O Goddess Dawn, much good you bring.

—the Rig Veda

Maid of the luminous grey-eyes, Mistress of honey and marble, implacable white thighs and Goddess, chaste daughter of Zeus.

—Hilda Doolittle

This Daughter, or Maiden, is the youthful aspect of the feminine Divine: We were all children once, and there are many situations throughout our adult life that require we both understand, and reconnect with, that child within. The Daughter or Maiden is there waiting with a helping hand for this journey. She also teaches us how to use youthful energy and outlooks to refresh our daily lives.

In Wicca, the Maiden is part of the threefold Goddess (the other two aspects being Mother and Crone). And while the ideals and traditions of Wicca are as yet still young, the human faith in a threefold Goddess is ancient, indeed. This trinity is found in many cultures and eras. For example, Carmenta (the Roman goddess of childbirth) is coupled with two sisters named Antevorta ("looking forward") and Postvorta ("looking back"). Antevorta is the Maiden, waiting for all that life has to offer, while Postvorta is the Crone who has the wisdom of perspective! Other examples of triune Goddesses who help us see the Maiden as she develops into womanhood and beyond include Zoryas (the Slavonic goddesses of dawn, evening, and midnight); Hera (the Greek patroness of marriage who had three temples—one for the Child, one for the Wife, and one for the Widow); and Bhavani (Hindu goddess known as the Triple Universe, and having three distinct forms).

As you're beginning to see, the Maiden Goddess is known by many names in a wide variety of cultures. Here are just a few:

☾ Artemis (Grecian)	☾ Renpet (Egyptian)
☾ Butterfly Woman (Native American—Hopi)	☾ Scota (Irish)
	☾ Siduri (Assyrian)
☾ Callisto (Arcadian)	☾ Uma (Hindu)
☾ Eostre (Anglo-Saxon)	☾ Ushas (Hindu)
☾ Kore (Grecian)	☾ Vesta (Roman)
	☾ Wah Kah Nee (Chinook)
☾ Persephone (Grecian)	☾ Yuki Onne (Japanese)

We will explore some of these young women and their myths in a moment. However, as a generalization, the Maiden appears in Classical art as a fresh, young woman just coming into her sexual maturity. What she holds or wears (or does NOT wear) depends greatly on the culture and era. Typically, if the Maiden is clad, it's in a white robe (implying purity but not necessarily chastity). If she's carrying something, it's often flowers or an implement that she uses (for example, the Huntress Maiden carries a bow). In all cases, however, the Maiden is very lovely and alluring, even as the craving for eternal youth allures humankind.

Historically speaking, perhaps the most common image of the Maiden we find is Artemis (Diana), with her bow and her dogs. Far more than just a huntress, Diana is associated with the moon, magick, and enchantment. What's interesting is that while we hear about Artemis the Chaste, her worship in the Mediterranean and Middle East seems more Mother-like; her images bear many breasts akin to the pre-Greek Great Mother. So, one might speculate that as with the moon, there was more to Artemis than simply a Maiden, but also the Mother (the full moon) and the Crone (the power of magick).

Maiden Myths and Legends

Any student of history knows that a great deal of humankind's feeling toward a topic is often revealed through regional myths and lore. This was the one place people could express their veneration of the Goddess freely and give more insights into her without fear because, after all, it was just a "story"! While there isn't enough space to share many Maiden myths, here are a few that have become widely celebrated.

Artemis

Since we spoke already a bit about Artemis, let's take a closer look at her. Artemis is the goddess of the wilderness and fertility. She was often depicted with the crescent of the moon above her forehead and was sometimes identified with Selene (goddess of the moon). She was also an Olympian, virginal goddess. Her main vocation was roaming mountain forests and uncultivated land with her nymphs in attendance, hunting for lions and stags. Artemis dutifully helped in protecting and seeing to the forest-dwelling creatures' well-being, along with their safety and reproduc tion. She was armed with a bow and arrows, both of which were fashioned by Hephaestus and the Cyclopes.

Legends claim that Artemis was born the day before Apollo, and even helped in his birth after safely assisting her mother cross the strait of Delos. This started the tradition of her being a guardian to young children and a protectress of women during childbirth. While this might seem an odd duty for the Maiden, it makes more sense when you consider that young women even today "baby-sit" and learn the art of childbearing/childcare from a Mother-type. In any case, Artemis reveals the independent nature of the Maiden, but one that has not abandoned her connection and responsibilities to family and the earth.

Kore/Persephone

A second well-known maiden from Greece is Kore (or Persephone). The word *kore* means "maiden" and it was Kore's mother, Demeter, who gifted humankind with the knowledge of farming and how to build a civilization. Kore loved to help her mother in various tasks, especially picking flowers. On one of her daily outings, she met some spirits who seemed to have no one to tend them, so she followed them to the underworld to give them attention. While Kore was gone, Demeter was terribly sad, and nothing on the earth grew. It wasn't until Demeter saw a crocus blooming that she knew Kore was returning, and thus blessed the land and crops once more.

As one might expect, this myth is all about winter and spring. It is a simple way of trying to understand that seasonal shift through storytelling, and it wasn't the only version of the story to be told! Homeric myths (which came later than the previous Kore depiction) talk of Persephone picking a narcissus, which was booby-trapped to transport her to the underworld. It was here that Hades took advantage of Persephone's innocence, tricked her into eating the fruit of the dead (the pomegranate), and then finally agreed to return the Maiden to her mother for six months out of the year so the earth would be fertile again.

Both versions of the Kore/Persephone myth illustrate a Maiden who loves beauty (flowers). It also shows that the Maiden, while helpful and exuberant, can often wander into a den of snakes without realizing it. This is one of the negatives of Maiden energy. When there's too much of it in a person's life, they often become unwitting and unwilling victims of their own trustfulness.

Vietnamese Dragon Maiden

Turning to another part of the world, let's consider the Vietnamese Dragon Maiden. A young man was walking the banks of a low lake when a maiden appeared. She said she was the daughter of the Dragon King, and that her father needed help. There was a hook in his mouth and she did not have the strength to remove it.

The young man agreed to help, so the maiden created a bubble of air in which she transported him to the sea. He carefully removed the hook, a service for which he was given a jug with a blue fish in it. The maiden returned him to the land and he said goodbye.

In the days that followed, the young man noticed something odd. His home was always clean upon rising. One morning, he got up early to try and see what was happening. The little blue fish turned into the maiden. He was so happy that he begged the girl to stay. She agreed and became his wife. Through this tale we see the maiden as helpful to her family—to the point of giving up a part of her life to serve them and repay a good deed.

Other Maidens

The stories of other maidens illustrate this Goddess-type's other attributes and associations. The Hopi Butterfly Woman, for example, is the young spirit of spring and an active participant in initiatory rights (the dawn of a new path). The Essene (Manichaean) Maiden of Light is radiant, a well-beloved daughter, and intensely passionate. There's also Uma, a gracious and virginal aspect of Parvati whose other manifestations as a determined wife and Kali the Black imply yet another triune Goddess; and Renpet from Egypt whose youthfulness stretched throughout eternity. In all of these women's stories and hundreds (if not thousands) more, we discover unique things about the Maiden, all of which we can remember as we work her magick in our life.

Activity: A Personal Goddess Myth

Our ancestors used stories to help them understand the powers of the Goddess. For this activity, I'd like you to try to write your own Maiden myth. If you were the Maiden Goddess, what would be your name and attributes? What kind of story would you leave behind to which future generations could relate and from which they would learn of you? Bear in mind this need not be a great literary work. What's important is the introspective process. This personalized story will begin to help you rediscover the Maiden within!

The Maiden's Attributes

Emotionally, the Maiden is naturally curious about feminine energy. This is, in part, why the season of spring and the Maiden are connected. Just as the earth is blossoming and developing out of its slumber, the woman within the Maiden begins to stir. A person of any age wishing to remember those first extraordinary hormonal surges and wonder at the incredible machine of his or her body would do well to seek out the Maiden for insight.

With the Maiden's steady growth toward womanhood, there are also new perspectives to explore, a sense of true liberation, and an intense exuberance for life. Everything is fresh, new, and interesting! If the Maiden gets something in her head, just get out of the way! With this in mind, she's definitely a good partner for new efforts; improving your appreciation for adventure; and for freeing yourself from anything old, outmoded, or unhealthy (especially ideas).

The Maiden's energy comes across as being beholding to no one but Herself, but also rather innocent and naïve in that air of confidence. This doesn't mean she will not help those who call upon her, but be aware that the Maiden has her own sense of order and priorities. This is actually very helpful for those of us who need a button that reads "stop me before I volunteer again." When we're ready to say YES, the Maiden shakes a wary finger and asks, "Isn't there something more fun you could be doing?"

Perhaps that sounds selfish, but there is a tendency among Neo-Pagans (especially our facilitators) to ignore the well of self. We are very often willing to give, but very bad about receiving. The Maiden, however, loves receiving (especially gifts) and teaches us how to do that gracefully, recognizing the necessity of it.

On another level, the Maiden represents the first seed of "genesis" (be that seed mental, physical, or spiritual). There may be risks in the generative process, akin to the fool about to leap, but the strength and autonomy of the Maiden is more than up to this challenge. So much so that in many cultures the Maiden eventually takes the Green Man or Horned Lord as her consort, thereby embracing, and eventually nurturing, all of Creation! Now that's a Lady with tremendous fortitude!

An additional attribute of the Maiden is the crescent moon, a sign of beginnings. As an initiator, she can really get things moving and shaking, making often swift and seemingly easy choices. This comfort and confidence makes her an apt lover, but one who does not fall in love for keeps (not yet, anyway—there's too much to learn and explore!). For those who have been abused or neglected in life, or those who love too quickly, this attribute speaks of true freedom to make completely personal, physical, and emotional choices without feeling tied to a person, family, job, ideology, or even your own bad habits. Through the Maiden, you can again learn to say "no" or "enough" and really follow through with that decision. In her, you reclaim your Sacred Self.

Now before going further, it's worth noting that not everything about the Maiden is proverbial sweetness and light. The darker side of the Maiden speaks to us of the feminine power lost due to a long, unbalanced patriarchal rule—the power from which we sometimes shy away. It has really only been a few generations in which the female cycle wasn't looked upon as a "curse" (for example). And, even now, many parents struggle with how to prepare their young girls for the realities of womanhood. The Maiden can be a helpmate in that journey. Because the Maiden is taking this journey too, she understands all the confusions and curiosities. If you're doing a rite of passage for a youth, call upon her to guide and protect that space.

Speaking of rituals, the dark Maiden also whispers about the power and customs of magick that were hidden in the darkness for safekeeping. The Maiden helps us reclaim the night, and bring spirituality into the full light of day. She tells us to embrace our magick; celebrate our spirit! And trust me, there is no sackcloth or ashes in the Maiden's faith. It is bright, joyful, and life-affirming. When your path has become long and hard, and you've lost touch with inner happiness, seek her out!

Finally, and perhaps most importantly, the Maiden is a trailblazer. You will never see her sitting on the sidelines regarding any issue, nor being a wallflower. True, the world was not quite ready for such a woman to storm onto the scene for quite awhile. Nonetheless, the Maiden bided her time, knowing full well that humankind would eventually be ready for her again. Meanwhile, each time a person stood up for true freedom and independence, she was there inspiring and celebrating that step forward. And each time such individuals died for their vision, she wept.

Who were the individuals that I feel the Maiden's attributes inspired? Well what about Empress Jingo (366 c.e.) who was pregnant when she invaded Korea and, therefore, had to have adjustable armor made (now that's not only courageous, but inventive!). Or what about Marie Gouze

(1748–1793), who under the name Olympe de Gouges, wrote *Declaration of the Rights of Women and Citizens*, thereby unwittingly condemning herself to the guillotine. Her story didn't end there, however. In the 19th century, when women faced the harsh reality of husbands and fathers at war, in an act of Maiden-like courage and confidence, they ventured into the workforce using Gouze's writings to guide the feminist movement. These women, and other people like them, illustrate the ways in which the Maiden's energy can touch us deeply, and motivate amazing social and personal change.

Activity: Maiden Meditation

Preparation: Wear comfortable, loose-fitting clothing for this meditation. Consider burning some incense that reminds you of spring. Light a white candle if it helps you focus. Make sure you're undisturbed, and sit on the ground (preferably outdoors if seasonally feasible).

Take three deep, cleansing breaths (in through your nose, out through your mouth). Release all your tensions and worries. Let them settle into the ground beneath you. Count backwards from 100 to one slowly with each breath you take. Drift gently—in a place that is not a place—and a time that is not a time—on the soul's horizon. Know that you are safe, secure, sensual, and sensitive. In your mind's eye, see yourself walking down a corridor of young trees, just beginning to bud with flowers of white, sparkling light. All around the light of dawn breakings across the earth, and spring is in the air. The birds are singing, the winds blow gently at your back, and the world rejoices.

The path is smooth ... very few stones or holes, and—as if yours are the first feet to touch it—it seems to sing with each step you take. The joy of that music fills you. Stop for a moment and listen ... listen to your heart beating and the whisper of life's blood within. Listen to the music of joy that is the youthful Goddess [pause].

Find a comfortable place in your mindscape to sit and enjoy the vividness of life's energy around you. Wait and watch. After just a short time you'll see a young, beautiful woman—so lovely, so filled with vitality that she takes your breath away. She wears nothing but an opalescent shift that plays around her body. There, in a meadow surrounded by trees, she will dance. Beneath her feet, flowers blossom. Above her head, the sun seems to reach down to embrace her.

After her dance, the young woman gathers one blossom into her hand with care. She brings it to you. Reach out and accept her gift, then listen.

Perhaps she has a message for you! When she turns to leave, tuck that flower in your heart chakra where its petals unfold with pure joy. This is how you felt the first time you jumped in a rain puddle or rode your bike without training wheels. This is the flower of your inner child, awakened.

You can stay here as long as you wish. When you feel filled to overflowing, adjust your breathing and slowly return to normal awareness. Don't move too quickly, nor try to rush. Do, however, make notes of your experience in a meditation journal or your Book of Shadows so you can refer to it later.

In review, go to the Maiden aspect of the God/Goddess when you need supportive energies for zeal; purity of intention in mind, body, or spirit; improved energy; youthful outlooks; renewed hope; a sense of wonder and appreciation (especially toward your own body); developing realness; inspiring connectedness and joy; improving health or vitality; expanding vision; stimulating boldness; learning flexibility; extending charisma or attractiveness; earning trust or trusting others; and applying effective enthusiasm to new projects.

The Maiden for Men

Remember that the Maiden (and the Goddess as a whole) is not simply a force for women. Although it's normal for most women to connect with this presence more easily (there are substantial archetypes in the energy of our gender), at least part of the purpose of this book is to encourage balance. I feel that men can benefit greatly from reconnecting with the Maiden, even as they benefit from their interactions with the God. Now, you might be asking yourself how? How do we get outside of our gender-specific reality to dance with the Divine Maiden?

First, if you look at your life, you'll probably see something of the Maiden already there. Perhaps you're adventurous, playful, or imaginative, for example. Those attributes are all Maiden-oriented, and through them you can more easily tap into her energies. Think about her when you're doing something that speaks to your spirit of Maiden energy and begin building that bridge—begin establishing a relationship!

Also, while one wears a cloth of gender in this life, there is certainly no limit as to how many masculine or feminine characteristics one person can have. It's highly likely that you've been another gender in another life—so knowledge of that experience is imprinted in the matrix of your soul.

This latent awareness will also help you in developing a relationship with the Maiden. You just have to be willing to think outside the box and release that inner child. Actually, many men seem to have an advantage in this.

The masculine gender, as a whole, seems innately capable of liberated play. I know in watching my children, they come to me for boo-boos and food, but go to their father for *play*, and this phenomena isn't limited to my home. This aspect of the male gender can help them keep in touch with the inner child, and through him, the Maiden!

Now, once you start developing this relationship, the next obvious question is how to apply it on a concrete level. For example, male friends come to me when they're having trouble understanding a young female companion, significant other, or mate. They don't quite understand what motivates this person, what really makes her happy and content. These questions represent an ideal situation with which the Maiden can help.

By getting to know her, you are indirectly also getting to know the women in your life similar to her (or men with similar young, feminine energies). In your interactive times with the Maiden, you can seek her council too! Although be forewarned that of the archetypes, I've found the Maiden to have a huge sense of humor. Expect a little cheekiness!

A Man's Prayer to the Maiden

Maiden Goddess, I would to know you. I welcome your presence in my home and my life. Every day, and in every way, help me celebrate my spirit and all those little moments that make up LIFE! When work threatens to overpower, remind me again to play. When duties seem heavy, remind me to put down the burdens and count my blessings. Let me see the world with your expectant eyes—those that see potential and beauty all around. Let me live each second fully, willfully and magickally, with your courage, your strength, your vitality as constant companions. So mote it be.

Common Symbols

Before we go on to look at more ways of connecting with and honoring the Maiden, or call upon her for assistance in specific spells, charms, rituals, and meditations, it helps greatly to know the symbols with which she is most often associated. Please note that each specific goddess typically has different sacred emblems, flowers, animals, and attributes (information along these lines is included in the correspondence list at the end of the book). What I'm providing here is "generic" in that it is intended to help invoke the Maiden archetype (no name, no cultural designation).

☾ **Colors:** White, silver, and pastels.

☾ **Moon phase:** Waxing.

☾ **Stone:** Clear quartz; any round, white stone.

☾ **Hours:** Dawn until noon.

☾ **Season:** Spring.

☾ **Plants:** Meadowsweet, thistle, and narcissus.

☾ **Other items:** Young animals; lightweight, playful clothing; or nakedness.

Let's take this information and transfer it into functional application examples. First, if you wished to make yourself a charm that would encourage Maiden energies and attributes in your life, you might bundle quartz in a white cloth with some dried meadowsweet blossoms. If possible, do this during the waxing phase of the moon. Bless and empower the bundle by adding an incantation such as:

Maiden of the morning, bless this crystal bright

That I might see a bit of you in me

Along the path of light

Maiden of hope and freshness, fill these petals now

That when given to wind, the magick begins

To me, your gifts endow!

Any time you have an immediate need for her assistance, open the bundle and sprinkle the blossoms about and refill the charm.

Or perhaps you're thinking of having a special Maiden ritual for the Spring Equinox. In this case it would seem appropriate to dress in something as light as spring itself, put down a silvery cloth on the altar, and mark the circle with white flowers or flower petals. All these things honor the Maiden and help invoke her presence. Also, begin the ritual at dawn, that way you can greet the Goddess as the light dashes across the horizon!

Celebrating the Maiden

We already know that the Maiden is associated with the entire season of spring. But what if you wanted one specific date to set aside to celebrate her energies? Of the festivals on the Wiccan Wheel, I'd recommend Imbolg

(Feast of Brid, also known as the Festival of Lights, Candlemas, and Groundhog Day).

As the story goes, the Old Woman of Winter (called Cailleach) travels to a magickal island where the Well of Youth lies. Come the first rays of dawn on the day of the Feast of Brid, she drinks of the well and becomes Brid, the Maiden of spring and promised bride to the Sun God. Wherever she walks, the earth is likewise transformed until scarcity becomes abundant life.

In Celtic mythology, Brid presides over poetic muse, creativity, and handcrafts, along with being a fertile maiden. As one of three daughters of Daghdha, the Great God, she also continues the tradition of triune goddesses. And as an interesting side note, a temple was erected in her honor in Kildare, Ireland, where the fires of the temple were maintained well into the Middle Ages!

If you'd like to consider some traditional customs through which to celebrate Brid and the Maiden today, here are some options:

(Place a corn doll in a bed of flowers, and carry it around the ritual space so each person can present a token to the Goddess.

(Make Brighid's Crosses from wheat stalks and exchange them with family and friends to encourage protection and prosperity for the whole year.

(Blow out a flame the night before, then relight it at dawn. Next, place a broom by your door to move out the old energies and welcome the fresh Maiden anew.

(Light candles in every window of the house the night before to show the Maiden the way (obviously, take care that curtains are pulled back and you have fire-safe containers). These should burn out naturally if practicable.

(Leave tokens for nature spirits, and do not pick any plants this day so that your gift can be received. In particular, a libation of milk or sweet cream is very apt.

Last but not least, let's not forget spring cleaning! Get rid of the old, welcome the new. As you go through your house, use specially scented cleaning supplies, chant, and sing to the Maiden! If there are miscellaneous items you find that you no longer use, give them to charity or someone who you know will enjoy them (particularly old toys since they reflect the Maiden's playfulness). This will also encourage the Maiden's abundance in and around your home.

2

God as Friend
Goddess as Friend

God as Friend

—A.J. Drew

Thou art God.

In the Koran, there is a word used to refer to Ibrahim. The word is Khalilu'llah, which means "friend to God." It is given to Ibrahim because he treated God as a friend, not as a ruler. While that might sound like blasphemy to a few, think about the way one might treat a guest as opposed to the way folk are inclined to treat a ruler. When we treat a guest well, it is because we *want* to treat that guest well. When we treat a master well, it is often because we do not want to suffer the consequences of not treating that master well.

But if thou be a king, where is thy crown?

My crown is in my heart, not on my head;

Not decked with diamonds and Indian stones,

Nor to be seen; my crown is called content,

A crown it is that seldom kings enjoy.

—William Shakespeare's *Henry VI*, part 3

In the relatively short amount of time that humanity has occupied this planet, we have worked our way right up to the very top of the food chain. We have been able to do so for one reason and one reason alone: we build interpersonal human relationships. Without that community-building skill, we would have gone the way of the dinosaurs.

As with most matters of survival, this skill is not one of choice. Doing so is encoded into the very substance that defines a great portion of who we are. Just as humanity has an opposable thumb because our DNA dictates that we do, so does humanity build interpersonal relationships because our DNA dictates that we do. Yes, we all meet folk that we simply do not like. But we cannot honestly deny that we are driven by our very nature to find like minds and bond as friends. Humanity is a communal creature.

This is the "crown" that Shakespeare called the "content" of our hearts, or perhaps that which causes our hearts to be "content." Either way, it is much more than wordplay. Call that of which I speak God or Goddess, King or Queen, or by any other name; it is the same. In the case of its masculine, half is the masculine principle of our soul (the content of our hearts). Now, certainly a man could rule as king with a firm hand. He could force his subjects into complacency with fear. But what kind of a king would that be? What type of a god would that be? Why are you reading this book?

Odds are high that if you are reading this book it is because at some point in your life you have become "discontent" with Christianity, Judaism, or Islam. I say "chances are" because these three religions are dominant in the culture in which this book will be read. In each of those three religions, God is presented as the king who rules with a firm hand, forcing his subjects into complicity with fear. In my particular part of the world (North America), this takes the form of repenting to a jealous God or receiving a one-way ticket to eternal torment (hell) without respect to the good that you did in your lifetime. Play by his rules or suffer the consequences of his jealousy. Now is that what you expect from a "friend"? A king? A god? If so, you need to seriously rethink your use of the words friend, king, and god.

Thou art indeed a king among men, but just what type of king you choose to be is entirely up to yourself. If you want to rule by force, so be it. If you want to be a friend to your subjects, then so be it. But remember that just as they are your subjects, so too are they kings and so too are you their subject.

This relationship works best when it is symbiotic. Ah, the golden rule that exists in just about every successful culture and religion this world has ever known.

Buddhist: "Hurt not others in ways that you would find hurtful."

Confucian: "Do not unto others what you would not have them
    do unto you."

Christian: "All things whatsoever ye would that men should do to
    you, do ye even so to them."

Hindu: "This is the sum of duty; do naught unto others which if
    done to thee would cause thee pain."

Islamic: "No one of you is a believer until he desires for his
    brother that which he desires for himself."

Jain: "In happiness and suffering, in joy and grief, we should
    regard all creatures as we regard our own self."

Jewish: "What ever thou hatest thyself, that do not to another."

Sikh: "As thou deemest thyself, so deem others."

Taoist: "Regard your neighbor's gain as your own gain, and your
    neighbor's loss as your own loss."

Zoroastrain: "That nature alone is good which refrains from doing
    unto another whatsoever is not good for itself."

Treat others in the way that you would like them to treat you. Friendships founded on symbiotic relationships are the best friendships a person could hope for. So what does this have to do with God?

The relationships that we form with all living things are the relationships that we form with the Creator. Here we see that separating the masculine (God) and feminine (Goddess) principles of the Divine is difficult.

It seems society has decided men do not form the bonds that women
do. I think this matter has been extended by the Feminist Witchcraft
movement, but please decide for yourself. Indeed, society is not only
determined to dictate how men express emotions, but with whom they
express those emotions.

Take a look at the lover's card in the Motherpeace tarot deck. There
you will find two women embracing in love and two men killing each
other with swords. I take that to imply that women show love with love but
men show love with violence. How dare they?

Then there is the current vision of Kwan Yin, who you probably
know as the goddess of compassion. She has become very popular in
recent times, but the modern concept of Kwan Yin is just as offensive as
the Motherpeace tarot deck.

Kwan Yin was originally Guan-yin, a Chinese bodhisattva. In Tibet,
he was Chenresi, whose name means "One Who Hears the Cries of the

World." Ah, but remember what I said earlier? Boys don't cry. It is true today just as it was in the eighth century when the male Guan-yin started the transformation into his current identification as female.

Fortunately, if we look past the surface of the current view of men as destroyers, we find deep, meaningful relationships formed by the examples of God found in the stories of a time before the great patriarchies ruled the world. A time when even though wars were waged, men relied on their relationships with other men.

Welsh mythology tells the story of Arawn (King of the Underworld) and Pwyll, who fell into dispute. As penance, Pwyll was forced to live as King of the Underworld (not a very pleasant place) for a year and a day while Arawn lived in Pwyll's place as king of a beautiful kingdom. The fix was in and nobody was able to tell that the switch had been made.

When the year and a day of penance was complete, Arawn discovered that not only had Pwyll fulfilled the tasks required of the King of the Underworld, he had refrained from one of the more pleasant aspects of that position. Although Arawn's wife had absolutely no idea it was not her husband who then ruled the kingdom of the Underworld, Pwyll refrained from going to her bed. As you can imagine, although Arawn and Pwyll started their relationship in dispute, they became the best of friends.

I chose this story to illustrate an important point: that although the following is a list of a few gods of friendship, as with most things, these archetypes are not simply givers of gifts. Friendships, as with most things, can be prayed for, but if you are not willing to live in a manner in which you are deserving of such gifts, you will not receive them.

Gods of Friendship

Airyaman: Persian god of friendship.

Damon: Few stories illustrate friendship better than that of the Greek Damon and his closest friend, Pythias. After Pythias was condemned to death, he was given time to set his affairs in order, but only if someone stayed in his stead and agreed freely to accept his fate should he not return. Damon accepted that role, knowing that if Pythias did not return he would certainly die. To the surprise of both young men, upon the return of Pythias, both were released because such a friendship as theirs could not justly be destroyed.

Mithra (also known as **Mitra**): Persian/Ancient Iranian god of not only friendships, but of oral contracts.

Wadd: Pre-Islamic moon god whose name means "friendship." His name is also sometimes translated as "love," but it is a reference to neither romantic nor family-centered love known as philia.

Friendships in Myth and Lore

Instead of focusing on the gods of friendship, let's look at some archetypes that matter a bit more. Let's look at the mythical relationships themselves. Here we see archetypes that are both gods as well as classic heroes mingle in the many acts of friendship.

Aeolus (Greek) was such a friend to Odysseus that just prior to Odysseus's departure on a sailing ship, he gathered up all the ill winds of the world and handed them to Odysseus in a bag so that they would not trouble his journey. While this might seem like common courtesy, one should keep in mind that Aeolus's name means "Earth Destroyer." Thus, his action to preserve and protect his friend was conducted in complete opposition to his very nature.

Apollo (Greek) was such a friend to King Admetus that when Atropos (one of the Moirae, or Fates) cut the King's thread, Apollo pled with the Moirae to restore his friend to life.

Ilmarinen (Finnish) was a god and protector of travelers who was rarely seen traveling without his good friend Vaiamoinen.

Iolaus (Greek) risked his life to help his friend Heracles kill the nine-headed Hydra.

Mentor (Greek) was such a close friend to Odysseus that when Odysseus left for the Trojan wars, he asked Mentor to not only watch over his kingdom, but also his son Telemachus. From that great act of friendship, we receive the modern use of the word mentor.

Pylades's (Greek) friendship with Orestes is so well documented that it is virtually impossible to find reference to Pylades without a reference to Orestes. When Pylades fell in love with Orestes's sister Electra, Orestes welcomed their marriage because he knew of no finer man to be his sister's husband.

Friendship Has a Price

Never a season with a fool shall ye spend
Less be counted as his friend

                                    —the Wiccan Rede

Make no mistake, friendship has a price. Particularly if you pick friends poorly.

Abderus (Greek) was eaten by the Mares of Diomedes. By some accounts, he was guarding the Mares for his friend Heracles.

Cuchulainn (Celtic) had a dear friend in a man named Ferdiad. Despite that friendship, Ferdiad fought for Queen Maeve against the forces of Cuchulainn. When Ferdiad was killed in that battle, Cuchulainn's heart was broken.

Pandareus (Greek) stole a bronze statue at the request of his friend Tantalus. That statue was in the temple of Zeus on Crete, so as you can imagine, Pandareus paid a good price for his friendship. By some accounts, he was turned to stone.

By now you are probably starting to see a pattern. Where elsewhere you may have read that friendships are always a good thing, here I warn that they are often detrimental to one's well-being. Where elsewhere you may have read about the giving nature of friendship, here I warn that friendship demands sacrifice. Before you decide that I am the ultimate pessimist, think back on the popular kids in school. How much was their friendships worth? Although they likely professed a large social group, was that social group structure on the natural bonds of give and take that a true friendship is? Or is it that the popular kids have great amounts of hangers-on who are there for the benefit of what social standings this "friend" could offer?

What, then, is your relationship with God? When was the last time you prayed without asking for a thing? When was the last time you lit a candle in honor of your patron deity without asking for a thing? When was the last time that you stopped suddenly, looked to the sky, and just said "thank you"? Certainly if you have purchased this book, you have a great amount to be thankful for. The great majority of people currently inhabiting this world have neither the freedom nor the resources to do so. Even if you are reading this book at your local library, you have the very fact that the library exists to be thankful for. Have you borrowed it from a friend? Well then, you have a friendship to be thankful for.

With the rise of interest in the old gods has come a silent plague. Instead of observing the ancient stories in the context of how they have been written, gods and goddesses have been taken out of context and presented as separate and unique objects. The result of this objectification of the gods is that we view these archetypes as if they alone, and not the relationships they participated in, are the focus of the ancient stories.

Ares and Eris

Ares, the Greek god of war, is almost always depicted with his friend and sister Eris, the goddess of strife. In the Roman pantheon, these are Mars (god of war) and Discordia (goddess of discord). In some depictions, Eris is seen in the entourage of her brother, following closely behind. But in most depictions, she precedes war—perhaps the most famous being the Trojan War.

Should we look at Ares alone, we see the Greek god of war. Should we look at Eris alone, we see the Greek goddess of strife and discord. But when we look at their relationship, we see the clear warning that strife and discord lead to war.

Thus when we objectify Ares, we see a god of war that one might call on to smite an enemy. But when we choose not to objectify, when we look at his relationship with his sister Eris, we see that although war may well be a necessary part of life, one might avoid it by avoiding strife and discord.

This is the way of virtually all stories found in our great and abundant lore. It is not the characters in the story, but the story itself that is important. When applied to friendships, especially those with our Lord, it is not the friend that is important, but the friendship, the interaction, and the story that is important.

So we see that being a good friend is not the whole of the subject, but neither is having good friends. For the object is not objectification. How one treats one's friends is not the key, nor is how one's friends treat you.

Objectification

If someone offers to "pray for your soul," are they doing so because they care about you or because they feel it is the right thing to do? If they do so because it is what a godly person should do, then that is *objectification*. If, on the other hand, they do so because they honestly care for your soul, then they are indeed being godly. Act for the appearance of the action, and you are objectifying the act. Act for the relationship between yourself and what or whom you are acting on, and you are not objectifying the relationship.

Hence, we cannot pick our friends because the true sense of being a friend is not a selection. It is not what a person can do for us, not what we can do for them. Even if one were to create a list of the attributes desired in a friend, that list would be useless because the very definition of a friend is found in the friendship (the interaction) and not in the attributes of any one person (the friends involved). This is why when we look at mythology we do not see archetypes of gods of friendship; instead we see stories of the great friendships (the relationships in action) that time will never forget.

The key is the exchange, the relationship between one person and the next. For this is your very relationship with God.

In the glory of our Lord and Lady, so mote it be.

Goddess as Friend

—Patricia Telesco

"The Temple of Friendship"

—Voltaire (François Marie Arouet, 1694–1778)

Sacred to peace, within a woods recess,
A blest retreat, where courtiers never press,
A temple stands, where art did never try
With pompous wonders to enchant the eye;
There are no dazzling ornaments, nor vain,
But truth, simplicity, and nature reign:
The virtuous Gauls raised erst the noble shrine,
And sacred vowed to Friendship's power divine.
Mistaken mortals who believed their race,
Would never cease to crowd to such a place!
Orestes' name, and Pylades' appear,
Wrote on the front, names still to Friendship dear:
Pirithous' medal of uncommon size,
Those of soft Nisus and Achates wise.
All these are heroes, and as friends renowned,
These names are great, but still in fable found;
The power to this remote retreat retired,
Nor Tripod boasts, nor priests with truth inspired;
She miracles but seldom can effect,
No popish saint e'er met with such neglect.
Still in her presence faithful truth attends,
And to the goddess needful succor lends:
Truth's every ready to enlighten all,
But few on truth for kind assistance call.

In vain she waits for votaries at her shrine,
None come, though all at wanting her repine;
Her hand holds forth the register exact,
Of every generous, every friendly act;
Favors in which esteem with friendship vied,
Received not meanly, not conferred with pride:
Such favors as those who confer forget,
And who receive, declare without regret.
This history of the virtues of mankind,
Within a narrow compass is confined;
In Gothic characters all these are traced
Upon two sheets, by time almost defaced.
By what strange frenzy is mankind possessed,
Friendship is banished now from every breast;
Yet all usurp of Friend the sacred name,
And vilest hypocrites bring in their claim.
All that they're faithful to her laws maintain,
And even her enemies her rights profane:
In regions subject to the pope's command,
Thus we see beads oft in an atheist's hand.
'Tis said the goddess, each pretended friend,
Once in her presence summoned to attend;
She fixed the day on which they should be there,
A prize proposing for each faithful pair;
Who with a tenderness like hers replete,
Amongst true friends might justly claim a seat;
Then quickly came allured by such a prize,
The French who novelty still idolize:
A multitude before the temple came,
And first, two courtly friends preferred their claim,
By interest joined, thy walked still hand in hand,
And of their union Friendship thought the band:
Post-haste a courier came and made report,
That there was then a vacancy at court;

Away each friend polite that moment flies,
Forsakes at once the temple and the prize;
Thus in a moment friends are turned to foes,
Each swears his rival warmly to oppose:
Four devotees next issue from the throng,
Poring on prayer-books as they pass along;
Their charity to mankind overflows,
And with religious zeal their bosom glows.
A pampered prelate one with fat o'ergrown,
Triple-chinned, much to apoplexy prone;
The swine quite gorged with tithes, and overfed,
At length by indigestion's force lies dead:
Quick the confessor clears the sinner's score,
His soles are greased, his body sprinkled o'er,
And spruced up by the curate of the place,
To go his heavenly journey with good grace;
His three friends o'er him merrily say prayers,
His benefice alone excites their cares:
Devoutly rivals grown, each still pretends
Attachment most sincere to both his friends;
Yet all in making interest at the court,
Their brothers downright Jansenists report.
Two youths of fashion next came arm in arm,
Their eyes and hearts, their mistress letters charm:
These as they passed along they read aloud,
And both displayed their persons to the crowd;
Some favorite airs they sing, while they advance
Up to the altar, just as to a dance:
They fight about some trifle, one is slain,
And Friendship's altar hence receives a stain;
The less mad of the two with conquest crowned,
Left his dear friend expiring on the ground.
Next Lisis, with her much loved Chloe came,
From infancy their pleasures were the same;

Alike their humor, and alike their age,
Those trifles which the female heart engage;
Lisis was prone to Chloe to impart,
They spoke the overflowings of the heart;
At last one lover touched both female friends,
And strange to tell! here all their Friendship ends;
Lisis and Chloe Friendship's shrine forsake,
And the high road to Hatred's temple take.
The beauteous Zara shone forth in her turn,
With eyes that languish, whilst our hearts they burn:
"What languor," said she, "reigns in this abode!
By that sad goddess, say what joy's bestowed?
Here dismal melancholy dwells alone,
For love's soft joys are ever here unknown."
Leaving the place, crowds followed her behind,
And struck with envy, twenty beauties pined:
Where next my Zara went, is known to none,
And Friendship's glorious prize could not be won:
The goddess everywhere so much admired;
So little known, and yet by all admired;
With cold upon her sacred altar froze—
Hence hapless mortals, hence derive your woes.

Taste this, and be hence forth among the Gods—Thysel f a Goddess.
—John Milton

In human interaction, our friendships are the most important type of relationship we build, and the need for friends does not diminish with age. In fact, research shows that people with good friends tend toward better overall health and well-being. Perhaps this is due to the emotional, mental, and tangible help that friends supply. From showing affection and providing various types of support, they also become guides, an extra pair of helpful hands, and important overall resources in our lives. Psychologists actually hypothesize that friends become a very real coping mechanism who offer the extra bonus of decreasing or alleviating stress.

Perhaps psychologists studied Aristotle, who tells us, *"Friendship is a thing most necessary to life, since without friends no one would choose to live, though possessed of all other advantages."* When asked, *what is friendship?* Aristotle replied, *"One soul in two bodies."* It seems, however, that no matter how much we might wish otherwise, it's not quite that simple to define friendship.

Depending on where one lives, friendship has unique implications. In Asia, for example, the role of a friend is often part of "family" (that is, you find that close relationship within the extended group of relatives). In Japan, a friend's behavior can affect your personal honor. And in some tribal cultures, a person's best friend has greater legal standing than some family members because of the implied trust in him or her.

There's also great differences exhibited in how various cultures and individuals define the parameters that constitute true friendship. Some determine it by common interests, whereas others measure it by attitudes or beliefs. These types of determinants are how Aristotle defined variances in friendships—namely by their goals (such as utility or pleasure).

I want to take the time to review this historical and psychological information because it gives us an important starting place for pondering the goddesses of friendship. We must understand the human element before we try to define the divine ones! So, which goddesses oversee this special relationship and how can we call upon them for help when a friendship gets damaged, or for building new friendships? Which goddesses teach us about being better friends? Well, there's a variety of multicultural references for us to consider, including:

⟨Amicitia (Roman)	⟨ Mary Magdalene (Christian)
⟨Amphictyonis (Greek)	⟨ Parvarti (Indian)
⟨Benzautin (Japanese)	⟨ Philia (Greek)
⟨Drvaspa (Persian)	⟨ Sekhmet (Egyptian)
⟨Kwan Yin (Japanese and Chinese)	⟨ Sif (Teutonic)

Let's take a closer look at some of these fine women.

Friendly Myths and Legends

Perhaps the most beautiful story of true-hearted friendship for all of humankind comes from the Far East. It begins with Kwan Yin, the goddess of wisdom, service, kindness, and benevolence. It is said that Kwan Yin was just about to reach the goal of Nirvana. As she stood at that incredible threshold, she heard the heart-wrenching sounds of crying. It was as if all the plants, animals, and people cried out in despair because someone of such virtue was leaving them. Without a second thought for herself, Kwan Yin turned back. In that moment, she determined to remain firmly on this side of Nirvana until every being (without exception) should precede her there.

To indicate her dedication, she openly exclaimed, "*If in time to come I am to obtain power to benefit all beings, may I now be endowed with a thousand hands and a thousand eyes.*" Her wish was immediately granted, giving her not only hands and eyes, but thousands of forms through which she could bring light to those in darkness, water to those who thirst, shade for those who are weary, medicine for the sick, a comforting presence for those who are sad, and generally be the best friend for which humankind could hope.

Upon having her wish fulfilled, she added yet more to her promises, "*A guard I would be to those without protection, a guide to travelers, and a bridge for the seeker of the Other Shore.*" The beauty of this promise is that the Pure Land, according to the Lotus Sutra, is actually within ourselves. So, to find our best friend, all we need to do is look within our heart where she manifests her many, many forms.

While it's hard to follow a performance such as that of Kwan Yin's, there is another goddess's story that caught my attention from Teutonic tradition. In it, the trickster Loki sneaks into Sif's bedroom and cuts off her beautiful golden hair. Thor was absolutely furious and made him promise to replace it. To fulfill this commitment, Loki gets the dwarves to make a magickal wig that would grow like Sif's natural hair.

Now, most folks wouldn't be too quick to forgive Loki, let alone offer him gentle hospitality, but not so with Sif. In the Elder Edda, we're told of Loki's return to a divine banquet even after being banished for killing one of the host's servants. Loki hoped to insult the gods, but before he could get a word in edgewise, Sif appeared. She brought him a cup of mead, offered civility, and basically told him to behave himself! It's uncertain whether Sif's efforts were for her friends at the party or perhaps because she had a soft spot for Loki, but in either case, this was an amazing gesture that speaks of handling difficult situations with friends with unique wisdom.

A third goddess whose story is rather curious is Sekhmet. The consort of Ptah and daughter of Ra, she is actually a much more ancient goddess than most, or as writings say, "One who was before the Gods, at the place of the beginning of time." She's generally characterized as someone who protects divine order, especially those things for which she is responsible. In addition, her actions seem directly motivated by devotion and love.

Now, on the surface that sounds like a perfect Divine candidate to govern over friendship—that is, until you find that she nearly destroyed all of humankind. Ah, but WHY did she do that? Well, it seems humans were conspiring to overthrow Ra and all the other gods (some her friends, others her family). She was absolutely furious to hear of this and wished to punish those with evil hearts and minds. So, every day she went out and killed those who were guilty. Sadly, so many had turned toward evil that it would not be long before there were no humans left.

Seeing this, Ra had a special beer made and poured 7,000 jugs upon the earth. When Sekmet saw it, she drank it up and found her heart filled with joy. From that day forward, she vowed never to slaughter again, and gained the title "One Who Comes in Peace." Other words used to describe her include beautiful, charming, and graceful! In fact, she bears some 4,000 names, including that of "fierce friend," because she can help us overcome physical and emotional harms and trauma in our life—effectively making inner peace. Having once seen how even the most justly motivated violence leads to no good, she helps us evolve past that in our spirits and our relationships, with total honesty as a guiding force.

Activity: Defining Friendship

Take a break from reading for a moment and get a notebook and pen or pencil. Now, go through the following questions and write down your answers. Let your mind and heart flow (be honest, after all, you're the only one who will read this).

1. How do you define true friendship?
2. On what do you base your friendships?
3. Do you feel the ones you have presently are equitable?
4. If your friendships are not balanced, what would it take to improve this situation?
5. When you think of your friends, do you mentally put them in different categories? If so, what? (For example, is one a "best friend" while another is a "dependable friend, but more distant"?) If so, how do you delineate those categories—by behavior, beliefs, etc?

6. What of your past friendships didn't work out or last (and why)?

7. Do you consider yourself a good friend (why or why not)?

8. Do you think you can improve the way you handle your current friendships, and if so, how?

9. If there is one person with whom you could develop a relationship, who would that be and why?

The answers to these questions will help you in many ways. For one (questions 2 and 4), it will improve the specifics of your rituals and spells (you can't get what you want if you're not clear about it!). Second (questions 3 and 6), if there are problems in your friendships, this list can become part of a "to do," with the Goddess as a helpmate in making personal improvements or changes, and in healing your relationships. Third, if you can identify why friendships didn't work in the past (question 5), it should help you avoid making those mistakes again. Lastly (question 7), why not work a ritual or spell that invokes a friendship goddess who can open the way for that relationship to blossom? Note, this isn't manipulating—but rather simply leaving out a magickal hand of welcome and waiting to see if it's accepted. You never know till you try!

Amiable Attributes

Now let's consider how these goddesses reveal to us some of the most important attributes of true friendship. Kwan Yin isn't difficult to perceive. Her endlessly giving nature speaks for itself. In this being, we come to see that true friendship often sets aside a person's shortcomings because it's guided by selfless love. When Kwan Yin looked upon humankind, she did not see our "sins" (if you will), but rather our potential, just as a good friend would. This doesn't mean necessarily allowing someone to wallow in negative behaviors, but rather emphasize and encourage the positive by word and deed.

Kwan Yin's friendship is not puffed up. She's a gentle guide and compassionate ally. So much so that she holds all things together in harmonious accord. Devotees claim they often feel her nearness, or see her in person. In this we see several more important facets of friendship—respect, equity, understanding, and staying close. Respecting your friends and honoring them in your life in both big and small ways is very important. This means knowing what's important to them, what hurts them, and what heals them (in other words, constantly bringing up past failures isn't a great idea!).

When friendships get out of balance or the people involved lose their ability to empathize, negative feelings can emerge and connections get lost. More importantly, in a world where people are often separated by hundreds (if not thousands) of miles, the last point of staying close is of ultimate value. Friendship takes time, effort, and communication if it's to last. The time and effort are really up to you, but open doorways for communication have been neatly provided by mail, phones, and the Internet! Who haven't you talked to in awhile? Give them a "ring" and re-establish that closeness.

Kwan Yin in Art

We learn a lot about this goddess from Eastern artistic depictions. A seventh century Tibetan painting, for example, shows her with a thousand arms with which to share blessings. The objects she holds include the dew of immortality, willow branches with which to spread compassion, the book of truth and honesty, and a jewel of wish fulfillment. In other pieces there are often children playing on her lap, suggesting not only real children, but the spiritual life that she nurtures in humankind. Her hands rest in her lap in meditation—thinking before acting, as a wise friend typically does. These same hands, palm held to palm, show a reverence for all things.

These depictions, and others like them, receive prominent displays in homes, workplaces, and even on the road to remind travelers of the invaluable worth of random acts of kindness and unselfish deeds. Is it any wonder that she was called the "Mother of 10 million Buddhas"—the idea being that from the feminine qualities of purity, compassion, and highest wisdom, Buddhas are born.

The beauty of Kwan Yin's example as a friend goes far beyond the emotional or physical level. Yes, she offers food, drink, comfort, healing, and other "mundane" assistance, but she also offers to be a bridge between the worlds. What a tremendous gift to give our friends—that of helping them achieve spiritual goals!

In this we see some comparative value to Drvaspa in terms of spiritual safety. In the book of common prayer of the Avesta we read, *"Unto the powerful Drvaspa, made by Mazda and holy, be propitiation, with sacrifice, prayer, propitiation, and glorification."* The reason Drvaspa deserved this honor had to do with her duties. It was her task specifically to help both people and animals and protect them from evil. In short order, the Persians dubbed her the guardian of children and friendship, who stood between them and any potential harm—as would any true friend.

This brings up another attribute of friendship to heed: that of safeguarding our friends and their loved ones from harm. While we can't always be present when danger arises, we can share with each other about those things worthy of concern. Mind you, a little diplomacy goes a long way in that regard. Your perception of danger and your friend's might differ dramatically, and you may find there are times to wisely "agree to disagree!"

Activity: Friendship Meditation

This meditation is designed for two or more people, the idea being to bring everyone into a closer rapport. To begin, have each person bring one candle to a nearby table, and have another larger candle central to represent the unification of everyone who participates. You can sit or stand, but hold hands. Begin breathing slowly in unison, in through your nose and out through your mouth. Become consciously aware of that breath as it spirals around the circle of your hands, joining with the heartbeat of the All.

Visualize a lovely pink-white light surrounding all present in a singular bubble. Within this space you are wholly safe, wholly united, wholly in symmetry. Sense the warmth being extended by your friend(s) and return it in equal measure. Think about what this person(s) means in your life, and what it would be like without them. As you do, let your spontaneous instincts guide you. You may wish to hold each other, share memories, cry or laugh—whatever feels right in this moment, celebrate each other— honor each other, and fill the room and your hearts with genuine love.

Moving along to Rome, we find Amica, whose name literally means friendship. Depictions of Amica show a beautiful woman clothed in green, her right hand bearing a full glass of wine, which is being offered to another. This offering of beverage is an ancient and fairly common custom of both hospitality and friendship, as it implies trust and welcome (even as we saw in the myth of Sif, earlier in this chapter). In fact, we see a similar custom with Amphictyonis (the Greek goddess of friendship and wine, as well as the motivator of international accord). While one might suspect that wine was offered by Amphictyonis to smooth global relations, the tradition stands firm. In both these goddesses' stories, wine symbolizes the joy of friendship and the laughter it brings to our souls. Bundled together, this makes a lovely reminder that friends open their doors and their hearts to each other—sharing in all the things that make us human.

The Friendship Goddess for Men

Friendship is not something unknown to men, but it's certainly an emotion they typically deal with differently than women. Friendships between men often exhibit some competitiveness, yet also a fierce loyalty that keeps things in balance. So, to which goddesses can men look to help them with their friendly interactions? One that comes immediately to mind is not a "goddess" per se, but an angel named Mihr who governs platonic love and companionship (this being is also said to help heal wallowing friendships). I have often found that men (not being quite as physically expressive) are more comfortable with a sense of personal space in their friendships, which makes Mihr's platonic aspect most appealing.

Two other goddesses that might prove more approachable for men are Artemis and Athena. Artemis was a goddess of the hunt, which was historically the men's venue. She was also someone who refused to follow traditional gender-oriented roles. Thus, Artemis can help both men and women overcome those boundaries that often hold back the expression of friendship, and a more complete understanding of the whole person(s) involved in any relationship. She is also an excellent goddess on which to call upon for insight if you're having trouble with a woman friend.

Finally, we come to Athena. In mythology, it was she who gave men a soul and helped Prometheus steal fire from the heavens (a friend in need is a friend indeed!). She is characterized as the goddess of war, courage, and friendship. Most importantly for men, during stressful times (even heated words), Athena tempers potential testosterone overload with gentle counsel. There are times to fight, times to flee, and times to simply wait. Recognizing the timing for right and proper action or inaction in our friendships will certainly make the road smoother.

A Man's Friendship Fetish

If you'd like to make yourself a portable token to help you connect with any of these goddess figures, you'll need a swatch of silver or white cloth (white is a traditional color for all these beings). Upon this, draw an upward pointing arrow (for Artemis and also a symbol that protects friendships). Also gather a small piece of lead, a pinch of sandalwood, turquoise, and a feather. Bundle these together on the night of a full moon while saying:

Goddess hear my wish and prayer

Where friendship grows, let my heart dare

To the foundations built by lead

By the aroma of sandalwood be staid

With a turquoise protect and charm

By the feather keep safe from harm

In all my true friendships guide and abide

In all my true friendships stand by my side.

So mote it be.

Carry this with you when spending time with good friends, or when wishing to build stronger friendships.

Common Symbols

Symbols for friendship goddesses aren't quite so easily defined. Unlike the Maiden, which has become a more universal archetype, the Friendship Goddess is a little more personalized. As we already noted in the opening of this chapter, her symbols might very well shift from culture to culture, depending on that society's prevalent traditions and customs. So, in giving you potential Friendship Goddess symbols, I'm also going to take a moment to explain the reasoning—from there you can tweak and personalize until it all fits together in your mind and heart.

☾ **Colors:** Yellow and golden orange. Yellow represents the sun and blessings, and friends are most certainly a treasured blessing. Golden orange, to me, represents the harvest. Because good, long-term friendships require hard work to maintain, this color supports the reaping of that labor!

☾ **Moon phases:** Use the waxing moon when you're trying to meet new friends or develop a new friendship. Use the full moon when working magick for your long-term friendships, and use the waning moon (or dark moon) to resolve the ending of a friendship in an amicable way.

☾ **Stones:** Chrysoprase (for selfless and tension-free friendships), lodestone (for attracting friends or making "connections"), turquoise (to protect your friendships), pink tourmaline (gentle love), any stones ruled by Venus (for happiness and

devotion), and stones ruled by the Water element (for compassion, peace, and reconciliation between friends).

(**Hours:** Dawn (for a newly starting friendship or renewal
within one), 2 a.m. to ease negativity in a friendship, 9 a.m.
for helpfulness toward others, 2 p.m. for improving your
overall relationship with each other, 7 p.m. for celebrating
differences and similarities between you, and 10 p.m. for
clear-headed decisions regarding your friends. Also the
month of August, for harmony and unity.

(**Season:** I always think of summer for its social nature.

(**Plants:** Sweetpea, rose (pink or yellow), lemon, passion
flower, ivy (friendship during adversity).

(**Other items:** Knots to symbolize unity and connection.

Celebrating Friendship

Throughout the world's history there have been some interesting ways
of honoring and celebrating friendship. Among the Balonda, when two
men agree to be friends, they have a ritual called "Kasendi." They sit opposite each other holding hands with a vessel of beer nearby. Tiny cuts
are made on each of the clasped hands, the face, and the stomach. Grass
gets pressed to each of these points, and then each man dips the grass in
his beer mug. These are exchanged and consumed, creating blood relations. After it has been completed, gifts are exchanged—both parties always give their most precious possessions. By tradition, these men are
now bound to assist each other in every way possible.

The giving of gifts to fulfill a pact of deep friendship isn't that uncommon.
We see it in the Bible between Jonathan and David. To quote from I Sam. 17:55:

> ...And it came to pass, when he had made an end of speaking
> unto Saul, that the soul of Jonathan was knit with the soul of
> David, and Jonathan loved him as his own soul. And Saul took
> him that day, and would let him go no more home to his father's
> house. Then Jonathan and David [7] made a covenant, because
> he loved him as his own soul. And Jonathan stripped himself
> of the robe that was upon him, and gave it to David, and his
> garments, even to his sword, and to his bow, and to his girdle.

Looking to yet another culture's means of celebrating friendship, Tacitus,
speaking of the arrangement among the Germans by which each military
chief was surrounded by younger companions and friends in arms, says:

There is great emulation among the companions, which shall possess the highest place in the favor of their chief; and among the chiefs, which shall excel in the number and valor of his companions. It is their dignity, their strength, to be always surrounded with a large body of select youth, an ornament in peace, a bulwark in war.

Further along we read:

...Elevated by friendship to the pitch of noblest enthusiasm, these were among the favorite saints of Greek legend and history. In a word, the chivalry of Hellas found its motive force in friendship rather than in the love of women; and the motive force of all chivalry is a generous, soul-exalting, unselfish passion. The fruit which friendship bore among the Greeks was courage in the face of danger, indifference to life when honor was at stake, patriotic ardor, the love of liberty, and lion-hearted rivalry in battle. "Tyrants," said Plato, "stand in awe of friend."

While I cannot say that most of what's presented in these three brief historical accounts is really suited to modern friendships, the stories illustrate that this particular relationship had its own rituals and customs even as did marriage. Thus, in considering the way you celebrate your friendships, my best piece of advice is to first consider your friend(s) and what might really tickle their fancy and their heart.

In particular, perhaps consider a semi-regular mini-ritual where you sit and share with each other in sacred space. You can invoke a goddess of your choice to bless that time, and come up with various activities that are truly meaningful to your relationship. Even if you can only do this once a year (or even once every few years), it will serve to keep the ties between you strong and healthy while you're apart.

To provide a personal example, I have friends in various states that I see very irregularly. Whenever we talk or write, I watch for unique pieces of information that show I'm really paying attention. Then, when we do get together, I'll pick out little gifts and plan a meal that reflects the information I've put together. It's really fun, shows how I feel, and supports the reconnection process (if you feed them, they will come!). Beyond this idea, there are so many other options, such as making two scrying mirrors through which you can communicate, carrying the same stone in your power pouches, keeping pictures on your altar, etc. Don't hinder your creativity here. So long as you find a way to celebrate your friends as the treasure they are, the Goddess will be pleased.

3

God as Lover/Husband

Goddess as Lover/Wife

God as Lover/Husband

Thou art God.

So, *which goddess is able to live with one god alone?*
The first goddess that comes to mind is Isis. Perhaps by choosing the quote from Propertius Sextus, my partner in this book did not intend to imply that a goddess cannot be monogamous. In fact, Isis was *not* able to live with one god alone: With the great love of her lord Osiris, they brought into manifestation their child, Horus. So I might go so far as to agree with my writing companion's choice of quotes in this case, but I choose to agree with only the second half of that quote (page 91). Which goddess indeed? Isis and many others.

Do I think all the gods and goddesses were heterosexual monogamists? Not any more than I think all of humanity is heterosexual monogamists. I bring this up because in our world we tend to make it so clear that the exception to the majority is welcome, that sometimes folk forget that the majority is also welcome.

When we look at the gods as lovers, we tend to have a very wide vision. Look at yourself as a lover. How many lovers have you had? Does that mean that you are not monogamous? I have had many more than a few; and yet, I consider myself monogamous because the very first definition of the word includes; "during a period of time" and during this period of time, I have "a single sexual partner."

Monogamy

1. The practice or condition of having a single sexual partner during a period of time. (*American Heritage Dictionary of the English Language, Fourth Edition.* ©2000 by Houghton Mifflin Company.) Now, please do not understand me to be the poster boy for monogamy. I have been involved in polyamourous relationships and I have broken the promises of monogamy on occasion. Like most folk, I have been with many people in even this short lifetime. Like a few, I have discovered that I like being the person I am right now. While that person happens to adore monogamy, I remember when I had other preferences and I would not dream of saying that any one way is right for another person.

Also, please do not think I am a spokesperson for white heterosexuals. Having been adopted, it is my understanding from having spoken to my birth mother that you can't judge a book by its cover. Insofar as the heterosexual part, I am sure I would be attracted to men if they weren't so, well, unattractive to me.

It is necessary to point out that when we examine lore, we are looking at a lifetime of an immortal. Finding references to a deity that has had multiple lovers does not mean that the deity was non-monogamous. Finding reference to a deity that has more than one wife does not mean that the deity was a bigamist. Finally, finding a deity that has had same-sex lovers does not mean that deity was gay. Yes, non-monogamy, bigamy, and homosexuality have been clearly recorded in Pagan lore, but none of these or their more vanilla counterparts are necessary, set-fast rules. If you disagree, find a gay man who has had sex with a woman and tell him that he is not gay because he once had sex with a woman.

These words—gay, heterosexual, and monogamous—are references not to the nature of a person's soul, but to a momentary state. Sometimes that state is a matter of a period in one's life. Other times it is a matter of a lifetime. I would hate to think that should I and my lover, who is currently female, be reborn as men, that we would reject each other simply due to our physical appearances.

This brings us to the next question: What is a lover? What is love for that matter? For the purpose of discussion, I will refer to the classic definition of Pagan origins. It was developed by the Greek and then incorporated and built upon by the Romans as having three parts.

Eros (Latin/Roman Amor): Erotic, carnal, sexual love. Eros is not only the word used to describe a type of love, but also a Greek god. Eros is most often cited as god of love, but he is much better cited as god of sexual desire. He is considered one of the oldest gods, perhaps of the same era as Chaos. In the mystery schools, Eros was considered "protagonus" or "first born." As his lineage is clearly given elsewhere, this is likely a reference to sexual love being a starting point and not a reference to the god Eros himself.

One of the lineages given for Eros is that his father is Erebus ("primal darkness") and his mother is Nyx ("night" or "darkness"). In reflecting on the creation myth in *A Wiccan Bible*, we understand the meaning of his name; 'desire.'

Philia (Latin/Roman Dilectio): Love of kith and kin. The epithet for Philadelphia is "the city of brotherly love." This is because its name comes from the term *philia.*

Agope (Latin/Roman Caritas): Divine love. Most often cited as the love a devoted member of a religion has for his or her deity.

Love and Wicca

When it comes to Wicca, love is where we split from many other religions. In other religions, the three forms of love remain separate. While some do teach that philia and eros can coexist, agope is always reserved for one's relationship with their god. That is to say, the love a person has for his god is taught to be of a higher nature.

In Wicca, there is no such separation. I have started each of the chapters I have written for this book in the same way because I want to drive home the idea that "Thou art God." In the matter of this chapter, it is how Wiccans understand the three seemingly separate categories of love.

In Wicca, as in other religions, agope is the word reserved for the love shared by a devotee to his deity. However, in Wicca, "Thou art God," and so is everyone else. Hence, because I am Wiccan, my goal is not to love my partner *as a goddess*, because it is not a simple matter of similes. My lover *is* my goddess and I her god, each sacred.

Hence, in Wicca, the art of being a lover is a threefold path. Please note that this does not address anything outside the art of being a lover. Philia can indeed exist outside the context of this chapter. Please also note that in the order in which these are presented, one can switch philia with eros because oftentimes good friendships come before sexual relationships.

1. **Eros** (Casual Sex): A sexual relationship in which your lover is not your friend.

2. **Eros and Philia** (Friendship): A sexual relationship
   where your lover is also your friend. This is either a sexual
   relationship that becomes a friendship or a friendship that
   becomes a sexual relationship.

3. **Eros, Philia, and Agope** (Divine Love): A sexual
   relationship in which your lover is not only your best friend,
   but the embodiment of that which you consider sacred.

Expanding on the principles presented in *A Wiccan Bible*, this three-fold path of love can be equated to the three aspects of humanity. The idea that each person is a combination of mind, body, and soul can be seen as the makeup of a lover as a combination of Eros, Philia, and Agope.

* Body (body/natural drive): Eros.

* Soul (nature/instinct): Philia.

* Mind (choice): Agope.

Love Knows Not Gender

You will note that within these definitions there is no reference to gender. Where there is great bias toward same-sex couples in our post-modern world, there is certainly enough lore to tell us that many of the ancient Pagan folk did not have such prejudices. Sure, there were certainly societies in which same-sex relationships were frowned upon, but remember that we are a post-modern religion. We get to decide who is who and what is what.

Dionysus (Greek): Described as very feminine, often wearing women's clothes, and had Adonis and Hermaphrodite as lovers.

Hyacinthus (Greek): Loved by both Apollo and Zephyrus, Hyacinthus returned the love of Apollo. In a jealous rage, Zephyrus (god of the winds from the West) blew a discus thrown by Apollo off its course. It struck Hyacinthus in the head, causing his death. From his blood, Apollo caused the growth of the flower that we today call the hyacinth.

Pan (Greek): Sometimes depicted in a randy chase of not only nymphs but of young male shepherds as well.

Ganymede (Greek): One of Zeus's many male lovers and cupbearer to the gods themselves. The story of Zeus and Ganymede was used for political purposes within Greek culture. Most notably this is found in Plato's use of the story to justify his lust for his male students. Thus we can be sure, as in modern society, homosexuality was not always welcome. After all, if it were accepted, then why would someone need to justify it.

This is why the Wiccan religion is absolutely clear that all acts of love and pleasure are sacred, otherwise the following line from the most popular version of the "Charge of the Goddess" would read just a bit different:

All acts of love and pleasure are my rituals.

You will note it does not say "All heterosexual acts of love and pleasure are my rituals."

In Perfect Love and Perfect Trust

Bide the Wiccan laws ye must,

in perfect love and perfect trust.

—From the version of the Wiccan Rede

copied into my Book of Shadows as a youth

I recall well a public ritual in which the guests were instructed that when they were challenged, they should respond with a scripted answer.

Guests were challenged: "It is better you rush upon this steely blade than enter this circle with fear in your heart. How do you enter this circle?"

Guests were to answer the challenge with: "In perfect love and perfect trust."

Setting aside for just a moment the ridiculous practice of putting a knife to the throat of your guests, let's look at the scripted answer. Remember, it is a public ritual. Are they expecting guests to have "perfect love and perfect trust" for perfect strangers? Or are they asking guests to enter their public ritual by first giving a perfect lie?

"Perfect love and perfect trust" is agope. It is the ability to love someone so much that you can get them so angry that they want to kill you, place a loaded gun in their hands, and have complete and total confidence that they will not pull the trigger. It is the unyielding belief that they would live, die, and even kill for you.

If you think that a willingness to kill for one's lover is a bit over the line, I am sorry you had such poor parents. You see, agope includes philia and all other forms of love. Thus with agope, motherly love is included. I have no doubt my mother and father were willing to kill to save their children, and because I feel that is a noble attribute, I welcome it in my lover.

Orpheus (Greek): Orpheus has been recorded as the greatest of the Greek musicians. Such was his talent that his songs could move inanimate objects to dance. Nothing did he love more than music, except Eurydice, the woman who had captured his heart. After Eurydice died from the bite of a snake, Orpheus confronted death itself (Hades) in order to return her to his arms. While Hades would have normally dismissed the demand as he had so many times, the song of their love was so great that even death could not refuse the request. There was, however, one condition. Hades sent Orpheus from the underworld with the assurance that Eurydice would be right behind him all the way to the surface, but that if he had any doubt, she would once again be ripped from him. As he neared the surface, Orpheus looked back only to see that his love was indeed right behind him. But with that expression of doubt, she was returned to the underworld, never again to be by Orpheus's side. This story warns us that without "perfect trust" there can not be "perfect love" (agope).

Pyramus (Babylonian): The story of Pyramus and his love Thisbe was likely the inspiration for Shakespeare's *Romeo and Juliet.* The parents of these two lovers refused to allow the two to see each other, so they decided to elope and meet in a secret place. When Thisbe arrived at that secret place, she encountered a lioness whose mouth was stained with the blood of a recent kill. She fled in fear, dropping the cloak that Pyramus had given her. When Pyramus arrived, he saw the lioness and the cloak that the lioness had destroyed and stained with blood. In sorrow, he fell to his knees and began to cry. Thinking his love was lost forever, he drove his sword (a gift from Thisbe) into his chest. Hearing his cries, Thisbe returned to that secret spot to find her love dying at her feet. She begged him to wait and then took her own life with his sword so they could enter into the afterlife in each others' arms. She fell limp, he embraced her, and they crossed to the next world in the way that they had hoped to live in this world, together in each others' arms.

Some of the Many Gods of Love

I remember sitting in a workshop being taught by the coauthor of this book, Patricia Telesco. I doubt it is a perfect quote, but I remember her firmly stating something in the order of *Love is the greatest magick of all.* So true is that statement, that throughout Pagan lore, we see time and time again that this thing we call love could not possibly be anything short of divinely inspired.

Aengus the Younger (Celtic): Also known as Angus, Anghus, Aonghus, Angus Og, and Oengus Mac Oc. The Irish Celtic son of the Dagda by Boann, Aengus is often depicted with four birds flying about his head. Those birds were said to be his inspirational kiss, which could fly off at any time toward potential lovers. It is easy to draw a connection between his birds and the arrows of Cupid.

Aizen-Myoo (Japanese): Also known as Aizen Myo'o. Japanese god of love who was worshipped by prostitute and musician alike.

Amor (Roman): So similar to the Roman Cupid that he is most often cited as being another name for the same god. Elsewhere, lore states that he is a predecessor to Cupid.

Cupid (Roman): As with Eros, his Greek counterpart, his name means *desire*. Cupid is most often depicted as a winged youth whose arrows pierce the heart to inspire love.

Eros (Greek): Described previously, but included here to further illustrate Divine inspiration. Eros is often depicted as Cupid is, with bow and arrows to inspire love.

Kama (Hindu): God of love who is depicted much as Cupid is, with bow and arrows that serve the same purpose: to inspire love.

Musubi-no-Kami (Japanese): Lore tells maidens that if they should happen to be walking by a cherry tree, Musubi-no-Kami might leap from that tree in the form of a beautiful young man offering cherry blossoms. Should she accept, her perfect lover will come into her life and later become her spouse. If she does not, she will be forever lonely. The message here seems to be that when true love is offered, jump on the opportunity because it probably will not come again.

Takami-Musubi (Japanese): The Shinto sky god said to be the source of divine love (agope).

And What of Love Scorned?

There is also lore that warns us against rejecting the potential of love. No, we should not accept every advance. If you want a warning about that, see the many lovers of Zeus. But neither should we close our hearts to the potential of love in its many forms.

Narcissus (Greek and Roman): In Roman lore, a beautiful youth was pursued by many a young nymph (one named Echo stands out), but he rejected them all. He chose instead to adore only himself. One day, while gazing into a body of water, he caught site of his own reflection. So charmed was he by that sight, he stood there gazing at it until he died. As he died, Echo watched, but was able to do nothing. As a result, in despair over the loss of her love, she faded into almost nothingness.

In the earlier Greek version, he is the same self-centered youth, but instead of being pursued by Echo or other women, he is loved by Ameinias.

Again, he rejects that love. So Ameinias, whose love is beyond infatuation, arrives at his doorstep with a sword and takes his own life, cursing Narcissus as he dies. That curse being that Narcissus will also know what it feels like to be in love with someone who refuses to return that love. Narcissus later finds that when he is unable to return his love in his own reflection.

In both the Greek and Roman depiction, the modern message is clear. In humility, I quote the very first thing I remember my young lady friend saying to me: "Get over yourself."

All of these examples and more are found in Pagan lore because humanity could not believe that something as sacred as love could find its origin in the human heart. Let's face it, humanity has not shown itself to be one of the finest species to have inhabited this world.

But that is what Wicca is all about. Yes, many say that Wicca was invented, but what religion was not? More importantly, what piece of art was not divinely inspired? Is not a religion an art unto itself? Is not the Wiccan Circle within which our rituals are conducted also called the Circle of Art? I believe very much that our religion is a post-modern recreation, but I also believe it came into manifestation right when it was needed and its creation was divinely inspired.

If I were to sum up Wicca in one line, it would be: "Wicca is the art of love."

In the glory of our Lord and Lady, so mote it be.

A closing note...

In 269 C.E., Bishop Valentine was beheaded by the Pagan Emperor of Rome. He was later made a Saint by the Roman Catholic Church and is today celebrated on "Valentine's Day" for his long-established work in helping Roman's (particularly soldiers) to write love letters.

It seems that barbarism has been the law of many religions, not just the ones we seem intent on claiming were barbaric. It is my sincere hope that this chapter will help us to see that the true nature of law is love itself. Love is the Law!

Goddess as Lover/Wife

—Patricia Telesco

"Hymn to Aphrodite (part 2)"

I

Peer of the gods, the happiest man I seem
Sitting before thee, rapt at thy sight, hearing
Thy soft laughter and thy voice most gentle,
Speaking so sweetly.

II

Then in my bosom my heart wildly flutters,
And, when on thee I gaze never so little,
Bereft am I of all power of utterance,
My tongue is useless.

III

There rushes at once through my flesh tingling fire,
My eyes are deprived of all power of vision,
My ears hear nothing by sounds of winds roaring,
And all is blackness.

IV

Down courses in streams the sweat of emotion,
A dread trembling o'erwhelms me, paler than I
Than dried grass in autumn, and in my madness
Dead I seem almost.

—Sappho

*Tell me who is able to keep his bed chaste, or which goddess is
able to live with one god alone?*

—Propertius Sextus

Throughout global myths and legends, the God and Goddess have
united in a variety of ways. Where they walk as lovers or life mates,
blossoms sprout and a font of creative energy wells beneath their feet.
Such stories imply that the union of the ultimate masculine and feminine
attributes was important to not only "genesis," but also to keeping time
moving forward. Among these tales, we find the following names appearing again and again as archetypal lovers or wives:

☾ Aphrodite/Venus (Greco-Roman)   ☾ Isis (Egyptian)

☾ Erzulie (Voudon)   ☾ Oshun (Afro-Caribbean)

☾ Freyja (Norse)   ☾ Parvati (Indian)

☾ Gauri (Hindu)   ☾ Pele (Hawaiian)

☾ Hathor (Egyptian)   ☾ Radha (Indian)

☾ Hera (Greek)   ☾ Shakti (Tantric)

Passion, love, and romance are, not surprisingly, also important to
humans. We need to feel needed, we need to understand our roles as
lovers, and if we so choose, to embrace the role of life mate. Perhaps
more importantly, we need to begin to clarify the difference between
intimacy, infatuation, passion, and true romantic love (as opposed to the
love of a friend or pet). Many experts on relationships feel that three out
of the four following characteristics must be present to maintain long-
term relationships:

☾ **Intimacy:** A sense of closeness, both emotionally and physically. Friendship and fellowship.

☾ **Infatuation:** A little too rose-colored, the original flush of
falling in love is often infatuation wherein the object of affection can do no wrong and everyone lives happily ever after.
While this gets a relationship up and running, it does not last.

☾ **Love:** An active emotion that cares for, and accepts, one's
partner in truthfulness and trustfulness. Love is a choice to
accept, and to work toward the sacred "we."

☾ **Passion:** Sexual behavior and drive, usually accompanied
by a feeling of lust. Note that passion occurs outside the
context of intimacy and love, and can be directed toward
an art, a hobby, etc.

Next comes the obvious question as to how various goddesses taught us about love, passion, and relationships. How can these beings help us reclaim love as a binding tie for couples of all types in the future? Before answering that question in detail, I have to bring up a minor glitch. Out of necessity, this chapter must look at love from the male-female union. Historically, there are very few archetypes of gay or bisexual love on which to draw. In addition, since the purpose of this book is to balance God with Goddess and consider them equally, it behooves me to approach the subject matter from a more traditional vantage point. Please know, however, that there is a little bit of God and Goddess in all of us. So as you read about goddesses and their male lovers, allow the lessons you find there to motivate your relationships in positive ways, no matter your choice of lifestyle.

Myths and Legends

While there are certainly many goddesses of love, and those celebrated as good wives and companions, perhaps the most widely known goddess in this category is Aphrodite. She appears repeatedly in Greek mythology and reveals a lot about the spirit of love, passion, and companionship at each juncture. For example, Aphrodite indirectly caused the Trojan War when she persuaded Paris to give her the golden apple, promising him Helen of Troy as a wife in return. What she neglected to tell him was that the dear woman was already married. When Paris whisked Helen away, her husband, King Menelaus, decided to attack Troy. I'd dare to say it was not the first (nor the last) war to be waged due to love.

It's important to note in our studies of Aphrodite that there seem to be two different beings in Greek literature. The first, reported by Hesiod, is the daughter of Uranus (Aphrodite Urania, the goddess of spiritual love). The other is the daughter of Zeus (Aphrodite Pandemos, the goddess of physical attentions and attractions). Somewhere along the line the stories of these two got rolled into one powerful goddess of love, beauty, and sexual rapture.

We're told that Aphrodite married Hephaestus, but both had many wild affairs. Ares, Hermes, and Dionysus all apparently loved Aphrodite, and she also enjoyed mortal lovers, including Adonis. In myths, it's not surprising to see such a being giving birth to Eros (erotic love), Anteros (god who punishes those who scorn love or do not return love of others), and Hymenaios (the god of marriage).

Along with this rather formidable entourage, the stories of Aphrodite often show her in the company of the Graces (or charities), the personification of charm and beauty in all things. It is they, along with the Muses, who bestow talent and inspiration to humankind. So here we find love in its many forms giving birth to the arts, which are celebrated by the Greeks as nearly sacred.

Activity: Give Form to Your Love

Make a list of about three to five people in your life that you love. Next to each person's name, qualify the type of love you have toward them (make special note if there's more than one kind of love involved, for a husband could embody both friendly love and erotic love). Now, get a piece of paper and crayons or any other artistic media with which you're comfortable and give form to your love. Think about how each type of love makes you feel. If it had a color or shape, what would it be? Bring that form, shape, color, sound, taste, or feel to life through the media you've chosen.

This activity serves two purposes. First, it gives you the chance to qualify your feelings in a different manner. We often find it hard to vocalize what we truly feel, but putting those emotions into another form can prove very revealing and helpful. Second, once this work is done, you can use it as an amulet or charm that protects and nurtures your feelings toward the person(s) about whom the initial word activity was directed. You can give it to them as a gift with an explanation, keep it in a safe place, or put it on your altar to receive ongoing blessings.

I find it interesting that in mythology, lover/wife goddesses often have connections to oceans and lakes. Consider that Aphrodite Urania was sea-born and Isis's Latin epithet was Sella Maris (star of the sea). It would appear that the Neo-Pagan correlation between emotions and the element of Water is nothing new whatsoever, but rather an ancient connection worthy of thought.

In Egypt and beyond, the name Isis became synonymous with the concept of a devoted mother and wife, and all that is best about the feminine aspect. Her devotion to Osiris became legendary. Isis had married Osiris and ruled Egypt with him, but Set was very jealous. He tricked Osiris into climbing in a box, which was then sealed with melted lead and tossed into the Nile.

Isis was both angry and grievous. She used everything in her power to locate Osiris's body, which was found in Byblos. Upon hearing word, Isis immediately traveled to Byblos hoping to use the magick Thoth taught her, to conceive Osiris's child, which she was able to do. But Set's jealousy was not to be undone.

When Set found the body of Osiris, he cut it into 14 parts, and scattered it throughout Egypt. Isis was horrified, but she set herself to the task at hand, namely reclaiming her husband's body. She searched high and low, finding all but his manhood (which was eaten by a crab). Assembling these together, she performed the Rite of Rebirth, beating the winds of immortality into Osiris's nose and mouth with her wings. This granted Osiris eternity, and he ascended. With such a story of fidelity, it's no surprise that she became known as the goddess of love, giver of life, divine healer, and protectress of marriage. And it would seem that many of these roles still pertain to lovers or wives—love can heal, and it can be fiercely protective.

Before we leave Egypt, let's not forget Hathor. This celestial goddess and mistress of heaven was also a deity of love, joy, music, and dance. Where Horus was the God-King, Hathor was the Goddess-Queen, also dubbed the Lady of Life, or more simply, Powerful One.

One story of Hathor reveals her more sensual nature, having it intertwined with a seasonal myth. When the Egyptian sun god Ra went off pouting for an extended time (likely an allusion to winter) because the baboon god taunted him, it was Hathor who coaxed him out of hiding. Her solution to his broodish state was to dance and strip before him. Not surprisingly, Ra quickly forgot his hurt feelings and rejoined the gods.

Depictions of Hathor show her as a woman with cow's horns and the sun between the horns (another potential illustration of her connection with Ra). She carries a sistrum, the sacred instrument of her priestesses. When sistrums were played correctly in Hathor's honor it was thought to invoke passion and fertility. This might help to explain her one rather brassy title—Lady of the Vulva!

Finally, let's turn our eyes toward India. Parvati is incredibly celebrated in the Hindu pantheon, having received a lot of attention from poets, musicians, painters, and dancers. She is nearly as complex a goddess as Isis, being adored for her spiritual love, her beauty, and her absolute sensual womanhood. Parvati was born specifically to marry Shiva and balance out his aloof ascetic life with dynamic activity and life-giving energy.

In traditional stories, Parvati's encounters with Shiva are filled with gentle and wise attentions. She takes great delight in listening to his deeds and in his handsome appearance. From the moment she knew she was to marry him, her response was one of grace and honor. Mind you, Parvati wasn't alone in making this fate possible. Kama, the god of love, helped inspire Shiva's lust. Shiva wasn't very happy about this and turned Kama to dust. Nonetheless, Parvati was determined and offered to perform ascetic austerities to win Shiva's love.

In Hindu custom, if one is heroic and persistent enough, a person's spirit generates so much heat that the gods are forced to grant that person a wish to keep the world from burning up. Perhaps more important in Parvati's story is the fact that this successful effort proved her very worthy. Parvati showed Shiva she could compete with him in his own realm, using control and fortitude to master her physical nature.

Once the marriage was performed, Parvati and Shiva went to Mount Kailasha to enjoy uninterrupted passion. As Shiva embraced her, the sweat of this divine body mingles with Kama's ashes and brings him back to life. In fact, so great was their lovemaking that it shook the cosmos. From here forward, Shiva and Parvati's married and family life is portrayed as harmonious, blissful, and calm. Iconography shows the two typically sitting in a happy, intimate embrace. But the relationship hardly ends there!

Shiva and Parvati enjoyed discussing philosophy, being both teacher and student for each other. She also loved to make him a special drink, prepare a quilt to keep him warm, and massage his feet. Truly anything that served her mate, made him happy and gave him pleasure or comfort wasn't overlooked. But don't be fooled. It is Parvati who upholds the order of dharma, who enhances the world's life, who protects both home and civilization with her presence, and who is credited with "domesticating" Shiva! It is even said that her tender care is what kept him from madness. In addition, she stresses the importance of custom to her husband whose ascetic nature often ignored such matters. Where Shiva is a god of excess, both ascetic and sexual, Parvati plays the role of modifier, as a good lover and wife might even in this world!

Attributes

Goddesses need their gods and vise versa. Perhaps more accurately, Goddess energy and attributes need God energies and attributes (and vise versa). No matter what skin you're in, we all have aspects of both mingling in our spirit. This is very important to remember as you read about these beings. Don't attempt to box in deity, or yourself, when it comes to the lover or "wife" that you could become.

In reviewing various beings and their choice of lovers or mates, it seems that both gain power and many other positive things from the union, in particular respect, joy, and a sense of wholeness. The relationships are not one-sided, nor does one master the other—as both are Divine! That, in itself, is a very good starting point for exploring the attributes of the Goddess as a lover and wife, being equally yoked. Our relationships, for them to be healthy, require some type of give-and-take—some reasonable balance point.

For insight into our inner Goddess as a lover, let's turn our attention to Shakti, who is the ultimate feminine principle of Kundalini energy. Shakti is personified as loving, playful, sincere, protective, and even somewhat innocent in her approach to sexuality. She embraces us in times of trouble, and teaches us how to channel our passions in the best possible ways.

To understand Shakti better, we must look at her aspects. The first is Sakti, the underlying divine power that inspires creativity (a great attribute in a lover!). There is active energy here on which we can draw and also a very real font of inventiveness to celebrate! In particular, come to Sakti when your relationship is getting dry or tedious. She'll spice things right up!

The second aspect of Shakti is Maya, the energy of delusion. At first this might seem very negative, but if we are to understand love and passion, we must also know its darker side. This shadow is one of selfish, self-centered ideas and actions, which are not part of any truly healthy relationship. Maya is also a goddess who will battle with our demons—deluding them so that light and life can be renewed. What demons might those be? Well, the memories of past hurts that keep you from true intimacy, a tendency to seek after unhealthy situations, a cycle of attracting the wrong type of companions, and other similar grey clouds come to mind.

Finally, the third aspect is Prakriti, who is the physical nature. All material things come to be through Prakriti, including our instincts. Prakriti also sustains and stabilizes the physical, offering us balanced passions that also bear a cosmic awareness of the spiritual connections implied in intimacy. This, I think, is very important. Many people have gotten very confused or emotionally damaged by not understanding that even the most playful fling can create spiritual ties between those involved. Prakriti is an excellent goddess to call upon in keeping your connections mindful, clear, and clean.

Against love and karma there is no defense.

—Hindu proverb

Activity: Your Lover/Wife Attributes

For this activity, I want you to think about what attributes of the Lover Goddess and the Wife Goddess you possess. This might be more difficult for men, but if you simply think in terms of characteristics and positive qualities, it should make the process easier. Ask yourself questions such as: Do you see yourself as nurturing? Are you inventive in bed? Do you inspire the best in your partner(s)?

When you're done considering those attributes, ask yourself what characteristics you'd like to develop. Make a list, and put the name of the goddess next to each item that you feel can most help you in those goals. Then, one at a time over the following days and weeks, develop relationships with those beings in your meditations. Call upon them in prayer, asking for help in the areas you've outlined while continuing to make honest efforts to develop new qualities on your own.

For example, if you want to be a more thoughtful mate, Parvati seems an excellent helper because she was ever-aware of her husband's needs. What are your mate's needs? What little things can you do to make him or her know how much they matter to you? Go to Parvati in thoughtfulness and ask for her guidance. Keep track of your progress, and celebrate even the smallest success as they will encourage ongoing positive transformation.

~❧❦~

Another Goddess who provides us with food for thought on being a lover is Oshun, the Nigerian and Brazilian goddess of love and happiness— indeed, everything sweet and good in life. Oshun loves to dance and play, she's very sensual and sensitive. Her followers leave her little gifts at riverbanks because receiving her blessing means life will be very worth living, indeed!

As the consort to the thunder god, Oshun teaches us the art of flirtation and its importance to both being a lover and a wife. In addition, her womanly wiles always accent the positive. In Oshun's realm, it's not about being stunningly beautiful by worldly standards, but about knowing how to use what you've got most effectively (again, this is where knowing how to flirt comes in handy!).

One story aptly illustrates Oshun's cleverness and charm. It begins with the blacksmith Ogun, who yearned to live in the forest. While he had been cursed to a life of hard labor, he felt himself strong enough to return to the forest and leave his troubles behind. It did not take long for Ogun's absence to be noticed, because the tools necessary for everyday life became less and less available. All of the Orisha (guardian spirits) tried to persuade him to return, even his previous wife, Yemaya, but no one had any success.

At this juncture, Oshun bravely went before the Orisha with a plan. Likewise, she wanted to try to change Ogun's mind and improve his mood. The Orisha laughed, thinking her much too young and inexperienced to succeed. Nonetheless, Obatala, one of the Orisha, felt it could do no harm to let the young woman make an attempt, perhaps wisely seeing something in Oshun that the others did not.

So, with determination wrapped around her waist, along with five yellow scarves and a container of honey, she advanced upon the forest. Oshun danced in earnest, revealing a little, then hiding a little, and all the while acting as if she was blissfully unaware of Ogun's presence. Ogun could not resist coming closer to look. Oshun pulled back ever so slightly. When Ogun got close enough, she smeared honey on his lips and retreated again. This routine, which acted as an enticing spell, continued, each time Oshun slowly moving Ogun closer to town. Before he knew any better, he was back in the city, surrounded by the Orisha. It was now a point of honor that he stay; otherwise he would appear weak or fooled. He also learned that sweetness was a powerful weapon, as was the clever ways of a young woman who knew how to put her best foot forward!

Another sizzling, sexy goddess is Freya from Norse tradition. This woman knew how to have lots of fun and lots of zeal in the bedroom. Considering she was the consort to both Odin and Frey (the chief of the gods and his brother), she had to be pretty energetic! All that sexual tension finds a balance point in Norse realms with Frigg, who is Odin's wife. Lest her husband get totally distracted by Freya, Frigg keeps a close watch over her relationships and all those of mortals. In fact, it's said she was the only person ever able to pull the wool over Odin's eye!

I find this acceptance of consorts rather interesting considering our times. Many people have taken on alternative lifestyles that include more than one intimate mate for long periods. In this, the individuals seem to cooperate; one balancing the other or inspiring the other, even as Freya and Frigg do here. These beings, therefore, offer a good option for patronesses for those who are polyamorous, part of extended family households, or other similarly unique love-styles.

For more conventional relationships, specifically marriage, let's look to Venus's attributes. Venus rules all aspects of love, specifically our sentiments and those things and people we truly value. Through her we learn about our tastes, what really pleases us, and what makes us truly happy, hopefully in the relationship we have at hand. She also reminds us to really *feel*, to really *experience* our relationships fully.

Venus stresses balance and refinement in our relationships. Every moment of every day, even the bland ones, are just as important as those big moments. She reminds us that if we don't do that daily bit of relationship maintenance, we're likely to find our loves and passions suffering. One of Venus's keywords is *unity*, but it's hard to remain united if you let weeds grow in love's garden. This was a harsh lesson that Venus herself learned while married to Vulcan, but knowing her true love was Mars (in fact, she had a child by him, the goddess of accord, Harmonia).

Now before you think this all sounds rather dull, there is nothing humdrum about this goddess's sexual prowess. Just because there's a long-term relationship here that will inevitably experience periodic difficulties, it doesn't mean that magnetism or attraction are lost! She simply tempers the passion of being "in love" (again, refinement) by removing the rose-colored glasses. Venus reminds us to see things as they truly are, and then either accept your partner as he or she is, or ask yourself if you're in the right relationship!

Interestingly enough, Venus also rules over money matters. In this, you can turn to her for guidance on creating a budget that includes enough bumper room for those little gifts and leisure activities that can mean so much when timed "just right!" This goddess has a natural appreciation for all the good things in life—romance, poetry, food, movies—those things that can sooth the heart or provide a mutually enjoyable outlet away from life's worries and responsibilities. In this, she gives us yet another lesson. The lover or wife who does not allow for time with his or her mate for "fun" will likely be unhappy and discontent. Playtime is one of the most important factors to long-term intimacy.

Lover/Wife for Men

As mentioned earlier in this chapter, when thinking about the Lover/ Wife Goddess in your life, the first step is to release yourself from the constraints of gender and simply be who and what you are. The Goddess's passion, her playfulness, her clever approach to both relationships and sex, can be of tremendous value to you. In addition, the Wife Goddess can help you become a better companion to your partner by bringing a wise, proactive energy to your relationship(s).

In heterosexual relationships, the Lover/Wife Goddess teaches you about your mate—specifically that most women want intimate connec tions, not necessarily just sex. On the other hand, one should not assume that the Goddess doesn't periodically have intense drives, even as you do. True sagacity comes in knowing the difference.

Activity: Honoring the Lover/Wife on Your Altar

Whenever you're making mindful efforts at connecting with the Lover/ Wife within and without, it's nice to have some sort of visual representa- tion of that effort on your altar (typically a Goddess image of some sort). Why do this? For one thing, it honors the deity with whom you've chosen to work. For another, it gives you a very important opportunity to learn more about this being (what items are sacred to her, for example) so those, too, can adorn your sacred space. For example, if you've chosen Venus, you might keep some salt water in your cauldron (since she was born of the sea). Finally, having this image in a visible spot serves as a daily reminder of what you're trying to accomplish. Stop here each morn- ing, light a candle, and whisper a prayer into the Goddess's ear. This acts as a morning letter of welcome that opens the door for her to share your home and your life.

~❧❧~

Some would claim that men will never truly understand the women in their lives. With the Lover/Wife Goddess as your helper, I think you might surprise a few people! The keynotes to remember about this aspect in- clude connection, presence, openness, and patience. Take the time to really get to know your partner—to really connect with them on every level possible. Be present and attentive, not off wool-gathering or think- ing of 101 tasks on your calendar.

Openness is a dicey topic for some men, yet if we look at our Lover/ Wife, they shared things with their mates from philosophy to learning what beer he might like! However, that kind of communication can't be a one-way street, or connection will never happen.

Finally, be patient. Be patient with yourself above all else. You're trying to look at yourself and your relationships in a whole new way. You're trying to tap into the Lover/Wife within and let that energy guide a bit of your sensitive, insightful self. And most importantly, you're reclaiming your relationships as sacred. These things take reverence, tenderness, and responsiveness—they don't just develop over night! Thou art God! Thou art Goddess!

Common Symbols

The Lover/Wife has many moods. Sometimes she is soft and subtle. Sometimes she is caring and compassionate. Sometimes she is fierce and frisky. So, in thinking of the symbols for the Goddess as Lover and Wife, we must consider all of these facets of her personality.

☾ **Colors:** Deep red (passion), pink (gentle love), light orange (intimate communications), blue (renewing peace).

☾ **Moon phases:** Full moon (fulfillment), moon in Aries (overcoming any barriers between people), moon in Cancer (creativity), moon in Scorpio (passion and sexuality), moon in Pisces (sensitivity or empathy).

☾ **Stones:** Amber or cat's-eye (attractiveness), amethyst or jade (love), rhodocrosite or Tiger's eye (physical prowess), carnelian or sunstone (sexuality).

☾ **Hours:** Six a.m. (improved insights), 2 p.m. (building relationships), 7 p.m. (compassion), 10 p.m. (handling emotional issues rationally).

☾ **Seasons:** Late spring (growing passions) or summer (passion's fullness).

☾ **Plants:** Herbs and spices associated with passion and love, including aphrodisiacs. Some known aromatics for these goals include: catnip (attractiveness), nutmeg (devotion), lavender (peace and joy), rose and berry (love), cinnamon or violet (lust), ginger or jasmine (to attract men), and musk or vetivert (to attract women). Some common aphrodisiacs are:

❖ American Ginseng (*Panax quinque folius*): Native Americans used this as a love charm.

❖ Anice (*Pimpinella anisum*): Has stimulating properties.

❖ Asparagus (*Asparagus officinales*): Eating this encourages many lovers.

❖ Arabian Coffee (*Coffea arabica*): Mix this with cardamom and honey for best results.

❖ Avocado (*Persea americana*): The flesh contains beauty-enhancing oil.

❖ Basil (*Ocimum sanctum* or *Ocimum basilicum*): Sacred to Hindus, one leaf a day improves creativity and stamina in the bedroom.

❖ Cacao tree (*Theobroma cacao*): Beloved chocolate, especially effective with honey or vanilla.

❖ Cardamom (*Elettaria cardamomum*): Add to coffee for erotic energy.

❖ Cayenne pepper (*Capsicum annuum*, Solanaceae): Used in limited quantities to improve your sex drive.

❖ Celery (*Apium graveolenns*): Eat this (fresher is better) to strengthen the organs associated with sex.

❖ Cinnamon (*Cinnamomum zeylanicum*): Use this spice to stimulate eroticism.

❖ Clary (*Salvia sclarea*): Add to wine as an aphrodisiac.

❖ Coconut palm (*Cocos nucifera*): Eat coconut or drink the milk mixed with honey

❖ Coriander (Coriandrum sativum): Mingling with wine is said to increase semen.

❖ Date palm (*Phoenix dactilifera*): Dates or palm wine both act as aphrodisiacs.

❖ Garlic (*Liliaseae*): Garlic juice and coriander is purported to increase your staying power in bed.

❖ Gingko (*Ginko biloba*): Excellent energizer for men.

❖ Horseradish (*Armoracia rusticana*): Forments love.

❖ Kava Kava (*Piper methysticum*): Increases your performance.

❖ Licorice (*Glycyrrhiza glabra*): in tea form, especially helpful to women.

❖ Lovage (*Levisticum o f ficinale*): Helps to open the heart and sexual chakaras.

❖ Mustard (*Brassica nigra*): For virility.

❖ Pimento (*Pimenta dioica*): Mixed with cocoa for aphrodisiac quality.

❖ Saffron (*Crocus sativus*): Increases sexual desire for women.

❖ Sassafras (*Sassa fras albidum*): The love herb of Native Americans. Excellent for a massage oil to heat things up.

❖ Sunflower (*Helianthus annus*): Both the seeds and oil act as sexual stimulants.

❖ Sweet potato (*Ipomoea batatas*): Improves sex drive for women.

❖ Vanilla (*Vanilla plani folia*): Best when blended with cocoa.

❖ Wheat (*Triticum aestivum*): Wheat germ contains natural estrogen and vitamin E, both excellent for women.

❖ Ylang-ylang (*Cananga odorata*): Aromatic oil that overcomes frigidity. Excellent component for massage oils.

❖ Yohimbe (*Corynanthe yohimbe*): Promotes potency in men.

(**Other items:** Other appropriate symbols for the wife include a wedding ring or knotted item (to imply the bonds between people). Representations for the lover might include erotic art, a phallic symbol, and a vulva symbol (such as the cup and dagger upon most magickal altars).

Honoring the Lover/Wife

The best way to honor and celebrate the Lover/Wife Goddess is through your relationships. Now, for any relationship to experience success, be it one of passion or a long-term commitment, the first step is that of knowing yourself in truthfulness. You cannot relate to your partner in any depth without first looking deep within. From that inner place of knowingness, the Lover/Wife Goddess teaches you to dance with another person in such a way that's both sexy and stable.

The next step comes from defining your partner—their wants, needs, desires, faults, and talents. Of which God or Goddess does this person remind you? If you can figure that out, then you can become the God or Goddess suitable to balance that situation. In such a relationship neither person loses himself or herself, but rather is nourished and fulfilled.

Now, it's not always easy to make the step toward awareness and developing that balance. That's where the sacred "we" comes into play. You celebrate your relationship in part by helping each other. Let new words unfold through the passions and/or love you hold for your partner. Be patient and open, and allow a little bit of the wild play along the edges of your times together. Blending with another person for life, or for a night, is very much like a waltz, you need to lead and follow, match movements, and slowly illustrate in motion all that you feel within.

Activity: Uni fied Breath

A fantastic way to attune yourself to another person is through unified breath, at least at the outset. Begin by sitting comfortably on the floor opposite one another. Shake out any tensions and simply begin to breathe deeply. Consciously strive for a pace that's comfortable to each of you—a pace you can mirror. When you get into that sync, continue for at least three minutes, slowly extending your aura toward each other. Reach out and stroke your partner's energy field. Get to know it intimately as your own. If it helps, take turns, but never actually physically touch the other person at this point.

Next, slowly work inward, coming closer and closer to the body with your hands and spirit. Remember to keep breathing together. When you get to the place of touch, touch very gently from head to toe. Get to know every inch. Memorize the areas where you sense a pleasurable response (you can come back to them later!).

Finally, indulge in giving each other all-over body rubs (still breathe in unison so you never loose that connection). Let nature take her course!

Another important aspect to honoring the Lover/Wife in your relationships is the concept of free choice. Love is a decision, and while we all want to give and receive love, love is earned. The best way to have that special "true" love develop is by remaining unattached. Attachment comes from ego—it's possessive and leads to jealousy and control issues. When love is elevated beyond the ego and selfishness, that's when you really connect and everything from a simple nod to the hottest night of sex has incredible meaning and power. The energy naturally begins to flow between the God and Goddess that you have become.

4

God at Work
Goddess at Work

God at Work

—A.J. Drew

Thou art God.

I have a very unique perspective on the Pagan community. As an author, I hear what most Pagans say during workshops and other opportunities for author/reader exchange. There I hear that most Pagans are not very concerned with matters of finance. But writing books is just my night job. During the day I run a Pagan shop in Columbus, Ohio. There I hear much the same story, but I see something completely different. There I see the best-selling products are those that claim to draw money. I firmly believe that such products work, but only when given a chance. Guess what? If you are honestly not concerned with drawing money, then you are not giving them that chance.

Let me tell you about the "R2B" society. At one point in my life, a friend and I were so frustrated with the question "what do you do?" that we agreed to always offer the same answer: "We are and encourage you to be." The title of the society, whose untracked membership is intended entirely as social commentary, comes from the shorthand of the statement: "v R n encourage u 2 B". Okay, it is silly. We were starving artists, so like most starving artists we sat around, drank wine, and tried to figure out two important matters. The first being the great mystery of life: Why are we here? The second being the great mystery of living: How are we going to pay the rent? Because our contemplation was not the answer people were looking for when they asked, "What do you do?" we created an entertaining answer: "We are and encourage you to be."

When someone asks you that question, nine times out of 10, they are really asking you how you pay your bills. I have great difficulty answering this question. I could say that I am a professional author, but that always invites trouble. The result is usually that someone receives an inflated idea of either my income or my ego. Other times they think I am telling a tale. What business is it of theirs anyway?

Maybe it is none of their business, but it is a valid question when one person seeks to learn about another person. Many of us spend more than a full third of our life at our work. If another third is spent asleep (oh, I wish), that means what we do at work is a full half of our waking hours. Toss in the time spent commuting to and from work, and guess what? Yep, we spend more time at work than we do at play. And yet most of us never think twice about inviting our Lord into the workplace. Why is that?

When I convinced a friend to make animal product–free soap for my Pagan store, I thought the product line would sell tremendously. But it was not until I convinced her to color a batch green and add a few select oils from a money-drawing recipe that the product line began to sell. Indeed, our most popular incenses, oils, and candles are the ones with the word "money" on the label.

With such little evidence of divinity in the workplace but so much hope of divine intervention in matters of income, I am starting to think that there are a great many people who have not found the connection between income and employment. The question "what do you do?" becomes "what do you do when you are not doing what you want to do?"

Question: Why can Pagan men make love all night long but Christian men cannot?

Answer: Christian men have to wake up and go to work in the morning.

If I were to create a practical line of prosperity candles, incense, and oils, I think I would start with titles such as Job Opportunity, Excellence at Work, Promotion, and Job Security. You see, I do believe very much that we have the ability to manifest our own destiny. I do very much believe that magick works and that we can work magick. But I also very much believe that in so doing, we invite our Lord into the workplace. Thus, if there is no workplace, then our invitation goes unanswered.

Here, too, we see objectification. In this case, it is the tendency to think the spell (object) is more important than the relationship to that spell. I have said time and time again that what we do in between ritual is infinitely more a part of being Wiccan than what we do in ritual. When it comes to such matters as money spells, what we do in between the spells is infinitely more important than the spell itself.

Now this is not to say that we should go to work with a hubcap-sized pentagram and read out loud the words from our Chant-O-Matic book. You see, neither magick nor divinity is the stand-out spooky things that they are often portrayed. In Wicca, both are seen as a part of the natural world. Nothing spooky to scare your workmates.

Instead, we invite our Lord into ourselves. We invite him to give us the inspiration and drive that is necessary to build prosperity. In our money spells, we thus see a prayer that asks those properties of our Lord that bring prosperity to become our own attributes; that we become the creators of our own prosperity.

Minimum-Wage Jobs

So, just how does one make a minimum-wage job a sacred place of work? To be honest, I do not know. While I am sure it can be done, I have yet to discover the method and thank the gods for that particularly lacking portion of my education. However, I can tell you how I made working at a convenience store sacred: I got out!

I am speaking of the job that directly preceded the worst moment of my life. Prior to taking that job, I had been so ill and disillusioned with my life that previously prosperous occupations had fallen away. And then, in what was probably a single instant, I discovered the secret, "thou art God," and understood that if I wanted a sacred workplace, that it was my responsibility to manifest it. That job at the convenience store where I was robbed at gunpoint so many times that I lost count; that job where I slaved for minimum wage, desperately seeking so much overtime that I would be able to put a little money aside; that job that many unemployed folk overlook out of some false sense of pride—that job was sacred! It was sacred because it put food in my belly. It was sacred because it was part of the path that gave me the ability to manifest the sacred workplace that I desired with all my heart—my own store.

No, I am not yet wealthy. Yes, I have experienced great setbacks. But with the exception of helping out friends who need trustworthy temporary employees at their business, I have been my own boss for more than 10 years. Sure, I work for an overly demanding slave driver. But that slave driver is me and I would not trade my boss for the nicest and most considerate employer. I am my own master.

This is not to say that all Wiccans should become self-employed. However, while it may seem at times that one can barely keep his head above water, this does mean that forward movement is an essential goal in the Wiccan religion. Even when we are just able to hold our ground, we do so because we aspire to do better in the future. Should we not hold that ground, then our aspirations will be, at best, more difficult to obtain and, at worst, impossible to obtain.

A Few Gods of Work

Understanding the idea of God in the workplace requires a bit of adaptation. This is because the Pagan god forms have not been allowed to evolve with humanity. Where once we grew, hunted, crafted, or in other ways acquired goods for ourselves and for trading, many of us do not have the hands-on experience of bringing a creation of work from birth to maturity. Most of today's jobs involve only a portion of that creative process.

As an example, this book is not the fruit of simply its authors. It is also the labor of its editor, copy editor, typesetter, printer, and let's not forget the folk in acquisitions and the owner of the publishing house. But instead of looking at this transformation and rejecting the gods as having no place in our work, we expand their role and see them as having evolved right alongside our work. As a result, the scribes become not only the gods of the author, but of the editors, typesetters, printers, and everyone involved in the process that was previously more of a one-man show.

Gods of Written Language

Patrons to authors, poets, historians, teachers, librarians, and anyone who works with the written word:

Nabu (Sumerian/Babylonian): Scribe to the gods as well as god of knowledge and the preservation of knowledge.

Nuada (Celtic): Also known as Nudd and Ludd. Irish god of poetry and writing.

Odin (Norse): Also known as Woden, Wodan, and Wotan. God of poetry who received the runes while hanging on the world tree. There is some dispute as to if the runes were initially used for magick or for writing. The argument is moot as the written word is magick.

Ogma (Celtic): The Irish Celtic god who created a written language called the Ogham.

Ogmios (Celtic): Also known as Ogmios Sun-Face. The French Celtic version of the Irish Ogma. Ogmios is said to have invented the alphabet of the Druids.

Tenjin (Japanese): Japanese god who taught humanity how to write.

Thoth (Egyptian): Inventor of writing in the Egyptian pantheon. Patron of authors and recordkeepers.

Wen-chang (Chinese): Also known as Wen-ch'ang. Taoist god of writing and literature. Patron to author, school teacher, and student.

Gods of Healing

Patrons to doctors, nurses, medics, veterinarians, and anyone working with medicine:

Apollo (Greek): Also known as Apollon. Greek god of medicine. But before calling on him for healing, I suggest you read the Appendix.

Asclepius (Greek): Also known as Asklepios and Aesculapius. Originally a culture hero, with time, Asclepius became one of the Greek gods of medicine and healing.

Enki (Sumerian): Keeper of the secrets of medicine, who shared them with humanity when needed.

Ro'o (Polynesian): Primarily a god of magickal healing.

Gods of the Smith and Forge

Patron of jewelry makers, smiths, and artisans who work with metal:

Funzi (African): Popular in the French Congo, Funzi taught the Fjort tribes how to work iron and copper.

Hephaestus (Greek): Also known as Hephaistos. Patron god of the blacksmith and, to a lesser degree, of all craftsmen.

Vulcan (Roman): God of not only fire, but the smith and craftsman's forge. Sometimes called by the more formal name Mulciber, which means "The Softener."

Gods of the Farm and of Negotiation With Nature

Patrons of farmers and those who negotiate with nature as an employment:

Basa-Jaun (Basque): The "Lord of the Woods" who taught humanity how to farm.

Buzyges (Greek): Culture hero who taught humanity in the use of animals to plough the earth.

Consus (Roman): Watches and protects stores of grain and food.

Gucumatz (Mayan): Also known as Kucumatz. Taught the Mayans the art of farming and negotiating with nature.

Nisse (Scandinavian): Also known as Gardvord. More of a house spirit that a god, Nisse is often described as a dwarf or short man who protects the farm and ensures a prosperous harvest.

Gods of Hunting and Fishing

Kat (Banks Islands): The god who taught the people of the Banks Islands the art of making canoes from logs. The Banks Islands are the westernmost islands of the Arctic Archipelago.

Kutkinnaku (Siberian): God who taught his people the art of both fishing and hunting.

Minga Bengale (African): An African god of hunting who taught humanity how to make nets and traps.

Tirawa (Native American): Pawnee sky god who instructed his people in the ways of hunting and fishing.

Gods of Various Other Occupations

Ambat (Melanesian): A potter himself, Ambat taught humanity the art of pottery and continues to lend his favor to those in that craft.

Marunogere (Melanesian): Instructed humanity on the art of home building.

Blood, Sweat, and Tears

You have read the list of gods at work, and chances are good that if you have spent any time at all in the "Pagan community" you know that the unemployment rate is greatly higher than in the greater community. By now, you have probably asked yourself why it is that our community seems so impoverished. On the other hand, you might be thinking just the opposite. Perhaps you have read a handful of spell books and you think that I am off my rocker to insist that work is sacred. Either way, you are probably wondering why it is that what I tell you here about the connection Wicca makes between prosperity and the workplace is so different from what you have read elsewhere.

The answer is that it is easier to be impoverished than to be wealthy or even financially secure. We see those green money-drawing candles and the books that tell us how to chant until we are knee-deep in cash, and we believe because we want to believe. The truth is that those green candles and books of money spells do work. After all, they are making a great deal of money for their creators.

Books of prosperity spells and books of money-drawing spells continue to litter the marketplace. The result is that folk honestly believe that this is what being involved in the Pagan community is. I am starting to sound like a scratched record, but this, too, is objectification. Instead of being concerned with the process of obtaining money (object), we are concerned with the object itself (money). In so doing, we have lost a very important part of prosperity. That important part is the concept that the process by which we improve our state of living is the process by which our soul is tempered.

Adversity is, for lack of a better word, good. It offers us the opportunity to overcome adversity. It is that by which the laws of nature improve the state of nature. One would think this would be a guiding principle in a "nature based" religion. Guess what? It is because "thou art God."

Now, if "thou art God," then that harvest god that you have been praying to for a bountiful harvest is the same harvest god that has to work and slave at the planting and tending of the crop long before that desired bountiful harvest. Those drops of blood, sweat, and tears are the implements of that prayer or ritual. They are that which the green money-drawing candle represents.

In the glory of our Lord and Lady, so mote it be.

Goddess at Work

—Patricia Telesco

Fires can't be made with dead embers,
nor can enthusiasm be stirred by spiritless men.
Enthusiasm in our daily work lightens e f fort and
turns even labor into pleasant tasks.

—James Baldwin

I would that our farmers when they cut down a forest felt some o f
that awe which the old Romans did when they came to thin, or let
in the light to, a consecrated grove (lucum conlucare), that is,
would believe that it is sacred to some god. The Roman made an
expiatory o f fering, and prayed, Whatever god or goddess thou
art to whom this grove is sacred, be propitious to me, my family,
and children, etc.

—Henry David Thoreau

In writing anything about the Work Goddess we face two small difficulties. First, there are a great many more gods written about in terms of
governing the trades and labor than goddesses. This isn't unexpected when
most of these myths began in hunter-gatherer societies.

The second problem is that most of the goddesses we do find have a
very specific role. Rather than have dominion over all trades or employment, they have but one or two focus points. Among the most common
are weavers, spinners and seamstresses, midwives, domestic artisans,
and healers. So, in writing this chapter I've had to get a little creative in
applying overall attributes of some beings to adjust with our modern,
workaday world where women do much more than just cook, clean,
gather, and mend!

115

The following are names from different traditions that are appropriate for the Work Goddess:

☾ Aphrodite (Greek)

☾ Brigit (Celtic)

☾ Chalmecacioatl (Aztec)

☾ Hestia (Greek)

☾ Holda (Teutonic)

☾ Isis (Egyptian)

☾ Mawshai (Assam)

☾ Minerva (Roman)

☾ Pecunia (Roman)

☾ Po Inunogar (Vietnamese)

☾ Shri (Indian)

☾ Ugadama (Japanese)

We will also be touching upon goddesses of excellence and skill (such as those listed in the following), since these two qualities dramatically influence human achievement in any career goal:

☾ Arete (Greek)

☾ Athena (Greek)

☾ Sarasvati (Jain)

☾ Sif (Scandinavian)

It would seem that the female Divine has much to teach us about making the most of our talents no matter where we may be, not to mention the most of our living situations 24-7. As spiritually minded folk, even flipping burgers has great soul-food potential if we just look at it in the right context. This is what Buddhists would call having right and proper livelihood and effort.

Specifically, pause for a moment to consider: what do you give your time? Is your labor something that nourishes wholeness? If not, how can you make it into something that will? Right effort recognizes that there are times to act and times to think. It also honestly appraises your abilities; we all have limits to our talent, depending on the setting. Don't have such lofty expectations that you continually fall short in your work, but instead approach your job honestly, stressing the positive and working on those things where you need to improve.

Right livelihood speaks to us of wants and needs. Even the most mundane of tasks *needs* to be done by someone. Perhaps that someone is you. You may not *want* to do that job, but it could prove to be a blessing not only to you, but those who also benefit from it. To provide an example, I hate doing dishes, yet it is a necessary task. In the setting of a Gathering, my doing the dishes can free up an elder or teacher to do something more important—their spirit-called jobs!

The message of the Work Goddess is relatively simple: Whenever you can, follow your bliss (do what you love and what you know you do exceptionally well). When circumstances make that impossible, BE the best you can be. Work joyfully and mindfully, allowing Spirit to flow through you and in you throughout the day. This, in turn, blesses others and cannot help but make your work environment a better place.

Myths and Legends of the Goddesses of Labor

It's kind of hard to imagine a god or goddess "working." In my mind's eye, I try to conjure the lovely Isis grabbing a briefcase or typing up a letter. It just doesn't quite seem apt. But if we consider that many deities were credited with Creation itself, one can certainly say that was a "work" of huge proportion. In fact, sometimes the Goddess is discussed as having labor during this mythical birthing process.

Still, God and Goddess are powerful. The work of keeping the universe moving isn't necessarily difficult for them. So how can we, in our workaday world, relate to beings who don't have to put in 40 hours to pay the rent and keep food on the table? To my thinking, the answer comes by focusing on those goddesses who taught humankind various skills, or who inspired excellence in their followers. By communing with the first, we can improve our skill sets, including transferable abilities. By touching the spirits of the second group, we move toward greater mastery.

We'll begin this quest by looking to Po Inunogar of the Cham people. This goddess is known throughout the community because of her legendary assistance in teaching the abilities necessary for creating a real civilization. Her story begins with her father, Po Kok, asking his daughter to go to the earth and rule over everything.

Together with the celestial, human, and earthly prince, Po Inunogar traveled and began setting up hamlets, villages, districts, and provinces. Once those were in place, she petitioned God to give the people annual festivals, to teach them how to cultivate rice, and also how to cure disease. So now the Cham had a place to live, food to eat, and ways to stay healthy! It's also worthy to note that she worked cooperatively with two other gods (Depatathor and Auloah) who assisted in common jobs and created religion among the people, which began with the writing of psalms! In this simple progression, we learn the value of organization and forethought in our jobs, and see that many hands can certainly lighten the load!

After introducing faith to the people, Po Inunogar taught the Cham all of the trades including land cultivation, fishing, the growing of grain, and even diplomacy! She strongly advocated having good foreign relations, especially with India. It seems this goddess was a global thinker who encouraged that approach in her followers and those she loved. In particular, she tried to convince her husband that invading neighboring nations was not a good vocation for a civilized country. Sadly, he did not listen.

One day while he was away from home on a conquest, she took a boat and sailed southward hoping to see her people once more. Upon arrival, she found her foster parents were already dead, which moved her to tears. In their memory, with her own hands, she built a shrine, cleared fields, and created gardens (almost as a living embodiment of the old saying, *if you want something done right, do it yourself!*). When these tasks were done, she also dedicated herself to seeing all of her country, developing its economy, and educating people about both virtue and customs. Again, there's much to learn here. Po Inunogar handled personal matters first, completed them with due diligence, then moved onto what she considered the next most important task. Her organizational skills rival some of the best executive assistants I've ever met!

Such was the service to the Cham people that Po Inunogar earned the title "Ana Celestial Jade Queen." It's interesting to note that in this part of the world jade is a stone of love, fortitude, and devotion. Every year, by the 10th month of the lunar year, people living in the vicinity of the Po Inunogar towers go there to present offerings on the goddess's altar and pray for her protection. In addition, in recent years, on the 23rd day of the third month of the lunar year, Brahminee monks of Cham cooperate with local people in organizing ceremonies of "ball dance" and "flower offering" to commemorate the goddess's ascension. These might be good alternative dates on which to honor the Working Goddess in your own life.

Activity: Past, Present, Future Employment

In reading about Po Inunogar, it would seem that her plans for not only her life, but those of her people, were well laid out. In order for the Work Goddess to manifest from within, we also need to consider our best laid plans. Consider for a moment the positions you've held in the past. Were they helpful to what you're doing now or what you hope to do in the future? Did you work in that position to the best of your ability, and if not—why?

What about your present working conditions? Are you making the most of them? Do you have a five-year plan in place for your career? If not, consider sitting down and thinking about specific goals to set for yourself. Don't be unrealistic (that will only discourage you). Instead, consider your time constraints and how you can best advance yourself without overextending your time budget. Put this plan in some noticeable location (perhaps the refrigerator door).

As you reach milestones, remember to stop and celebrate them somehow. Internalize what you've learned from that accomplishment. Light a candle and thank the Working Goddess, and pat yourself on the back for a job well done!

The second myth I'd like to explore is that of Yelamma because it resulted in an interesting ritual that dedicates young women to being sacred prostitutes! Now, at first you might wonder why we would look at such a thing, but as the world's oldest profession among women, it certainly bears consideration in our exploration of the Working Goddess! In addition, the stigma we associate with prostitution didn't occur nearly as much in countries where it was regulated as a profession.

Yelamma was a young woman from a lower caste household who was brought into another family's quarrel. Her story begins with Parasurama's father, who was enraged because his wife, Renuka, had impure thoughts—she had become attracted to another man. In his rage, he ordered Parasurama to cut off the head of his mother, which he did obediently. Out of sympathy, Yelamma took the dead Renuka in her arms. Because she was an outcaste, and therefore not allowed to touch someone of caste, Yelamma also had her head cut off.

The father now promised Parasurama a reward for his extraordinary fidelity. The son, in turn, asked to have his mother restored to life as his reward. The father approved and told him how to put Renuka's head back on her body. In his eagerness, Parasurama accidentally mixed up the heads. Since this mix-up, the woman with the high-caste head and the outcaste body has been worshipped as Mariamma (or Mari), the goddess of smallpox. The woman with the outcaste head and the high-caste body is worshipped as goddess Yelamma, to whom prostitutes are dedicated.

For centuries after this story was popularized, people brought their daughters twice a year and offered them into service as devadasis (the sacred prostitute). The ritual was basically a symbolic marriage of each girl to the goddess, which allowed her to hope for a fate similar to Yelamma, which was the improvement of her caste. The costs of temple dedication were often met by a man who wished to employ a particular devadasis favors after she had attained puberty.

After initiation, the new devadasi (or devadasi) returned to her home where she stayed until she reachedher maturity. On reaching puberty, she would go through another ceremony, giving herself to someone who could adequately pay for her services. Once again, she returned to her home briefly, and then the girl typically moved to the temple, or to the home of a specific man as a concubine.

While this sounds rather crass to our Western minds, for many girls, this represented a way to monetarily support her family while they could not have otherwise done so. For lower castes, in particular, it meant the untouchable becomes "touchable." Such women lived a relatively normal sexual life and exercised a fair degree of choice in choosing her sexual partners; and although he was not a husband, the relationship would often continue on a long-term basis. The professionalism of the devadasi became legendary.

In addition, it's important to note that those women within the temple walls performed useful functions such as cleaning, lighting lamps, dressing the deities, etc. They sang devotional songs and danced in celebration to the Goddess. They taught music and dance to other young girls to the point of keeping alive various classical Indian music and dances. Effectively, the devadasi became an integral part of all large Indian temples!

Sadly, in modern times the role of devadasi has transformed from one that was honored (to the point where every bride hoped to have a bead from a devadasi necklace as a blessing) into a dirty, back-parlor type industry. It is one that, outside the context of sacredness, played into human failings such as greed and unhealthy lust. Nonetheless, this negativity doesn't erase what Yelamma originally embodied.

So, what exactly is it that Yelamma teaches? For one, compassion toward others in our line of work. There are real rewards in so doing. In Yelamma's case, she earned the status of a goddess. The next thing Yelamma illustrated through her worshippers is that work can be a sacred thing if we but look at it differently. No matter in what position we begin our life, if we work with the best possible mindset and devote ourselves earnestly, we, too, can improve our figurative caste!

Finally, I'd like to look briefly at Arete, who will also appear again in the attributes section of this chapter. In Greek tradition, Arete attends the hero Menoikeus when he sacrifices himself to save Thebes. Her presence there speaks of his gift and his great talents. She and the goddess of virtue appear in the Greek stories together frequently, implying that excellence and virtue go hand in hand.

In addition, one myth tells of Arete becoming a Theban seeress. This temporary disguise allowed her to speak wisdoms from a softer visage without making people afraid because of her divinity. So now we have the sense that excellence not only begins with virtue, but also has sagacity and insight to guide it. No matter what your career, these are truly wonderful attributes for which to strive, and for which to seek out the face of the Working Goddess to assist in their development.

The Working Goddess's Attributes

Arete has already provided some wonderful insights into what constitutes the Working Goddess at her best, which is to be expected of the personification of valor and distinction. In the *Greek Lyric III Simonides* we read:

> Arete dwells on unclimable rocks and close to the gods tends a holy place. She may not be seen by the eyes of all mortals, but only by him on whom distressing sweat comes from within, the one who reaches the peak of manliness....

Lyric IV of Bacchvides goes on to say:

> If their bodies have perished ... their fame still lives; for Arete, shining among all men, is not dimmed, hidden by the lightless (veil) of night: flourishing constantly with undying fame she ranges over the land and the sea that drives many from their course. Look, now she honours, the glory-winning island of Aiakos and with garland-loving Euckleia (Good Repute) steers the city, she and wise Eunomia (Good Order), who has festivities as her portion and guards in peace the cities of pious men.

While this might sound lofty, this concept of excellence was among the most important focal points of the Homeric age. Those who strive for perfection help drive all of humankind toward an ideal. Thus, leadership was inseparable from true excellence. Ability feeds self-actualization, which in turn attracts people by its assurance. What was most interesting to me, however, and something that feeds into our discussion regarding excellence in our jobs, is the idea that those who are striving for these goals also have a real duty to others—a duty to maintain a certain nobility of action and thought. In other words, Arete challenges us to grow into our potential and become good role models not simply for our coworkers, but for everyone we meet!

And what about Sif, another goddess of skill and perfection? Here we have a very powerful warrior in her own right. Yet unlike some warrior beings, Sif retains all of her femininity and beauty. She's also a fabulous wife to Thor, and a goddess who grants improved skills to her followers if they're worthy. In Sif we discover that we need not give up any aspect of true self for our work, or to excel in our chosen life's path. We also discover that beauty need not be weak, and it need not be something that implies a lack of intelligence or ability (as we often see with the modern blond jokes).

Activity: Developing Your Excellence

For this activity pick out one aspect of your career in which you'd like to pursue greater skills to the point of achieving excellence. On a mundane level, ask yourself what you can do to improve. For example, do you need to take a night class or practice more? Whatever it is, decide how much time you can dedicate every week to giving of yourself to your goal.

Next, choose a Working Goddess to help you with that aim. You'll be invoking her in a spell. The spell begins by writing your goal on a piece of paper. You'll also need a small brazier or fire-safe container, a candle dedicated to the Goddess, and an aromatic that matches your goal. For example, if you need to improve your personal appearance on the work front, anoint the candle with lavender, primrose, or heather.

Place the candle on your altar or in a place where it can remain undisturbed for about one hour. Wait until the waxing to full moon if possible. Light the candle and invoke your chosen goddess with words meaningful to your situation. Ask her to bless and energize your efforts. Light your wish in the flames of her candle and let them burn to ashes in the brazier. The smoke carries that desire to the four winds. Use the ashes in a plant potter or other gardening effort to give strength to "growing" energy for your wishes. Blow out the candle after you've finished taking care of the ashes. Light it again any time you're going to study about or work on that particular attribute. This supports the original spell and provides more power with which to work.

A third goddess who teaches about work is one that you might not expect. In Rome, Hestia is the goddess of the hearth, home fire, and consequently, of domestic life. So where do the trades come into play? Well, in order to understand this, first you need to know that the ancient Greeks built the hearth in the center of the courtyard of the home. Around the edge of the courtyard was a porch. This arrangement allowed domestic life to proceed regardless of the weather, including the baking and the warming of wash water. Central to our focus, however, this was the fire used for all those things that fell under the category of home trades, which were indispensable. To me, this speaks very strongly of the ability to balance home and work on one platter, something with which many of us struggle. When work becomes overwhelming or stresses our relationships, Hestia is there to restore the symmetry.

Fourth in our exploration of the Work Goddess and her attributes, we come to Brigit, a Celtic sun goddess who also presided over inspiration (or the "fire in the head," as described in the "Song of Amergin"), battle prowess, goldsmithing, healing, and midwifery. In these skills we see that Brigit embodied both Fire and Water elementally, and it's interesting that her sacred springs and wells were used to bathe men and restore them to wholeness so they could go about their normal tasks! Turn to Brigit when you feel like your ability to enjoy your job has grown cold or your place at work is stagnating. Also call upon her when you need healing so you don't miss extra time on the job!

Last, but certainly not least, we'll examine the Indian goddess Lakshmi. The worship of this goddess is quite common in the Jain community of India (the merchants). The oldest known depiction of Lakshmi is found in central India dating to about the first century B.C.E. It shows her being anointed by elephants while sitting on a lotus. As the daughter of Indra and the wife of Vishnu, it is said that the power to uphold and protect the world comes through her.

More important to merchants, however, this plentiful goddess brings us both prosperity along with a sense of responsibility for appreciating and using our blessings wisely. Seek out this being especially when you need your job to provide adequately for you and/or your family, or name her as the patroness for a self-owned business. For verbal invocations or prayers by which to honor her, here are samples of hymns to Lakshmi from the "Sri Sukta," which is considered the ultimate hymn for honoring this goddess. The letters, syllables, and words in the 15 verses collectively form what is called the "sound body" of Lakshmi; in other words, the words are thought to carry her divine vibrations:

> May that divine Lakshmi grace me. I hereby invoke that Shri (Lakshmi) who is the embodiment of absolute bliss; who is of pleasant smile on her face; whose lustre is that of burnished gold; who is wet as it were, (just from the milky ocean) who is blazing with splendour, and is the embodiment of the fulfillment of all wishes; who satisfies the desire of her votaries; who is seated on the lotus and is beautiful like the lotus (Verses 3–4).

> O Lakshmi! I am born in this country with the heritage of wealth. May the friends of Lord Siva (Kubera, Lord of wealth and Kiriti, Lord of fame), come to me. May these (having take their abode with me), bestow on me fame and prosperity. I shall destroy the elder sister to Lakshmi, the embodiment of inauspiciousness and such evil as hunger, thirst and the like. O Lakshmi! Drive out from my abode all misfortunes and poverty (Verses 7–8).

Tuck one of the previous verses in your wallet, purse, or checkbook to keep money where it belongs!

By the way, Lakshmi is also an excellent helpmate when you need to improve your appreciation toward your work, or your culpability regarding how you spend the money you make.

The Work Goddess for Men

In seeking out a Work Goddess for men, the best choice seems to be Athena. Here you have a goddess of wisdom, war, the arts, industry, justice, and skill. In other words, she has a marvelous blend of the things that can make you more effective in the workplace, and also a lot of attributes to which men naturally relate.

Consider for a moment the number of heroes Athena assisted in their jobs throughout Greek mythology. First there's Asclepius. Athena favored him with the blood of Medusa, which could give or take life. With that gift in hand, Asclepius became known for his skills and was named the Patron of Healing!

Next we come to Hercules, who always seemed to have Athena helping him. During his sixth labor, she scared a flock of birds. During the 11th labor, Athena returned the Hesperidean apples back to the island. During the 12th labor, it's believed that she escorted Hercules out of the underworld, and finally when madness threatened him, she knocked him out, which prevented him from killing his mortal father. It would seem that as a patroness, one could do little better!

Odysseus is another example. Athena appeared throughout the *Odyssey* any time our hero faced certain danger in his journeys. So if your work entails any type of travel, Athena can be an apt protectress.

Fourth, we have Orestes. The Delphic Oracle of Apollo tells Orestes to kill his mother in order to avenge the death of his father. The Furies, however, did not take kindly to the killing of kin and they hounded Orestes endlessly. Realizing he must take some action, Apollo arranges to have Athena judge the case, and she favors Orestes, feeling that the influence of the gods had left him very vulnerable. In this, you can look to Athena when you're asked to perform tasks at work for which you feel unqualified, or called upon to act unethically in any way. In particular, the unwilling warrior may find real comfort in Athena in dealing with both duty and humanity.

Activity: Work and Play Spell

As Stephen King's character discovered in *The Shining*, all work and no play makes "Jack a dull boy." Athena seems to remind us that we need to keep our personal and professional time neatly balanced without losing anything in either space. This spell invokes her blessing on a charm that you can carry with you. To begin, pick out something that symbolizes your job (but it needs to be portable). For my work, for example, I chose a special pen that I use for signing books.

Wait until the day before (or days of) the full moon, as those days are sacred to this goddess. Take the item you've chosen beneath the lunar light and hold it up to the heavens saying something such as:

> Athena Ergane, Great Goddess of skill and labor
> See this emblem of my career
> In it my security and prosperity rests,
> and I would to do my job well
> Bless those efforts
> But in the times away from tasks, also inspire my humanness
> The child within who laughs and wishes
> Pour your energies into this token,
> and release them as needed into my life.
> By my will and your power, so be it!

Remember to carry the token with you regularly so it can influence the energies in and around your life.

Lastly, we consider Perseus as a fifth example of someone Athena assisted (albeit for her own purposes). When Perseus was sent on a nearly impossible quest to get Medusa's head, it was Athena and Hermes who provided him with the helmet of invisibility (used to trick three Graeae). They also got a wallet and winged sandals from the nymphs. It was the wallet into which Perseus would deposit Medusa's head so he wouldn't risk seeing it at any time in his journey. So, when you're feeling overexposed at the office or in the field, turn to Athena to grant some respite. Also call upon her when you need to move swiftly and safely about your work tasks.

In closing this section on Athena, I leave you with this excerpt from the "Hymn to Athena" by the Pagan writer and worshipper of the Ancients, Apollonius Sophistes:

> And since that time whene'er we want to please
> Her heart, we pray to Her in words like these:
> "Athena, hear me, Aegis-bearing maid,
> Thou daughter of the Mighty Father, aid
> In every bold endeavor, standing by,
> Companion on whose guidance I rely.
> Thou knowest I've forfilled my every vow,
> So please, I pray, be friendly to me now,
> And hold thy hand above my works and give
> Success on this and all the days I live."
> So hail to Thee, Athena, Wisdom's child,
> The source of thought and action reconciled,
> The bright-eyed bringer of abundant wit,
> Effective action's first prerequisite.
> And hail to all the Goddesses of yore,
> To all the ancient Gods that we adore!
> Perhaps my song hath pleased thine ears; if so,
> Thou might on me thy fruitful gifts bestow."

As it was written, so let it be done!

Common Symbols

As one might expect, the emblems for the Working Goddess varied by trade and her other attributes. As you create spells, charms, and rituals, think not only about the specific goal you have, but also the goddess upon whom you're calling for blessings as a good starting point. To this foundation, you can add these generalized symbolic components:

(**Colors:** Red (activity), yellow (communication-oriented jobs), green (prosperity and personal development), orange (the harvest of diligent labors), blue (motivating peace or joy in the job that you have).

(**Moon phases:** Waxing to full moon (for performance related magick), moon in Aries (developing skills and personal attributes), moon in Leo (learning or improving talents), moon in Virgo (financial boost), moon in Scorpio (developing a passion for your job), moon in Aquarius (benefiting from your labors).

(**Stones:** Bloodstone or malachite (success in business), carnelian (communication), amethyst (contentment), fluorite (improved focus), coral or salt (financial improvements), sunstone (energy), chrysoprase (success), sugilite (wisdom).

(**Hours:** Three a.m. (determination), 6 a.m. (tenacity), 8 a.m. (empowering your conscious mind), 9 a.m. (focus), 4 p.m. (timeliness and scheduling), 10 p.m. (clarity).

(**Season:** Spring (for growth and change).

(**Plants:** Pecan (attain or maintain a job), celery or lily (mental focus), alfalfa or tomato (prosperity), cinnamon or ginger (success).

(**Other items:** Varies by the goddess. Items that symbolize your job—for example, weaving and spinning goddesses such as Azal Uoh (Mayan) and Holda (Teutonic) might well be honored with yarn, needles, and other tools of their craft. Chalmecacioatl (the Aztec goddess of merchants and traders) or Pecunia (Roman goddess of tradesman's profits) might well be represented by the first dollar you earn, while His Shih (the Chinese goddess of perfume sellers) is best symbolized by aromatics!

Remember that this list is only a starting point. Use it as an idea-inspiring source rather than something to be followed unerringly. The two most important keys for success are trust in your own instincts and the voice of the Working Goddess with whom you're developing a relationship.

Celebrating the Work Goddess

Okay, let's face it, most of us don't often think about doing a song and dance to honor our job. Work is, well, work! Even so, without gainful employment, life would be much different and much more difficult. So it's good once in a while to stop, give thanks, and celebrate whatever jobs exist in our lives.

For timing of such rituals or activities, we can look to the ancients for assistance. For example, in ancient Egypt, the spring harvest festival honored the goddess Isis (the goddess of all trades), and it began on March 20. It was not uncommon for trade persons to bring their tools to a temple for blessing during this celebration.

Later in the year, on May 23, we find the people of Marta, Italy, honoring another goddess. Known as the Madonna of the Mountain, she watches over trade folk in a similar fashion as Isis does. And also similar to Isis's festival, everyone brings their tools to shrines to be blessed that day.

A third potential time frame is during October (the first 10 days of the fortnight following the autumn new moon). At this time, the goddess Saraswati is celebrated and worshiped. In particular, those pursuing excellence in learning new skills come to the goddess for her aid. All factories and workshops receive a sprucing up, and the tools with which a person works receive veneration for the service they provide. Overall, her festival day is excellent for spells or rituals focused on improving your knowledge of your job, or increasing your skills (particularly if you work in the arts).

And what might you do on your day of celebration? Well, cleanse, bless, and reenergize the implements of your trade. Perhaps you can meditate about your work, and how to improve yourself in that setting. Light a candle and say a prayer for your employer's continued success. If you're unhappy in your job, this is a good time to work magick for new opportunities, while also bolstering tenacious energy to continue effectively where you are until you can find another job. All in all, the best way to honor the Working Goddess in your life is by giving 100 percent to your job while "on the clock." That makes her smile, and often brings success quite naturally.

5

God of the Hearth and Home

Goddess of the Hearth and Home

God of the Hearth and Home

—A.J. Drew

Thou art God.

I have to tell you about the condominium complex I once lived in. It was called Hearth Stone Condominiums. After living there for about six months, I noticed something very odd. I had not seen a single chimney. In the entire complex, there was not a single hearth, or was there? A quick check of my dictionary and I discovered the word *hearth* is often synonymous with the word *home*. This is because before electric and gas heating, the hearth was the source of both hot meals and warm conversations. Every home had one, and beside its warmth was where the family would often gather. The hearth and the fire within it became the symbol of the spirit of the home. Okay, maybe the condominium complex can get away with using the word *hearth*, but I am still confused about their use of the word *stone*.

When you think of the word *Wicca*, what comes to mind? Maybe the casting of enchantments to win love. When you think of the term *Wiccan Ritual*, what comes to mind? Did you know that the word *pagan* comes from the Latin term for "country dweller"?

Many of today's Pagans live in the city, commute to work via mass transportation, and communicate via the Internet. Not exactly the life of a country dweller is it? Words change with lifestyles, and today those folk who live off the land are probably in the minority. But that does not mean that their way of looking at life needs to be in the minority. The ancient country dwellers must have been tremendously dedicated to the family, because without that family, they could not have survived. In today's modern world, is it any different?

In a conversation with my young lady friend, I made a joke about creating a new religion. "You already have," she told me. Where I believe all I have done is recite that which I have learned about Wicca in the context of how I have understood and applied it to my life, she believes I have described Wicca in such a way as to bring an entirely new meaning to the word. Her brother calls it *Familial Wicca.*

Invented? How could anyone *invent* something that has been so ingrained in the human experience that it is found again and again in Pagan lore? If Wicca is a modern reconstruction of ancient Pagan religions, then of course it is family centered. Not because your coven (or whatever fanciful word you wish to use) becomes closer to you than your family as some will lead you to believe, but because your coven *is* your family. For example, my father who was Lutheran is more of a Wiccan High Priest than any Wiccan High Priest I have ever met.

This is because it is more important that we *be* Wiccan than *play* Wiccan. Our Lord is much more than some stand-in during a ritual conducted by your local Pagan bookstore owner. My Lord is alive and well and living in my memories of a great man. My Lord is alive and well and living in the many great men this world has afforded me the opportunity to have known. All without respect to my religion, their religion, or anyone's religion.

If such a view gives you the opinion that I am not really Wiccan, so be it. I feel that what is in a person's heart is infinitely more important than what is on their lips. But at the same time, please do not consider yourself Wiccan unless you have entirely invented your image of our Lord. For as Wicca is a post-modern religion, each and every god form taken from Pagan lore is in fact a god form taken from another religion.

We are the old gods!
We are the new gods!
We are the same gods!
Some will never die!

—A modern Pagan chant

Likewise, I do not have to visualize the casting of the Circle that matters. Yes, I do so in ritual, but that ritualistic casting of the Circle dims when compared to what it represents—the finding, building, and maintaining of the home for the purpose of providing a safe place for the gathering of the family (ritual) and celebrations of life (the living of that life).

Circle strong and circle bright!

Merry meet! Enjoy the night!

The ancients knew that home and family were important. So rather than placing their many incarnations of God strictly in the heavens, they opened their doors and let him into their homes and lives rather than keeping him pinned up in some bookstore, waiting for the next opportunity to make the owner a buck or two.

Agni (Hindu): As the spark of life itself, he is alive in every living thing. However, his fires burn the brightest in the hearth and hearts of the home and family.

Domovoi (Russian): Also known as Domovoy. Sometimes called "the Grandfather," Domovoi is the spiritual master of the home. He lives in each home, or perhaps there is a separate Domovoi in each home. He is good spirited, watching over both home and residents, but he is also quite the trickster. His presence is often known by the rattling of hanging pots in the kitchen, the slamming of a window someone left open, or maybe the mystery of the hiding car keys. All ways to remind you that he is there.

Kamado-gami (Japanese): The Japanese protectors of the home. The Kamado-gami are said to be the very spirit of the hearth.

Penates (Roman): Also known as Di Penates. Their name means "The Inner Ones," and they are the Roman protectors of storerooms, root cellars, cupboards, and the stocks necessary to maintain a home. They are worshiped in the home with sacrifices from daily meals, which are cast into the hearth.

Svarog (Slavonic): Also known as Svarozic and Svarozits. He was once the highest god in the Slavonic pantheon. Originally a sun and fire god, as other gods grew in favor, he retained his connection to fire, but to the fire of the hearth in particular. As state grew more important than the home, he was vilified. As a result, he is sometimes cited as a fire demon despite his long history as a family guardian.

Thab-lha (Tibetan): A fierce fire god who, according to lore, will cause great suffering to anyone who would take action against the hearth and home.

Zao-jun (Chinese): Also known as Tsao-chün. His name means "Lord of the Hearth," but his attributes are not limited to the structure itself.

Rather, his name is a reference to the protector of the family. In accordance with Chinese lore, his image or idol is placed above the fireplace (hearth) so that he might watch over and protect the family. He is often depicted surrounded by children, given offerings of honey, and praised on New Year's eve.

The Man About the House

Of course, the ancients did not have to contend with some of the stereotypes and social settings that we as post-modern reinventors of Pagan ways must. In just a couple of generations, we have seen the role of the head of a household/home change wildly. Just a few decades ago, the maintenance of the home was the job of a woman. A housewife was the norm and a house husband was seen as a sissy. Then the women's movement came along and decided that a housewife role model was a patriarchal attempt to suppress women, so women took to the workplace. Wait a minute; stop right there. If both men and women left the home for the workplace, who was left in the home? Aha!

In our headfirst rush forward to acquire greater wealth to secure, furnish, and better the home, we have forgotten that a secure, furnished, and improved home is useless if it is not the center of our family. Personally, I would rather live in a shack warmed by the love of kith and kin, whose company I can enjoy, than a mansion where I never see kith and kin, who are only the mildest of acquaintances. I am not saying that it is necessary to forsake work to have a good family life. But neither am I saying that for a good income one must forsake family. In this and all things, the Wiccan seeks balance.

Certainly the lives of the ancient Pagans were more readily centered around the home, but there are clear steps that can be taken by modern Pagans to reestablish the home and family as sacred. Steps that invite not only or Lord into our home, but his Lady as well. The idea is to use that invitation to cause interaction between the lords and ladies of your home (you and the ones that you love).

What About the Hearth?

In our modern world, fireplaces are often few and far between. But in the same way that Wiccan rituals are to Wiccan lives, the fireplace is only a symbol of what is really going on. In days of old, the fireplace was the central heating system of the house, and so it became the central gathering point as well. For that reason, it became the symbol of home and its flames flickered as a representation of the spirit of that home. The household gathered before the flames for interaction, and thus the fire was seen as the family.

In modern times, the flickering of those flames has been replaced by the flickering of the TV. While discussion might come from what is seen there, I am sure you can see how replacing the representation of the spirit of the house with a TV can be damaging to that spirit. Please do not get me wrong, I adore *Will and Grace*, but using them as the spirit of my home just will not do. So, to further the interaction between the gods and goddesses of the home, one should turn away from that soul-sucking device and instead turn to the other members of the home for interaction and entertainment.

Activity: The Bardic Circle

Better yet, turn it all off! Once a month (and better it be when the moon is full), make the preparation of a meal a household event. Once that meal is ready, turn off all the electricity. Gather at the dining room table by only candlelight. Share a meal and a tale.

The host begins by telling a tale or joke, maybe singing a song or doing anything to entertain the table. When he is done, move clockwise to the next person seated at the table. Repeat until each person has provided a wee bit of entertainment and then begin again if you like. If you would like comedic relief at the end, conclude with the assurance that "Thou art Will and Grace."

Home Dedications and Blessings

Moving into a new home is a sacred occasion, but so is the realization that a home is sacred. So there is no need to up and move to dedicate and bless your home. More so, there is ongoing reason to do just that again and again, although perhaps one formal dedication and ongoing blessings is more in order.

Dedication: The home is the center of the family. As the family is the single most important thing in the Wiccan heart, the dedication of the home is one of the most sacred celebrations in our religion. It should be participated in by not only the kith and kin who will dwell within it, but by all those who share kinship and friendship with those who will. But if you are looking for some great secret ancient rite, you are reading the wrong book. You see, the modern term for a *home dedication* is a *house-warming party*. So send out those invitations, gather up the folk, and let's get started.

If you have land on which you can plant, establishing gardens in each of the four quarters of that land will bring the blessings of the four quarters to each. With respect to what will and will not grow in your climate, attempt to select plants that correspond to the elements associated with those quarters. A quick reference can be found in the back of *Wicca Spellcraft for Men* (I hope to provide a much larger reference at a later date). If space affords the opportunity, trees planted at each quarter are a great idea. Make the planting and tending of the gardens and trees a family event.

Mirrors placed on the outside of the front door are considered powerful wards against forces baneful to the home. Instead of purchasing a complete mirror from a department store, why not purchase the makings from your local craft store? With a few ribbons and a hot glue gun, you will be surprised at what you can create. Mirrors are also used as wards in the windows of the home.

Remember that the home warming party is just that, a "home" warming party. While the event might flow with spirit, letting the spirits flow can sometimes remove the focus from the event. In attempting to design activities and plan the party, try to remain centered on the event at hand.

Ongoing Blessings: Because the home is sacred in the Wiccan religion, Wiccans often take an extra step in assuring that our everyday lives are filled with reminders of that view.

The Grunge Box or Bottle: Oftentimes, something as simple as having a box or bottle next to the door will remind us to leave the outside where it belongs—outside. This is in the order of leaving work stress at work so that it will not infringe on the home. I have seen some really elaborate work utilizing stained glass and mirrors to create a kind of reverse Pandora's box, but something as simple and stylish as an old metal milk jug on the porch will do just fine. The idea is that before entering the home, one is visually reminded to leave the outside influences behind. So just before the entrance to the home, many Wiccans place an object to remind us to take a moment and visualize the emotional grunge of the day leaving the body and entering the grunge box or bottle.

Sage Smudging: Others choose to use a more formal device. It is widely believed that the smoke of sage (smudge sticks) and a few other herbs can be used to cleanse the body of negative energy. Keeping a smudge stick and a fire-safe bowl by the front door is always useful in protecting the home from outside influences that might find their way into the home on the shirttails of a bad day at work.

Sweet Grass: Although often cited as sage is (for purification), burning sweet grass in a similar manner is said to call and welcome beneficial spirits and uplift the soul.

Holy Water: Some shy away from the idea of keeping holy water by the front door because it reminds them too much of Roman Catholic traditions. But water combined with sea salt is a symbol of the union of the masculine and feminine principles of the universe, and thus life itself. Keeping a bowl of Wiccan holy water by the front door can go a long way towards grounding negative energy. Prior to entering the home, dip your fingers into the water and bring your fingers to your left shoulder to remind you of our Lady and the receptive energies of the universe, on your right shoulder to remind you of our Lord and the projective energies of the universe, then to your forehead to remind you of the intellect/mind by which you choose to accept these forces, and finally to your genitals to indicate that you are part of this creative force. Yes, the action is similar to a Christian crossing him- or herself, but the symbolism of the cross has a much longer history than Christianity.

Rethinking Our Religion

Despite the fact that Wicca is often cited as a "family religion," upon reading the many books offered by today's market one can easily miss that point. We are told that the gods are this and the gods are that, but we are rarely reminded that the gods (and goddesses) are us. In reference to the home, it is said that man is king of his castle. If "thou art God," then I ask you, are you not god of your home? If so, then is not that home intended to be thy heaven?

In the glory of our Lord and Lady, so mote it be.

Goddess of the
Hearth and Home

—Patricia Telesco

"Homeric Hymns to Hestia"

Hestia, in the high dwellings o f all, both deathless gods and men who walk on earth, you have gained an everlasting abode and highest honor: glorious is your portion and your right. For without you mortals hold no banquet—where one does not duly pour sweet wine in o f fering to Hestia both first and last.

Hestia, you who tend the holy house of the lord Apollo, the Far-shooter at goodly Pytho, with soft oil dripping ever from your locks, come now into this house, come, having one mind with Zeus the all-wise—draw near, and withal bestow grace upon my song.

This was an airy and unplastered cabin, fit to entertain a travel-ling god, and where a goddess might trail her garments. The winds which passed over my dwelling were such as sweep over the ridges o f mountains, bearing the broken strains, or celestial parts only, o f terrestrial music. The morning wind forever blows, the poem o f creation is uninterrupted; but few are the ears that hear it. Olympus is but the outside o f the earth everywhere.

—Henry David Thoreau

When you think of the word "home," what images immediately come to mind? Is it a safe haven that nurtures body, mind, and soul? Is it warm and welcoming? For spiritually oriented individuals, it's very important that our homes somehow reflect us as whole people, and also nurture our magick in substantive ways. Effectively, this sacred space is the center of your universe, so it's an area well worth our attention, and one to which we should be directing spells and rituals that evoke ongoing blessings.

So how do the hearth and home goddesses come into this picture? Well, it's interesting to note that in nearly every ancient community, the first part of a village, or the first part of a home that was built was the hearth. The fire represented life, warmth, safety, and love. People regarded the loss of the binding power of that light as a very ill omen, indeed. So it's not surprising to discover that many ancient goddesses cast a watchful eye on the home, the ovens, or fireplaces (which were often one and the same). Among them are:

(Aspelenie (Lithuanian)   (Hulda (Teutonic)
(Chinnintamma (Eastern Indian)   (Kamui fuchi (Japanese)
(Ghar Jenti (Asian)   (Kikimora (Slavonic)
(Hestia (Greek)   (Nantosuelta (Celtic)
(Hlodyn (Germanic)   (Vesta (Rome)

Now, some of you may be thinking that you only have a microwave or a toaster oven, so how does the Hearth Goddess affect you? Well, quite honestly, the Hearth Goddess should be part of any magickal home already, be it a hovel, hotel, high-rise, or houseboat! Every day when I light my Spirit candle, that action welcomes the Divine into my home and life. The Goddess isn't a pushy broad. She likes feeling welcome! Showing Her ongoing hospitality cannot help but improve the atmosphere of any home. So, if you haven't done so already, consider ways in which you can bring the Hearth Goddess back into your living spaces to reclaim their sanctity.

The Hearth of Myth

We'll begin our mythic adventures with Hestia. Of all the goddesses of Greece, the stories of Hestia reveal her as being the mildest, with a loving and tender heart. In the "Homeric Hymn to Aphrodite," Hestia is described as a queenly maid whom both Poseidon and Apollo sought to wed. Their passions for her would have easily caused a huge disruption on Olympus; thus, with wisdom, she refused both offers. Because of this staunch and insightful stand, her father (Zeus) gave her a much greater honor than any such marriage to another deity. She became the heart of every home and the protectress of family unity.

It's not surprising that lore credits her with being among the most ancient of Greek goddesses and having taught humans the skill of how to build houses. This is implied heavily in the Greek proverb "Start with Hestia," which basically means begin at the beginning! In fact, whenever a new town was developed, fire from Hestia's public hearth was used to start the ovens in the new community, thereby assuring unity.

Activity: The Sacred Flame

In the Greek tradition of fire-starting, we see a hint of something we could integrate when moving from one residence to the other—namely the keeping of an original flame or coal that's safely kept and protected. Now, since not everyone has a fireplace, we might have to get a little creative in applying the concept. Perhaps your sacred flame is a favorite lamp that you've had with you since you moved out of your parents' house. Perhaps it's a large pillar candle that was among your first magickal tools. Whatever you choose, find something that you can easily retain no matter where you live.

Once you've chosen this item, call upon the Hearth Goddess to bless and empower it. You might use an invocation such as:

Life of fire, Light of love

Send your blessings from above

By this item that honors Thee

Protect all within, your goodness freed!

Or if you'd like something more traditional, here are two samples from "Homeric Hymns":

Hestia, Thou who tends the holy house
of Lord Apollo, Pythian, Shooting Far,
Thou having hair that drips with silky oil,
approach this house and enter, of one mind
with All-Wise Zeus; and for my song grant grace.

Thou, Hestia, in ev'ry lofty home
of deathless Gods and folk who walk the Earth,
hath gained a seat eternal, honor grand;
Thy prize is fair and noble; lacking Thee,
feast not we mortals, if both first and last
we offer not sweet wine to Hestia.

Hestia protects all suppliants at every private house and city hall. None may be turned away lest the Goddess find offense. Her fire is sacred, being the center of Greek life. As goddess of the hearth, Hestia also presided over matters of personal security, joy, and hospitality. When a child was born, the parents walked them around a symbol of Hestia while reciting prayers so he or she would be accepted as a full part of the family. I rather like this tradition because it introduces the child to the spirit of the home, and the Hearth Goddess who protects it!

A second hearth goddess is Hulda, who is of Teutonic tradition. Her name means Sacred Spirit, which equates to the flame of life in every human being. Without Hulda's fires, without that spark, everything is inert. In fact, it was strongly believed that every cooking fire, which warmed the family, contained Hulda's life-giving spirit.

Hulda's myth mingles with the very beginnings of time when Hulda's energy spun out to create life. This energy left a trail that we now call the Milky Way, but which was also called Hulda's Road (or the Road of Souls). By this path, all beings can find their way back to the Monad, to the original hearth! Perhaps in Hulda's case "home" is where the hearth is!

Third we come to Nantosuelta, the Celtic goddess of the home. This goddess is described in myths as having various attributes including a little house, a bird, a beehive, a saucer or cup, a small cooking pot, and a honeycomb—in other words, all things associated with a happy and prosperous dwelling. Nantosuelta's stories indicate she also presided over areas of nourishment and health, and even sometimes carried a cornucopia! Thus, in this lovely woman we find energies that sustain and heal our sacred spaces and fill them to overflowing with peace and joy.

Nantosuelta's blessings seem very reminiscent of our fourth Hearth Goddess—Brigid (Brighid or Brigit). Having dominion over all fires (both in the physical and spiritual realms), this goddess of the home keeps the family warm by night and sustains them by day. Among this goddess's many abilities we find inspiration, creativity, healing, midwifery, and domestic arts, all continually stewing on her well-tended coals.

Brigid was active in promoting the welfare of livestock, especially cattle, which were very important to an agrarian community. She also seems to be a bit of a peacemaker, as she mediates in great conflicts between the Tuatha De Danann and their enemy, the Fomorians, for the possession of Ireland in the Battle of Magh Tuiredh. If that weren't enough to endear this goddess to human hearts, she was also married to the Fomorian king, Bres. Thus Brigid becomes an ancestor-deity, a mother-goddess whose main concern was the future well-being of Ireland (her HOME!).

"Blessings of Brigit" (Traditional Celtic Prayer)

Brigit daughter of Dugall the Brown, son of Aodh, son or Art, son of Conn,

Son of Criara, son of Cairbre, son of Cas, son of Cormac, son of Cartach, son of Conn

Each day and each night that I say the Descent of Brigid

I shall not be slain, I shall not be sworded

I shall not be put in a cell, I shall not be hewn

I shall not be riven, I shall not be anguished

I shall not be wounded, I shall not be blinded

I shall not be made naked, I shall not be left bare

Nor will Christ leave me forgotten

Nor fire shall burn me, nor sun shall burn me

Nor moon shall blanch me

The stories of Brigid became so powerful throughout Celtic lands that with the advent of Christianity she was portrayed as the midwife and foster mother of Christ. She is the perpetual friend and helper of Mary. Out of this sainthood, the feast of Imbolc became what Christians call her Feast of Purification. Nonetheless, this celebration mirrors many Pagan customs for the Goddess. Milk was poured out as an offering, special cakes were baked, and dolls in Brigid's image were created with loving care.

The girls of every household carried Bride dolls throughout town. They stopped at each house, where the women would present a small gift along with one of the cakes to the image. Finally, the girls ended up at one house where the Bride dolls were set in a window, followed by dancing until dawn and singing hymns to this goddess-saint. While there was more to the overall event than what's shared here, it's an amazing testament to the influence that this goddess of hearth and home wields, even to this day!

Attributes of the Goddess of Hearth and Home

The mingling of hearth goddesses with the home seems perfectly natural in that fire was integral to every part of our ancestors' lives. And while the connections are not always clear, it's important to explore the attributes that both offer to our homes. We'll begin this exploration with a hearth goddess strongly associated with all sacred fires, and also domestic fires—Vesta in Rome. We know that historically, the hearth and the family unit were the core of Roman society.

The priestesses of Vesta became the handmaidens of the hearth, and given charge of the Vestal fire so that it would never go out. To fail in this duty was sure to bring all manners of terrible luck to Rome—an unthinkable sin—so the Vestal Virgins attended their tasks with all due diligence (even as we should tend our homes!). Chosen between the ages of 6 and 10 years old from Rome's elite families, a priest would take the new Vestal in hand, saying: "I take you, you shall be the priestess of Vesta and you shall fulfill the sacred rites for the safety of the Roman people."

Each girl gave 30 years of her life in service to the Goddess (as many women give their families, if not more!). While this might sound like an arduous life, the Romans rewarded the Vestals with honors and privileges during service so long as they remained chaste, and after service they could become a private citizen. At that juncture they could now accept legacies, create wills, testify in court, and even free an accused person if she wished.

Activity: House Cleansing and Blessing

As we are talking about maintaining balance in our sacred spaces, this is a good moment to share more about house cleansing and blessing. Would you really want to welcome a hearth goddess into a home in spiritual or physical disarray? That's one of the reasons why churches are kept in good order—people want the God and Goddess to be pleased!

Now, the concept of cleansing and blessing doesn't mean you have to suddenly become the Martha Stewart or Miss Manners of Neo-Paganism! Trust me when I say that the Hearth Goddess is very pragmatic and understands each person's limits. What it does mean, rather, is that you should be mindful of the space you're in and make sure it's not collecting psychic dirt. This dirt might get left behind by you after a bad day, by friends who visit while under stress, and even by an angry stranger driving by (if your magickal defenses aren't wholly charged). So, regular cleansings and blessings are a really good idea through which you can invoke the Hearth Goddess and honor her too!

I usually combine spiritual cleansing with weekly chores. For example, you can add a bit of lemon juice or oil, or even plain salt, to water for washing the floors. Stir this counterclockwise (to decrease negativity) and say something such as:

Goddess of my home and heart,

Through this water, blessings impart

Wherever negativity and sadness lay
Gather and wash them neatly away!

When you dispose of the wash water, you dispose of the non-constructive energies!

If you want something more formalized you can certainly have a house blessing ritual, but I suggest everyone in the home take part if possible. It improves your overall results if all members support this goal in word or deed. Hold house blessings during the full moon, for all good things. Choose a Hearth Goddess on whom to call for blessings and ongoing protection (preferably one with whom you have an established relationship—your house patroness is ideal). While the ritual can take any form you wish, I recommend that you move through every room of your living space (going clockwise as much as possible to generate more positive power).

When done correctly, ongoing cleansings and blessings generate what I call the "ahhh" effect in a home. When people come to visit, their tensions seem to slip away and they sigh with comfort. In addition, you'll find this makes the inside of your house feel like a safe, private haven, even if you live in the middle of the city!

Last in our series of goddesses to look to in understanding the domestic goddess's attributes comes from Slavonic tradition. Her name is Kikimora, and she has an amazing sense of humor and duty. If a house-person is lazy, Kikimora tickled their children at night, whistled, and caused other little disruptions. If the house-person was diligent, on the other hand, she would spin and look after other small tasks on their behalf. When someone wished to please her, they would wash pots and pans in fern tea, and leave a bit of this in the cellar or behind the stove (her living spaces).

I like this goddess for two reasons. First, she rewards the diligent, but doesn't become overly harsh with those who have gotten off track. Rather, she uses small hints to remind them of what's important, of what *needs* doing. Second, she illustrates a sense of humor, which is an amazing coping mechanism and teacher for any household. Humor can make the hardest of days and lessons seem much less difficult. Embracing Kikimora keeps us on track, and in a very good head space!

The Hearth Goddess for Men: Cardea

While many men may not think themselves very domestic, I think that many men can still relate to the Hearth Goddess with little difficulty. Why? For two reasons. First, the God aspect is no stranger to fire (just ask Prometheus or Vulcan!). Second, because the ancient art of fire tending and keeping for a tribe or village was often performed by a man, who might also be the wise person or shaman. This fire was the heart of the community, and its lighting was an act of facilitation—be it facilitating warmth, protection, or celebration. By working with the Hearth Goddess, men can reclaim this aspect of their ancient past and then take those fires to rekindle their hearts and homes.

For this purpose, I've chosen the goddess Cardea. Ovid speaks of this goddess of doorways as having the power to *open what is shut and shut what is open* (an act of facilitation). From this unique vantage point, Cardea looks both forward and backward in time, offering us the gift of perspec tive. Roman mythology tells us that she lives at the hinge of the universe, keeping the four winds in her protective care. This is very interesting because wind feeds fire, and fire offers protection when well-tended.

Activity: The House of Self

Since one of Cardea's functions is to allow us to see ourselves and our home life in a unique light, we can use this activity as a means of tapping into her perspectives. You need nothing for this activity other than about 20 minutes of undisturbed time. Begin by getting comfortable and breathing deeply.

Now close your eyes and get ready to paint an image in your mind. See yourself walking down a road. It's very familiar and worn, as if you've walked this way hundreds of times before. Along the road, you see a house. Stop and look at this house very closely. What condition is it in? What kind of landscaping does it have? What's inside? Explore the house completely from top to bottom, and try to remember as many details as possible.

Just as you're about to exit, you notice a secret door. Open it. Walk in that room and see what's inside. Again, try to remember all the little details, then head out of the house, moving back down the road you just traveled, back to your normal mental space. Open your eyes and either tape-record or write down everything you experienced in the visualization—including colors, aromas, textures, and so on.

Now, psychologically speaking, what you have just seen is either a representation of self, or of your home. If it's in disrepair, what needs to be fixed? For example, if the kitchen needs work, it represents emotional issues (the heart of the home). If the attic has holes, consider your thoughts and how they're affecting you or those with whom you live. Windows are like eyes, so if they're dirty, perhaps you're not seeing things clearly!

By the way, the word *cardinal*, meaning "very important," is connected to Cardea, as well as the Latin *cerdo*, meaning "craftsman"!

As the goddess of the hinge and turning seasons, another gift from Cardea is an awareness of time and cycles. I know in my own home that there are many moments that go by unnoticed, and suddenly I see that one of my children has grown an inch or learned something new months ago! Cardea helps us be more alert with regard to these things so we can appreciate them, and honor each moment as sacred and special.

Common Symbols

As with the other goddesses thus far explored in this book, the Hearth Goddess has several different functions, each of which can be represented by a variety of symbols and items. In particular, one should be mindful of not simply the Hearth Goddess's fire, but her warmth, hospitality, healing power, and love when choosing suitable items for spell and ritual work.

(**Colors:** Red and orange (fire, passion, protection, love), yellow (a solar fire color that inspires improved communication), green (healing).

(**Moon phases:** This would depend on what you most need to do in your home. For positive energy, you want to work with the waxing to full moon (the full moon, in particular, helps manifest loving and hospitable energy). For decreasing negativity, work with the waning to dark moon. In addition, look to the moon in Aries for cleansing, moon in Gemini to balance out diverse energies in a home, moon in Libra for discernment and balance, and the moon in Aquarius for an appreciation of little things.

(**Stones:** Lava or eye agate (protecting your space), turquoise (encourages kinship), obsidian (strong foundations), amethyst (a happy home), amber or coral (healing), jade (love), cat's-eye (providence), carnelian (blessing), and salt for cleansing.

☾ **Hours:** Two a.m. (banishing negativity in the home), 7 a.m. (perspective), 8 a.m. (rational thinking), noon (the fire of the hearth), 2 p.m. (relationship building and strengthening), 7 p.m. (healing differences).

☾ **Seasons:** I tend to think of the Hearth Goddess in spring (because of spring cleaning) and in the winter when there's a lot of communal activity in the house, but really (since we are living in our homes year-round) she is a goddess for all seasons.

☾ **Plants:** The Hearth Goddess in her fire aspect may be represented by all hot or intensely flavorful plants, including allspice, basil, bay, cinnamon, ginger, and pepper. For warm feelings in the home, look to lemon (which is also a good cleanser). To promote joy consider lavender, marjoram, or saffron. When pursuing ongoing health in the home try coriander, geranium, or thyme. Use alfalfa for providence, birch or basil for protection, and sage for wisdom.

☾ **Other items:** Small fire sources such as a brazier; all cooking appliances; doll houses (and their accoutrements); pineapple, coffee, or wine (hospitality); milk, bread, or rice (providence); barley or corn (blessings); bee imagery (for kinship or community); honey, garlic, or onion (for fire).

Please bear in mind that the Hearth Goddess is really with us whenever we think of her, especially in the pantry or kitchen. Historically this is where many people placed items honoring her—as close as possible to the hearth fire.

Celebrating the Goddess of Hearth and Home

In addition to having a small altar in one's home, there are various times in the year when different traditions revere the Hearth Goddess. On February 1, for example, the Irish celebrate Brigid's Day. Traditional food includes bread with raisins, currants, and candied citrus rinds, often served with ale (a beverage sacred to this Hearth Goddess).

If you'd like to participate in Brigid's day, make equidistant crosses out of yarn or any other material and hang them around the home. This brings luck, health, and the blessings of the Goddess. By the way, this is also the date on which Candlemas is celebrated. Traditionally, candles burned all night to give strength to the sun (and likewise to the hearth fires!).

Activity: Goddess House Candle

This is a very simple activity in which you're going to create a candle that represents your Hearth Goddess and the spirit of your home. To begin, you'll need a form into which to pour melted wax. I suggest using a milk carton because it's actually similar in shape to a house. You'll also need wick and a knife or pencil that reaches across the entire mouth of the milk container.

Melt the wax in a non-aluminum pan, adding herbs that represent your chosen Hearth Goddess, or the energies to which you wish to bring your home. If using dry herbs, grind them very finely (powder is best). If adding oils, do so sparingly and check the resulting scent regularly until you achieve a pleasant blend. Stir this clockwise while invoking a blessing. One blessing I like that you could easily adapt comes from Cherokee tradition (the original is in normal text, and an adaptation is in parentheses):

May the warm winds of heaven

(May the warm winds of the Goddess)

Blow softly upon your house. (Blow softly through this house)

May the Great Spirit   (May She and the Lord)

Bless all who enter there. (Bless all who enter here)

May your moccasins (May all who live here)

Make happy tracks (Walk in beauty)

In many snows. (Through all of life's storms)

And may the rainbow (And may hope and light)

Always touch your shoulder. (Always be our guide)

Let the wax cool a bit while you tie one end of the wick to the pencil or knife and drop the other end down so it nearly touches the bottom of the container. It helps to attach this to a paperclip so the wick stays centered in your candle. Pour in the wax, let it cool, then unmold and decorate in any way you wish.

In the future, light this candle whenever problems, sadness, or other stresses begin to disrupt your home. When you get to the point where there's nearly no candle left, remelt the original wax, adding more as needed, and make a new house candle out of it.

Toward the end of February, Romans celebrated the goddess Fornax, who ruled over the baking of bread and was responsible for providing bread for the circuses. Her name actually means oven, and her festival date was February 17. Obviously, if youd like to celebrate this goddess, bake some bread that day or buy fresh bread and share it with family and friends! Also scatter the crumbs to the birds with your wishes for health, prosperity, and a happy home!

Similar to Fornax is Matergabiae (woman of fire). This Lithuanian goddess rules over the house and cooking. The first new loaf of bread for any batch was offered in part to her, and it was even marked with sacred emblems. This is certainly an easy custom to recreate. You can either cut an emblem into the surface of your bread as it bakes, or use an egg white wash in the last few minutes (apply with a paintbrush) to create browned emblems.

Next, consider Kamui Fuchi, a Hearth Goddess to the Ainu of Japan. This supreme ancestress is the Tribal Mother and the Lady of the Home. To honor her, people recited prayers and gave offerings while cooking rice and brewing beer. If you wish her to scare away evil spirits that bother your home, give her an offering of mugwort or the first sip of beer from a freshly poured glass. Note that libations to the Hearth Goddess are nearly as common as food offerings, the most prevalent liquids being milk, beer, or wine. As with many such hearth goddesses, Kamui Fuchi was often venerated at or near the hearth.

Last, we have Anna Purna, the Indian goddess of food. As the ultimate provider, her symbol was often a simple silver vase. By uttering her name in the morning and evening and offering her rice and milk every Saturday, Monday, and Thursday, your home will never want for food. Again, this returns us to the tradition of giving to receive, and being mindful of the Goddess on a daily basis. When it comes to our homes—our sacred space—there is no greater partner for whom we could wish than the Lady of the Hearth!

6

God as Father

Goddess as Mother

God as Father

—A.J. Drew

Thou art God.

Let's start this chapter with a bit of an exercise. Find a pen and piece of paper. Fold the paper lengthwise to create a crease and then unfold it. Now, on the left half of the paper, write down the name of every Mother Goddess you can think of before reading anything else from this chapter. When you can think of no other names for our Mother Goddess, fold the paper back up and set it aside.

Our father who art in heaven,
Hallowed be thy name.
Thy kingdom come,
Thy will be done
On Earth as it is in Heaven.

—The Lord's Prayer

Has A.J. lost his mind or have we lost "Our Father"? History books tell us that about a thousand years ago, the Vikings converted to Christianity. Shortly thereafter, the view of Christendom had of the Vikings changed. No longer were the Vikings 'the barbaric Pagans," they were now good Christian souls with whom Christendom could do business. As the Vikings had a long history as merchants and tradesmen, the conversion must have seemed like a profitable idea. But don't think this was not a bloody conversion. Yes, a great many people suffered and died, but generally speaking, it was at the hands of other Vikings. Convert or die, convert or die. Although it is a familiar story in the history of Christian domination, in this case it was not an invading Christian force that brought about the conversion. And yet, many people just experienced a knee-jerk reaction to my citing of The Lord's Prayer.

Eventually, the conversion was near complete and the All Father (Pagan/heathen term) was replaced with the Our Father (the Christian term). Another thousand years went by and we find that the religion of the Viking was defeated, but not destroyed. The name Odin is once again spoken openly and the fires of the Norse gods have been rekindled along with the heathen heart. But that has not been the only thing that has been burning. Reports of the burning of Christian churches in the name of the old Norse gods has become so prolific that Viking lightbulb jokes are now heard about the Pagan community.

Question: How many Norsemen does it take to screw in a lightbulb?

First Viking: We don't need lightbulbs. We read by the light of the burning churches.

Second Viking: Lightbulb? Read?

Laugh all you like. I know I did the first time I heard this joke. But there is nothing funny about it. No religion should be punished for the actions taken in their name a thousand years prior.

Yet here we sit: Wiccans call themselves Pagan. Norse folk call themselves heathen. Christians call us all Satanists. As a result, the world starts to look a bit more like it did back in an era when we killed each other with sticks and stones, the difference being we have become much more proficient killers. One is forced to wonder what our Lord in his aspect as Father thinks of what his children have been doing these last few thousand years. Which father am I speaking about? *Our* Father!

God, protect me from your followers.

—A popular bumper sticker

Ah, that bumper sticker says it all, doesn't it? One father and many children who bicker and fight over which one is his favorite. Enough! I talked to Dad just the other day and he wants you to know that if you don't play nice, he is going to take your toys away.

While this warning might sound trite, the father gods have little in common with the whimsically romanticized views presented in most pop Pagan literature. Like our earthly fathers, they both reward and punish, depending on our conduct. Why? Because that is what a caring parent does. So for just a moment, let's put down those glowing crystals and look at Father as he was and as he is.

Father as Creator

The first role of Father is as Creator. This is, after all, how he becomes a father. While pop Pagan lore tells us that the traditional view of the Creator was Goddess and that it was not until Christianity became popular that the Creator was viewed as male, a realistic look at history tells us that this simply was not the case. Yes, there were indeed female Creators who were said to have brought the world into existence without the help of a man, but there were also many male Creators who brought about existence without the help of a woman. You see, there was a time when we did not realize that sex led to pregnancy.

But none of these many stories can be successfully used in the context of the Wiccan religion. They are not forbidden, hidden, or in any way prohibited from Wiccan study, in fact it is greatly important that Wiccans understand other cultures. But the use of a monotheistic image of the Creator is simply not the Wiccan way of looking at things. You see, Wicca is a nature-based fertility religion. As such, we view the creation of life in the way that humans create life. I am, of course, talking about the sexual union between men and women. Now in saying this, I am not excluding gay and lesbian folk from the ranks of the Wiccan. Just the opposite. Remember, when we are talking about such matters as the Creator, we are talking about constructs for understanding. Yes, I believe our Lord and Lady are very real, but the way in which we see them is a human construct because we see them through human eyes. It would be rather pompous to state that we can see them for the total of what they are now, wouldn't it?

Homosexuality and the Father God

First, we must get one thing absolutely clear. There is a distinct difference between gender identity, sexual preference, and what is on a person's driver's license. These are three distinctly separate subjects. A gay man is not generally a woman trapped in a man's body nor is a lesbian a man trapped in a woman's body.

A gay man can be "all man" and a gay woman can be "all woman," but that does not mean that either can be completely masculine or completely feminine. But neither can people who are heterosexual. Every man and woman is a composite of masculine and feminine. Sexual preference is simply a remark on the gender a person prefers to have sex with and not one's own gender identity. Gender identity is what gender a person identifies him- or herself as being. Finally, what is on your driver's license is how the government has assigned gender identity for each individual.

Any combination of these three is possible, but only one denotes a person's gender as far as I am concerned: gender identity. If it calls itself a duck, then it's a duck. Who am I (or you) to say it is not? Okay, maybe the duck analogy isn't a good one, but I am sure you understand what I mean. One's gender identity is a matter of *personal* identity. It is not something that is assigned based on your driver's license or who you choose to welcome into your bed.

If humanity is the child of our Lord and Lady, then each human is created of our Lord (masculine principle of the soul) and Lady (feminine principle of the soul). Thus, each human soul is both masculine and feminine. In Wiccan ritual, the use of symbolic heterosexual sex is not the praise of heterosexuality, but rather the praise of that which the act creates, the magickal child.

Truth be known, the world has never known the conception of a physical child by only two women. It is even harder to imagine that such a phenomenon could take place by two men. But that does not mean that a 'magickal child' can not been created by a same-sex couple. You see, any interaction between individuals is an interaction between the masculine principle of the soul (God) and the feminine principle of the soul (Goddess) because each person is a composite of these two principles.

So although the rituals of Wicca are indeed symbolic acts of heterosexual union, what is really being marked is union between the masculine and feminine principles of the soul. The offspring of that union is the "magickal child." A prime example would be a handfasting of a same sex couple. In that example, the magickal child is the marriage that is produced by the ritual of handfasting.

Adoption and the Father God

There is no part of thee that is not of the gods.

This brings us to the Father God and adoption. While the majority of Wiccans were raised by their natural parents, most of us were not raised in a Wiccan household. In effect, our entrance into Wicca is the act of being adopted by the Wiccan views of the gods. Know first that the idea of adoption has been provided by many Pagan cultures. Notably, adoption was illustrated in ancient Greek law, which included the registration of adopted children on the seventh day of the Greek month of Thargelion.

Here, too, we see that what is found in the heart is more important than what is found in the act. In the same way that what takes place between Wiccan rituals has more to do with being Wiccan than the rituals themselves, what takes place in the raising of a child is more important than the conception of a child. Adoption (a labor of love) is just as sacred as conception, birthing, and all that comes between. If we were to believe any other way, just how sacred would the relationships be that we form with our Lord as Father if we were not born into a tradition that praised those gods?

Wicca and the Father God

With the issues of homosexuality and adoption addressed, I can tell you that Wiccans view the Father as just that—a father. I grit my teeth when I hear folk claim that *The Spiral Dance* is a good introduction to Wicca. While it is an excellent book on Goddess-centered spirituality, Wicca is not a Goddess centered religion. Let me repeat that again and invite you to quote me:

Wicca is not a Goddess-centered religion.

Nor is Wicca a God-centered religion if the word *god* is used in a masculine sense. Instead, Wicca centers on the union of God and Goddess (Lord and Lady). So although we have made clear provisions for adopted and homosexual Wiccans, when we consider the gods as parents, we do not see a goddess laying a great cosmic egg. Nor do we see a god masturbating a pantheon into existence. Sure, there is historic Pagan lore that does state that some ancient Pagan folk used these constructs to under- stand Creation, but there is also historic evidence that states many Pagan cultures practiced human sacrifice. Neither of these are Wiccan. Instead, Wiccans view the Creator as the union of our parents because that is how we create. It's really a simple concept, our Creator is Mom and Dad.

Father- and Mother-Centered

If we were to say that a religion centers on its view of the Creator, then we would state that Wicca is centered on our Lord Father and Lady Mother. Yes, we do see these aspects of the Creator in many other capacities, but when looking to the Creator, we see how we create.

Generally speaking, that relationship is defined as Father Sky and Mother Earth. Here, too, you will find lore that states that the earth has not always been personified as feminine and the sky has not always been personified as masculine. Indeed there are earth gods and sky goddesses. However, the balance between the masculine (Father) and feminine (Mother)—all of what has been created by these parents—has been best represented by the principles that would indicate such a construct.

The Genderification of Earth and Sky

Science states that neither energy nor matter can be created or destroyed. They can simply trade states. Another commonly accepted scientific theory states that the creation of the universe began with the big bang. If these principles are correct, where, then, did the matter and energy for the big bang come from? That is the puzzle of the great cosmic egg I mentioned earlier. Where did it come from? Here is the punch line: We do not know.

Pan-gu (Chinese): Also known as P'an-ku. According to early Chinese lore, Pan-gu was born of that great cosmic egg. As he grew, he pushed the top half of that egg upward to form the sky (yang) and the bottom half of the egg down to form the earth (yin). Some Taoists tell the story a bit differently, stating that Pan-gu was created by the five elements and then in turn created the sky (yang) and earth (yin).

Yo (Japanese): The Japanese equivalent to the Chinese yang. The Japanese equivalent to yin is "In."

The Union of the Lord and Lady

That great cosmic egg is all that is. It is the material and energy that existed before the big bang. It is the yin and yang, Yo and In, masculine and feminine, Lord and Lady, sky and earth, all undivided. In Wiccan terms, the symbol represented here is life itself. It is our beloved Father Sky reaching down to Mother Earth and Mother Earth rising to meet his embrace.

The Final Portion of the Exercise

On a piece of paper, trace the symbol of the Union of Lord and Lady. Thinking on what I said about humans being a composition of the masculine and feminine, see if you can use a ruler or other straight edge to separate that symbol into equal halves so that either half is entirely yin or yang. It cannot be done, which is the very message that symbol is intended to convey. Even if we were to divide the symbol along the curved border between the yin and yang, we still have a dot of the yin within the yang and a dot of the yang within the yin.

So, knowing that all of creation is a combination of both the masculine and the feminine, we look to the Creator as masculine (Father God) and feminine (Mother Goddess). Because the genderification of sky as masculine (yang) and earth as feminine (yin) best suits our needs as well as the ancient lore on which we have based our modern religion, we see Father God as Father Sky and Mother Goddess as Mother Earth. Or do we?

Take out that list of mother goddesses that you created as this chapter started. To the right of the fold, write down the names of the corresponding father gods. If you are like most Wiccans, chances are that you have had the names of those mother goddesses practically drilled into your head. But recalling their partners will be next to impossible.

A Few of Our Father's Many Names

Apoyan Tachi (Pueblo Zuni): Father to all the life on earth in the same way we humans father life. He and Awitelin Tsta (earth mother) are an excellent example of the Wiccan view of Father Sky and Mother Earth.

Dyaus Pita (Hindu): Also known as Dyaus. Hindu All Father and Sky God of Vedic times. With the earth mother Prthivi, they are another classic example of the Wiccan concept of Father Sky and Mother Earth.

Mu Gong (Chinese): Also known as Mu Kung. He is the Taoist personification of the yang (the masculine principle/element). His wife is Xi Wang-mu (also known as Hsi Wang-mu), who is the personification of the yin (feminine principle/element). Together, they created the heavens and the earth.

Odin (Norse): Also known as Woden, Wodan, and Wotan. Historically referred to as Alfadir (meaning All Father), Odin is a sky god and is considered the Father of the gods in the Norse tradition. By his wife Jord (a personification of the primitive earth) he fathered Thor. By his better-known wife Frigg (also known as Frigga) he fathered Balder, Hod, and Hermod. He is also the father of humanity, having carved the first woman from an elm tree and the first man from the ash tree.

Uranus (Greek): Also known as Ouranos. He is an All Father and sky god. Brother and husband to Gia (an earth mother). Together, they parented the Titans and many other children.

Xpiayoc (Myan): Myan sky father similar to the Greek Uranus. His wife is the earth mother Xmucane.

There Is No Mother Without Father

Some people are quick to point out that occasionally men often leave pregnant women, who then become single parents. This is true. And some women use abortion as a form of birth control. Both men and women have been, are, and will be irresponsible. This is one of the many reasons we have archetypes. In this case, the archetype serves as an ideal.

Now, I am not saying that we should all wear wristbands that read W.W.O.D. (What would Odin do?), but if that is what you have to do to remember the principle, then so be it. But it is the principle itself that is important. Just who is this Father God? He is us as the fathers we would like to be. He is the fusion of not only lore (archetypes) but the knowledge or memories we have of our own fathers.

Activity: Reminding Ourselves of Who We Wish to Be

Again, fold a piece of paper in half. This time, on the left side of the paper, write every attribute of your own father (or memory of your own father) that you want to bring into yourself. On the right side of the paper, write down every attribute of your father's that you do not want for yourself.

Fold a second piece of paper in half. This time, on the left side of the paper write every aspect of yourself that you believe will help you to be a better father. On the right side of the paper, write down each aspect that takes away or inhibits you from being a good father.

Tear or cut the two pieces of paper in half. Staple the left halves together and the right halves together. Fold them and place the left half in your left pocket and the right half in the right pocket. Carry them there for a week. Whenever you interact with your children or in any capacity as a father figure, remove the two slips and see from which list you have drawn to cause your action in that capacity.

Gradually, you will begin to remember those lists and think about them before you interact. With any luck, you will begin to act more in accordance with your mind and conscious choice. That is the difference between our Lord as Father and our Lord as Master. Where the Master acts more out of instinct, our Father acts more out of mind and conscious choice. Sure, some of those acts might seem a bit mean, but it is all in the role that a father must play to protect and educate his children.

In the glory of our Lord and Lady, so mote it be.

Goddess as Mother

—Patricia Telesco

"Hymn to the Mother of the Gods"(Aztec)

This hymn was written for Teleoinan, who was considered the Mother of all Gods and the Hearth of the Earth.

Hail to our mother, who caused the yellow flowers to blossom, who scattered the seeds of the maguey, as she came forth from Paradise.

Hail to our mother, who poured forth flowers in abundance, who scattered the seeds of the maguey, as she came forth from Paradise.

Hail to our mother, who caused the yellow flowers to blossom, she who scattered the seeds of the maguey, as she came forth from Paradise.

Hail to our mother, who poured forth white flowers in abundance, who scattered the seeds of the maguey, as she came forth from Paradise.

Hail to the goddess who shines in the thorn bush like a bright butterfly.

Ho! she is our mother, goddess of the earth, she supplies food in the desert to the wild beasts, and causes them to live.

Thus, thus, you see her to be an ever-fresh model of liberality toward all flesh.

And as you see the goddess of the earth do to the wild beasts, so also does she toward the green herbs and the fishes.

I will sing of well-founded Gaia, Mother of All, eldest of all beings, she feeds all creatures that are in the world, all that go upon the goodly land and all that are in the paths of the sea, and all that fly: all these are fed of her store.

—"Homeric Hymn"

The mystery of new life must have been awe-inspiring for our most ancient ancestors who understood very little of how the body works. To see this miniature human issue forth from a woman, alive and alert, was indeed miraculous. As the bearers of new life, women became associated with fertility and the drive to sustain humankind. It is but one short mental leap from that thought process to seeing God as a woman who is the creative force in all things, who births the world. It's interesting to note that in many cultures, the Mother Goddess is often reflected by a name that has a prefix or suffix of Ma or Am, similar to the sounds a child makes when suckling and first learning to talk.

It is also interesting, although not overly surprising, that we began calling the earth *Mother!*

Thus, in considering the Mother Goddess, we need to look at her from two perspectives. The first is that of one who sustains and nourishes—that is, as the earth goddess, who provides and from whom all life (that we presently know) originates. The second is the Maternal Lady, who watches over mothers and families, cares for children, and may have even given birth to the universe itself. Her names are many, including:

(Amaterasu (Japanese)   (Ishtar (Babylonian)

(Cybele (Anatolian)   (Isis (Egyptian)

(Demeter (Greek)   (Kali (Indian)

(Gaia (Greek)   (Mut (Egyptian)

(Inanna (Sumerian)   (Oya (African)

One of the most famous depictions of the Mother Goddess is the *Venus of Willendorf*, which was found in Austria in 1908. Dated to 25,000 B.C.E., this pregnant figure is but one of many uncovered in regions as diversified as France and Egypt, featuring large breasts and hips. While there is some controversy as to whether these were meant to be goddesses or simply fertility charms, other archaeological and written evidence has led to a common acceptance of the imagery as the Mother.

The Mother Goddess isn't always portrayed in art as pregnant. Sometimes she has a small child (often a boy, who, in mythology, might become her consort). This imagery seems sweet and loving, but the Mother Goddess is not always benign. Just ask any mother bear defending her cubs how much warrior energy comes with motherhood! This brings us back to the human element of this exploration.

When we choose to bring new life into this world the learning curve for adults becomes amazing. There is nothing that stretches us as people more than sharing our space with children and attempting to bring them up as best we can. The adjustments that go alongside parenting aren't always easy to make. So we're left to ponder what the divine mothers have shown us through their stories and attributes that can help us in our task. What exactly did the Mother Goddess stand for in various cultures?

Mythic Mother

The first step in getting to know the Mother is to listen to her stories. Just as a child sat in the kitchen while mom recounted various family memories, myths are our Mother Goddess's memories as imprinted in human awareness. We'll start with Gaia, the spirit of the earth.

In the beginning of this charming Greek story we find nothing but darkness. Nyx, a bird with black wings, was all that existed in this empty realm. Nyx laid a golden egg upon which she sat awaiting life. Eros, the god of love, was born from that egg, and its remnants became the air, sky, and earth, which he named Gaia. Eros then used his power to inspire love between the sky and the earth, who (through their passion) gave birth to all humankind. Through this story we see that love is a creative energy, and an important part of the Mother archetype.

Activity: A Personal Creation Myth

For this activity I'd like you to get either some paper, a tape recorder, or paint and paper (whatever medium feels most creative). You'll want to do this at a time when you won't be disturbed. Get into a light meditative state, and release all your tensions.

Next, think about your mother or someone who you feel personifies the best in mothers everywhere. Bring that person's face into your mind. Now pretend for a moment that she is a powerful goddess—how would this woman have gone about the task of Creation? Would she have birthed a cosmic egg, baked life into existence, or sung the song of life? Create your own Mother Goddess myth in celebration of this individual and her positive influences on your life. The creation can be in any artistic form with which you're comfortable. Write a song that tells her story, carve her story into three-dimensional reality, or whatever! When you're done, you may want to present this person (if possible) with the item you've created as a Mother's Day gift!

Next, consider Amaterasu. This sun goddess of the Japanese pantheon radiated with life and hope, blessing Japan with her beauty. Through her, all people (her children) learned about their loveliness and potential.

Her story begins with Amaterasu and her brother (Susa) making children who would rule Japan wisely. From their union, three beautiful goddesses and five gods were born, all charming and powerful. Sadly, Susa was overly proud of his part in Creation, and began to think that Amaterasu didn't appreciate him enough. He unleashed his wrath in several successive acts of spite, the last of which frightened Amaterasu's oldest friend to fall dead from shock.

Amaterasu ran as fast and as far as she could to a cave in a corner of heaven, then blocked the door with a stone. It was quiet and safe in the cave and she planned to stay for a long time in the darkness. Meanwhile, in despair, Susa began the journey to the underworld alone.

Amaterasu's time in the cave allowed her to think about things between herself and Susa. She wondered if perhaps she failed her brother by not loving him enough. In her fear and anger, her ability to see clearly had been lost—her light had grown dim, but this darkness didn't compare to the dark earth. The people and the land had lost their shining Mother. They had to remain in their homes without light or hope, and the world began to die.

Things looked pretty bleak, so the other 800 gods gathered together to try to find a solution. They got a cock to crow before dawn and hung mirrors, bright cloth banners, and jewel strands on the tree just outside Amaterasu's cave while uttering sacred words. Once the tree was ready, Ama no Uzume came forward and began to dance uproariously. It was such a dance that all 800 gods laughed.

Inside the cave, Amaterasu was confused. She'd never heard such a noise and couldn't resist looking out. When Amaterasu emerged, she saw her reflection in the mirrors and realized that she'd been neglecting her children of the warmth and joy of her life-giving light. She immediately returned to heaven and vowed never to be frightened again by any storm or ill will. In this act, we see the tenacity of a mother to do what is right and best for her children, even when it means overcoming personal fears or dangerous circumstances.

It's interesting to note that other mother goddesses go through a descent cycle (a time away) during which the earth and its people suffer. We see it with the Babylonian Ishtar who goes into the underworld. While she is there, all fertility on the earth ceases. When she emerges again, the entire earth rejoices in her splendor. A third example is Demeter (Greece), whose sadness leaves the earth barren while her daughter Persephone is trapped in the underworld. This theme stresses the life-giving energy of the Mother, and her importance in life's web.

Sumerian mythology talks about the birth of vegetation, which begins with sweet waters and a goddess named Ninhursag, who was the earth. Once the waters brought life to Ninhursag, the next goddess (Ninnu) was born (she who makes things grow). It was also Ninhursag who fashioned people and animals. There is similarity to this basic story to those told in Babylon. A Babylonian Creation poem says:

The goddess they called...the mother

The most helpful of the goddesses, the wise Mami;

Thou art the mother-womb,

The one who creates mankind,

Create, then, Lullu and let him bear the yoke,

Let him be made of clay, animated by blood.

Here we're seeing the Mother as the creative force behind all things (the birth-giver). In effect, the drive of the Mother goddess is very similar to the desire many women experience when they begin to yearn for children.

Moving to Egypt we discover perhaps the most complex goddess in history, Isis. Isis, as mother of Horus, was by extension regarded as the mother and protectress of the pharaohs. In fact, she was the mother and protectress of all Creation. The relationship between Isis and Horus may also have influenced the Christian conception of the relationship between Mary and the infant Jesus Christ. The depiction of Isis with a suckling or seated Horus is certainly reminiscent of the iconography of Mary and Jesus, and Mary is certainly another Mother Goddess archetype.

Isis is not alone in her mothering influence in this region. Mut is also well worth considering. As the Queen of the Gods, she symbolized the Eye of Ra, which could see all things. Her name, *mut*, means "mother," and it is the same term used for earthly mothers in the Egyptian language of the time.

I have given unto thee the sovereignty of the father Geb, and the goddess Mwt, thy mother, who gave birth to the gods, brought thee forth as the first-born of five gods, and created thy beauties and fashioned thy members.

—*The Book of the Dead*

There's an interesting link between Mut and vultures in both Egypt and South Africa. In the latter, the term for vulture is the same as one applied to lovers, because they are always seen in pairs. This bonding is the same as that for mothers and children—being protective, powerful, and loving, with wings that encompass a child and keep them from harm.

Similarly, in the regions of Tanis and the Oases of Kharga, her followers saw Mut as the Great Mother. From her all things were created, and as such she was sometimes portrayed as having male parts (it's said she conceived life itself). Her formal title was *"Mut, who giveth birth, but was herself not born of any."*

Finally, in our mythic exploration of the ancient mother we turn to Kali. The Western mind finds it difficult to comprehend the typically frightening image of Kali as having anything to do with motherhood, yet it's very common to hear her devotees call upon Kali-ma (*ma* meaning "mother").

O Kali, my Mother full of Bliss! Enchantress of the almighty Shiva!
In Thy delirious joy Thou dancest, clapping Thy hands together!
Thou art the Mover of all that move, and we are but Thy helpless
toys.

—Ramakrishna Paramhans

Kali-ma's dance is that of Creation itself. She represents the part of life that is somewhat unpredictable and wild. And as with life, all things eventually come to an end, which is where her destroyer aspect comes into view. Kali's destruction is not aimless or without purpose, but rather a cleansing so all things become new again, and again she will dance the Mother's waltz to give life reborn.

Motherly Attributes

Everyone has an earthly mother from whom they were born. Those who grew up with a mother typically saw this person as having many roles—that of nurturing and loving to chastising and correcting! Divine Mothers are no different, and that's part of what makes the Mother Goddess so important to our fractured society. We need a positive model for "tough love" that asks the best of us, but also understands when we fall short in our humanness.

It's obvious in looking at our world today that there's a yearning to touch the Mother intimately again, yet this yearning isn't really anything new to humankind. In fact, this prayer written in 150 c.e. by Lucius Apuleius aptly describes the feelings of our forebears.

O blessed Queen of Heaven,

whether you be the Dame Ceres,

original and motherly source of all fruitful things in the earth,

who after finding your daughter Proserpina,

through your joy caused barren and unfruitful ground to be
cultivated,

and who now inhabits the land of Elusie;

Or whether you be the celestial Venus,

who in the beginning touched all things with engendered love,

who is now worshipped within the Temples of the Isle of Paphos,

being the sister of the God Phoebus provider of meat for so many,

now adored at the sacred places of Ephesus:

You who are terrible Proserpina,

whose deathly cries have the power to preserve us from the
dark spirits and ghosts which appear before men,

keeping them bound within the earth;

You who are worshipped in diverse ways,

you who illuminate the very ends of the earth with your feminine shape,

you who nourish the fruits of the world by your vigour and force;

Howsoever and with whatever name it is right to call upon you,

I pray to you to end my travail and misery,

deliver me from wretched misfortune which has pursued me for
so long.

In Wicca, the Mother aspect is represented by the season of summer
when the earth is ripe, the sun is high in the sky, and all life is cresting to a
pinnacle of activity. In Western traditions, the Goddess remains pregnant
until the Winter Solstice, at which time she gives birth to a sun god of some
kind. (Note the adaptation by the Christian church. The symbol of a reborn sun certainly wasn't lost on ancient theologians!). But let's look more
closely at specific mother goddesses to discern even more of this being's
attributes than what we've seen in mythology.

One of the oldest figures to come forward as a mother goddess is
Cybele. Her image appears on Smyrna's coins, and she was regarded as
not only Mother Earth, but also the protectress of the city. Interestingly
enough, she was represented by a simple black meteorite, implying her

raw, foundational energy. The Romans adopted Cybele into their pantheon around 200 B.C.E., naming her *Magma Mater Deum Idea* (Great Mother of the Gods).

Cybele's worship reminds us that mother goddesses were not regarded simply as overseeing matters of birth, but had the power of entire tribes and villages in their hands (after all, we do have eyes in the back of our heads!). As the point of origin for all, this makes sense. I am also fascinated by the use of stone and the term Magma in Roman custom, alluding to the very womb of Earth. This is important in magickal practices because it is from all life that energy flows, and the earth is our spiritual classroom.

Activity: Choosing a Mother Goddess

At the outset of this activity, make a list of what you consider to be the best attributes of a mother (both mortal and divine). Put them in order by what you feel is most important to least. Refer to that list as you read this chapter, or while looking through any book of goddesses. See if you can't find one being to whom you strongly relate in the Mother role (perhaps a goddess from the culture where your path originates, or one attuned to your family tree by country of origin).

Once you've found such a being, develop a relationship with her (so doing often heals many mother-child issues and arguments, by the way). Set up a special surface honoring this person, and keep something of your own mother (if possible) along with those items. Remember to pray for mothers everywhere, calling upon your Mother Goddess for blessings. Also remember that if you still have a mother on this plane, all that you do for her uplifts the Mother Goddess and manifests with joy.

In India we find an interesting approach to the Mother, who is known as Maha Devi or Uma Devi. This goddess birthed all things and has many incarnations including Durga, Kali, and Parvati. This goddess is depicted as gentle, watching ever over nature, bringing rain, and protecting all things from disease. And as we saw in Kali, she is also the mother of death! Overall, the Devi speaks of the power of the Mother, and the importance of the feminine aspect in the universal balance in every part of life's network—both human and nature, as well as the preciousness of our time in this world. The Devi's rain also alludes to a fertilizing aspect.

Third, let's look to Inanna (Sumerian) and Ishtar (Babylonian). The beings in these regions often tie together and overlap. Inanna was a mediator of differences (as a good mother does between siblings) and the source of all joy and fertility. A traditional Sumerian blessing expresses this very well:

May (the goddess) Inanna cause a hot-limbed wife to lie
down for you;
May she bestow upon you broad-armed sons;
May she seek out for you a place of happiness!

Ishtar was another name for Inanna, celebrated as the Great Mother with life-giving power. The interesting thing about Ishtar is that she retains an independent position. Even when Ishtar is a gods consort, her personality is unique and apart from that association. This is extremely interesting considering the womens liberation movement. With Ishtar, we see that wife and mother need not be dependent or secondary to her mate, and indeed has a life worthy of recognition. There is no such thing as "just a housewife" in this Goddesss vernacular!

From Incan tradition we discover the image of the contented mother, who is calm and focused. Her name is Pachamama, the companion of all women. And not surprisingly, this goddess lives inside the earths womb, being a primordial Mother image. Pachamamas lesson is quite simple: There are both happiness and rewards to mothering, even when its a difficult job. Nonetheless, even the most experienced of mothers often meets situations that challenge the ability to keep that calm demeanor and attentive focus!

Last but not least, Id like to return to Kali. The maternal nature of this goddess is the defining aspect for even her modern-day devotees. The love that exists between parents is generated in Kali-mas heart, and extends to her children with all tenderness. Devotees reach out to nurture this relationship, but never forget that Mother has a very real temper, and a heavy hand when needed.

Kalis lesson is not simply one of motherly love, but of appreciation for the life we've been given by our mortal and divine mothers. The fabric of life has pain and ecstasy, decay and birth, darkness and light—and Kali encourages her children to explore everything up to and including confronting our mortality. In that moment, one can begin to truly let go and revel in the ways of the Divine Mother.

The traditional image of Kali stresses many of her lessons and attributes. Full-breasted in the pose of a dance, her Creation is ceaseless. Her hair is the very fabric of the cosmos—from chaos emerges order. The garland of 50 heads represents the Sanskrit alphabet, where wisdom and knowledge lie. The girdle of hands represents karma—the work of our hands, what we bring to our own life. Finally, her white teeth offer purity balanced against a long tongue, illustrating the intense enjoyment of all that life has to offer. In all this, Kali challenges us to take what we have been given in life and approach it with gusto—knowing that the Mother Goddess does likewise!

Mother Goddess for Men

Jungian psychology espouses the Mother Goddess as an archetype—a touchstone in the collective consciousness of which all people should be mindful. Carl Jung theorized that "the feminine principle as a universal archetype, a primordial, instinctual pattern of behavior deeply imprinted on the human psyche, brought the Goddess once more into popular imagination." More importantly in experiencing fulfillment and wholeness, one must come to understand the Mother Goddess within.

Many men have expressed the need to return to the Goddess, indicating that this is not simply a woman's issue. Having a vital connection to the ultimate female principle helps men relate to their mortal counterpart more easily. In turn, there's less fear and resentment of what's regarded as female power. And while most men in the Neo-Pagan movement find sexism distasteful, they also have the reality of women's life-giving power staring them in the face. No matter how much we might dislike it, sexism is part of our culture and sexist myths take a very long time to weed out of our behavior and thoughts.

This leads us to the nagging question of how men can release themselves from their own gender framework to understand what it's like to be a "mother," let alone reconnecting with the Mother Goddess. Now, if you have children, the parental feelings you have are very similar to other mortal mothers and offer at least a hint of the Divine ones. Nonetheless, it's still not quite the same as having life grow within you, then birthing it, feeding it from your own body, and so forth. If you don't have children, you might consider pets, plants, and projects as figurative kids.

Perhaps the key is to find something toward which you have a strong emotional attachment, someone or something you want the very best for—that you want to nurture into maturity. Dedicate yourself to that end, and each time before you go to do a "motherly" task associated with that person, situation, or thing, stop and reconnect with the Mother Goddess through the following visualization.

Activity: Visualizing the Mother Goddess

In your mind's eye, visualize a place that's wholly comfortable and safe. It's just a distance away from you, so you'll need to move yourself through the visualization to reach it. As you get closer, you notice someone is waiting for you in that protected haven. You can't be sure who it is, but you know you feel totally at ease—there's a familiarity about her.

You get closer and notice the woman smiling. It's a warm, welcoming image that seems to embrace you even at this distance. All around her, a gentle white-pink light radiates outward in all directions. As it touches on a sprout, it grows; as it reaches a tree, it bursts forth with fruit. As it fills your spirit, your hunger and thirst are wholly filled.

It's only now that you realize this woman is larger than life itself. As you come up to her, the aura greets you—gathering you into loving arms. That energy overflows, saturating your aura with the Mother's attributes you most need. Hold these tightly, knowing them as part of yourself, and thanking her for her gift. Then, slowly return to normal awareness, trusting in the Mother to manifest through you.

Symbols of the Mother

There are some general shapes and items that have long been associated with the Mother Goddess. In particular (and somewhat obviously), anything bearing a womb-like shape can represent her. Bowls were among the favorite items, often being used in temples to hold sacred water (the water of life and blessings, which also connects to the birth-giving energies of this goddess). More recently, cauldrons are popular in Neo-Pagan traditions because many have three feet, alluding to the triple goddess of whom the Mother is the second aspect.

Other common symbols for the Mother are seas, fountains, ponds, and wells (living water). The great number of wells dedicated to Brigit (another triple goddess) in Ireland stands as a living testament to this connection. Just as the Mother's love is vital, water is essential to all life, fertility, and inventiveness. Without it our world would be a wasteland, and it's worthy to note that a newborn's body is nearly 75 percent water!

Here are more Mother symbols for your reference:

☽ **Colors:** All those that are rich and full, in particular dark red, forest green, vivid yellow, and royal blue.

C **Moon phase:** Full moon, moon in Cancer (fruitfulness, providence), moon in Pisces (mother's intuition, Water element).

C **Stones:** Geodes, any round stone, pumice (child bearing), jade (love), amber (protection and healing), selenite (settling sibling disputes), sodalite (wisdom).

C **Hours:** Noon to sunset, 7 a.m. (hope), 4 p.m. (common sense), 8 p.m. (sound guidance).

C **Seasons:** Summer to mid-fall.

C **Plants:** Cinquefoil, cowslip, parsley, pomegranate, tansy. Also, geranium (fertility), nutmeg (devotion), marjoram (health), rose (love), violet (peace), clove (protection), and cinnamon (psychic alertness).

C **Other items:** Labyrinths, ovals, cup or chalice, baby imagery (both human, plant, and animal), bread or rice and grains, rich soil, caves.

While each mother goddess will have emblems and items sacred to her apart from what's on this list, this gives you a good starting point for creating a Mother Goddess altar, or calling on overall maternal energies for spells and rituals. For example, if you want to make a Mother Goddess charm that will inspire her attributes in your life, you might wrap a simple round pebble in an oval, dark-blue cloth. Hold this in the palms of your hands, making a little womb into which you can direct an incantation, such as:

Blessings great, troubles few
Mother Earth, in this cloth of blue
From Gaia's heart to my hand
In this charm, your magick stands!

Carry this with you. By the way, when you really feel like you need to "ground out" and reconnect with your earthly Mother Goddess, take the stone out and put it into the ground. Meditate on that spot, feeling the energy of Earth through your belly button, and visualize an umbilical cord connecting you to the stone, and thus to the world!

Celebrating the Mother

Throughout the world, various peoples have set aside special days to honor the Mother. In India, that day comes in September or October with the fast of Navratri, followed by a day of celebration for Durga—the divine shakti energy that gives life. Typically, the fast days include special dances called Garba, which take place around a symbolic item that represents the Goddess (often a pot with a lamp inside). *Garba* translates as "womb," and the lamp in the pot symbolizes life in the womb.

Another activity that takes place during this festival in certain regions is the conveying of heat to a goddess image. This is followed by pouring milk over her to lovingly cool her down. Here, heat represents the normal trials of life, and the milk (or coconut water), of course, washes away those problems with the Mother's love and attendance.

The 10th day—celebration day—is filled with feasting and thanksgiving, and sometimes includes a parade to the Goddess's temple. Why fast? Giving up a little of the Mother's abundance is a type of offering to her. Why feast? Because providence is one of the most important functions of the Divine Mother! In particular, sweets are often favored because they represent life's sweetness!

In Western society we have two days that immediately come to mind as ideas for honoring the Mother—Earth Day and Mother's Day! Mother's Day seems obvious—you celebrate the Goddess by doing special things for her counterparts here on Earth. Now, for those of you who are separated from your mothers (due to death or other situations), how about doing something nice for someone you regard as an excellent mother, or a mother figure (or perhaps making a donation to a children's medical facility in the name of that person)? And if you have an altar, don't forget to light a candle and thank the Mother of us all for your life and blessings today!

As for Earth Day? While it has been said (and rightfully so) that we should be making every day Earth Day if we care about this planet, having this date set aside gives us pause to feed Earth's spirit—Gaia. This poem from ancient Greece seems apt for such an occasion:

> Mother of all, Foundation of all
> the oldest one, I shall sing to the Earth
> she feeds everything that is in the world
> whoever you are
> whether you live upon her sacred ground
> or whether you live along the paths of the sea
> you that fly.
> it is she who nourishes you from her treasure-store
> Queen of the Earth through you, beautiful children

beautiful harvests come
The giving of life and death both are yours
Happy is the man you honor
the one who has this has everything.
His fields thicken with ripe corn
his cattle grow heavy in the pastures
his house brims over with good things
These are the men who are masters of their city
the laws are just, the women are fair
happiness and fortune richly follow them.
Their sons delight in the ecstasy of youth
their daughters play—they dance among the flowers
skipping in and out
they dance on the grass over soft flowers
Holy goddess you honored them
ever flowing spirit
Farewell mother of the gods
bride of heaven sparkling with stars
For my son, life allow me love of the heart
Now and in my other songs
I shall remember you

Whenever you celebrate Mother Earth, plant some seeds in the soil of her womb so new life can grow. Reach out with your mind and heart to Gaia's aching spirit and offer her comfort and nourishment even as she has so graciously given us. Enact spells and rituals for global healing, and dedicate yourself anew to being a good caretaker of this sacred space of Earth.

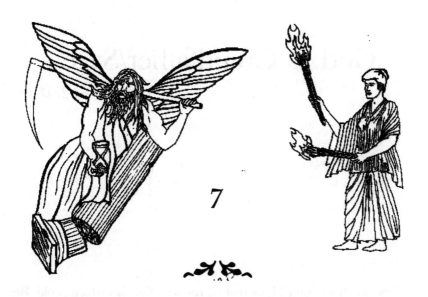

God as Grandfather/Sage

Goddess as Grandmother/Crone

God as Grandfather/Sage

—A.J. Drew

Thou art God.

Time and time again I hear that we do not value that which is old. But then there is wine, art, and all the many other things that appreciate with age. I do not believe our society has an issue with age, I believe our society has an issue with self-importance.

Consider the lack of extended family households in Western culture. Do we put our grandparents in a nursing home because we do not value them, or because we don't want folk to think we have lower value because we live with our seniors? Now I am not talking about the challenges of fulfilling the medical needs of the sick. I am speaking about the emotional needs of both young and old.

Although I have not raised a child myself, I am certainly well into the father stage of my life. I mention this because my moving into the father stage means that my mother has moved into the grandmother stage despite the fact that she does not yet have grandchildren to play with. She is Grandmother despite the fact that she is not yet an unpaid baby-sitter.

Call me a mama's boy if you like; I consider my relationship with my mother to be one of my greatest strengths. Second on my list of strengths is the driving force of my father's memory. I will never forget the look on his face when I graduated from basic training at Ft. Leonard Wood. That pride that he showed for his son has caused me to do things that some folk only dream of, such as writing books for a living.

So, I don't believe for a moment that we do not value age; I believe that we do not recognize that value because we feel it somehow takes away from our own. For some odd reason, folk tend to think that if we have received advice, inspiration, or a helping hand in our accomplishments, that those accomplishments are somehow diminished. Here again we see objectification. Instead of looking to the process and the relationships that brought about the accomplishment, we see the accomplishment (object) itself. However, one must wonder what, if anything, we are if not the result of the relationship between us and our seniors. What does one create today that is not a result of work that was done yesterday?

This is the glory of our Lord and Lady, that they are forever changing, growing, and maturing. As Father, he is the son who has grown. As Grandfather, he is the father who has grown. Am I not the child of my mother and father? Are they not the children of their mother and father? Thus, am I not of my father's father and my mother's mother?

Lo there do I see my father.
Lo there do I see my mother.
Lo there do I see my brothers and my sisters.
Lo there do I see the line of my people back to the beginning....
—"Ibn Fadlan's Account of Scandinavian Merchants
on the Volga in 922"

These are the first four lines of a prayer as recorded by Ahmed ibn Fadlan in 933 C.E. Ahmed attributed it to the "Norsemen" that he had encountered on a journey that brought him in contact with the Pagan Norsemen just southeast of Russia (near the Volga River). These lines were recorded in a time when both the extended family and the ancestors were seen as one of man's greatest strengths.

Lo there do I see the line of my people back to the beginning....

Indeed, in cultures where the extended family was considered a strength rather than an embarrassment, connectivity with our elders ran much deeper than it seems today. But not because we no longer value our elders, but rather because the culture in which we live seems hell-bent on placing value only on individual accomplishments and not on the strength one can find in his or her family.

This is where we can excel as a religion and a community. Where the larger community fails to recognize the strength of the extended family, Wiccans can become strong by accepting that strength. Where the larger community fails to recognize the strength of our grandparents and ancestors (our line), Wiccans can become strong by accepting those strengths.

Our Personal Grandfathers

My mother tells me that on the day she brought me home, my grandfather was waiting. She describes the joy in his eyes as something she had never seen there before. It did not matter that I was not of his blood, I was of his heart. Although I do not remember this first meeting, what I do remember of my grandfather was filled with equal joy.

So when I think of our Lord as grandfather, it is his face that I see more than any other. Sure, I have looked at Pagan lore. But in seeing those many examples of our Lord as Grandfather/Sage, I see the face of the man who called me Grandson.

Akba-atatdia (Native American): The Grandfather and Creator god of the Crow. Similar to Old Man Coyote.

Chronos (Greek): The Grandfather of Time. He is depicted with a long grey beard and is often cited as time itself. Note: Not to be confused with Cronus.

Domovoi (Russian): Also known as Domovoy. A house spirit called "Grandfather."

Elli (Norse): Also known as Elle. Norse personification of old age itself. It is said that Elli beat Thor in a wrestling match. This is perhaps a comment on how old age can not be defeated.

Es (Siberian): Creator and Grandfather god of the Ket.

Gama (Japanese): Depicted as a joy-filled old man with several scrolls, which denote his great wisdom.

Jurojin (Japanese): Shinto god who brings with him a happy tone to old age. He is depicted as a smiling sage/elder who rides atop a white stag. When walking, he is often depicted with a cane and a turtle (itself a symbol of great age).

Kaakwha (Native American): Also known as Hawenniyo. A Grandfather Sky god of the Seneca.

Nereus (Greek): The Greek Grandfather of the sea. He and his wife, Doris, were the parents of the 50 Nereids (beautiful women of the sea), so you can imagine how many grandchildren were in need of free baby-sitting services.

Old Man Coyote (Native American): Also known simply as Old Man. Common to the Plains and Western Tribes, Old Man Coyote is a more mature, less trickster-like incarnation of Coyote.

Tecciztecatl (Aztec): Also known as Tecuciztecal. An Aztec Grandfather Moon.

Our Cultural Grandfathers

Lo there do I see the line of my people back to the beginning....

—Ahmed ibn Fadlan

This brings us to our cultural grandfathers, or "the line of my people back to the beginning." Perhaps it is because I am an adopted child, but I see absolutely no reason to base one's pride in a bloodline. Sure, a person is a member of a bloodline, but what has that person done to deserve the pride that accompanies the lineage? Now, please do not misunderstand me as saying that I would not be proud to be a member of my family even if they were blood relatives, but that pride is based on my interaction with them. It is based on being a part of that family in deed, not in blood. Think back on Odin, the All Father of the Norsemen. Was he not the All Father to a culture rather than a specific bloodline? Is this not true of most of our images of deity?

For this reason, although I have discovered that Sicilian, German, and Irish blood pump through my veins, I am not proud of the accomplishments of the Sicilians, Germans, or Irish any more than I am of any other tribe of humanity. I do not count them as the line of "my people" at all. Instead, I am an American, and damned proud to be. My cultural grandfathers are the men who conceived the idea for what I feel is the greatest nation on Earth.

> *We hold these truths to be self-evident, that all men are created equal, that they are endowed by their Creator with certain unalienable Rights, that among these are Life, Liberty and the pursuit of Happiness.*

—from the Declaration of Independence
of the United States of America

Think about that for just a moment. It reads "endowed by *their* Creator." Not by the state sanctioned, common view, or democratically elected Creator. They were very specific in their use of words. I am endowed by *my* Creator as I view the Creator (the union of male and female). My mother is endowed by *her* Creator as she views the Creator (something that transcends gender). Wow, one of the core ideas behind the Wiccan religion (that all paths are valid) was included in one of the documents sacred to my nation. Now *that* is something to be proud of!

This melting pot of a country, this is *my* people. While I certainly have a personal family lineage, when "I see the line of my people back to the beginning," I see not only those members of my family who have served this nation, but also those who might not have connections to my immediate family. I see the cultural grandfathers of my nation. You see, when asked who my people are, I do not speak of some genetic link to any ancient people. I see a direct link to the here and now. I am an American! Thus, my cultural grandfathers are the great men who founded this country.

Here, too, we see objectification. Instead of seeing these cultural grandfathers in the context in which their actions were taken, people have objectified those actions, looking at the deed itself and not the context in which the deed was done.

Objectification and Relationship Views

Where I see the grandfathers of this nation as having made clear and deliberate steps to ensure that slavery would be abolished, there is a wave of young folk who contend that those great men were devils in disguise. As evidence they often present the following:

Objectification view: The founders of this nation were evil because slaves were considered by our cultural grandfathers as only three-fifths human.

Relationship view: The founders of this nation were great because from the very beginning they wanted to abolish the institution of slavery. To that end, they struck a compromise (relationship) with forces that wished to continue slavery. That compromise was the very instrument that abolished the practice.

You see, the slave states wanted slaves to be counted as full citizens because that would help perpetuate slavery by giving those slave states more representation in Congress, and thus a greater influence in matters of maintaining the legal status of the slave trade. The non-slave states did not want to count slaves at all. If that had been the case, the non-slave states would have received greater representation in Congress, and thus a greater influence in matters of abolishing slavery. The three-fifths concept came about as a compromise, helped the Constitution get approved by all states, and led to the eventual abolishment of the slave trade in the United States of America.

So, from the viewpoint of objectification, our cultural grandfathers were monsters. But seen in the relationships that brought about the actions that are now being objectified, they were great men.

The truth is, without regard to religion, this is a Pagan nation. Its very structure being developed by the ancient Greek Pagans, refined by the ancient Roman Pagans, and then brought into manifestation by a group of people who challenged the head of the Church of England, King George III.

Good and bad, this is "the line of my people back to the beginning." Good and bad, the cultural grandfathers of the United States are my cultural grandfathers.

What Is a God?

What does this have to do with God as Grandfather and Sage? Again, I have begun each and every chapter in my half of this book by saying "thou art God" in the hopes of driving that message home. If you and those who have come before you are God, then your earthly grandfather (living or not) is God. If you and those who have come before you are God, then your cultural grandfathers (living or not) are God.

In the glory of our Lord and Lady, so mote it be.

Chapter Commentary

In this chapter, my praise of the masculine portion of the soul has been great. Of course it has, I am speaking of Grandfather archetypes of which I am greatly proud. Please do not consider this chapter as a statement about men having a greater role in the foundation of my great nation. My role in this book is to discuss my Wiccan view of the masculine principle of the soul (God), and so have remained thus focused in this discussion.

Goddess as Grandmother/Crone

—Patricia Telesco

"Grandmother Moon"

Grandmother Moon
shine brightly on me.
Let my heart be open
to the joy that you see.
Take these worries and fears
from my mind that runs wild.
Let me dance in your moonlight
and again be a child.

—White Owl

Hekate the Beauteous, you I invoke: You, of roads and crossways, of heaven, of earth, and sea as well. You, the saffron-clad, among the tombs, dancing with dead souls the Bacchic rite. You, daughter of Perses, lover of desolation, taking joy in deer and dogs, in the night. You, terrible Queen! Devourer of beasts! Ungirded, possessed of form unapproachable! You, bull-huntress, universal sovereign Empress: You mountain-roaming guide, and bride, and nursemaid, I entreat, O Maiden, your presence at these sacred rites, with grace to the Oxherd and a joyful heart eternal

—"Orphic Hymn"

In an era when the word *old* has often come to mean "useless," this may be the most important chapter of this book. In some areas of the world, such as the Far East and among Native Americans, the aged among them are honored as being wise. In fact, the elderly everywhere are a precious resource, in my opinion. It's very unfortunate that we've given in to thinking that such knowledge and experience has no value. We often say those who do not learn from history are doomed to repeat it, yet our elders represent that very history from which we could learn!

Why is it that we seem to shun or fear old age? In part, it's the natural human uncertainty toward death and what (if anything) lies thereafter. If you don't believe it, just look at how youth and beauty are worshipped in the media. Also, look at how often humans are kept alive long beyond the time the body can support quality life.

Yet more evidence of the deep-seated fear toward mortality comes in how we treat the elderly in the West. When such individuals could easily be appreciated for their vast life experience, we see a disdain for having to "take care of" them, which in turn takes away human dignity. Rather than being given liberation and a chance to live without the other constraints life places upon adult life, many of our elders end their days in loneliness, frustration, and fear. This should *not* be so, and it's something with which the Grandmother stands ready to help.

The elder aspects of the goddesses represent power and wisdom, but not in a physical sense. Rather, these beings rely on adeptness, wisdom, and cunning. Mind you, the shift away from the physical does not mean these beings lack strength or power. They have the infinite knowledge of the ages at hand to draw upon! Her names are many, including:

(Aju (Hindu/Buddhist)	(Edda (Scandinavian)
(Amma (Norse)	(Hanna (Asia Minor)
(Anne (Syrian)	(Hekate (Greek)
(Baby Yaga (Slavonic)	(Papa (Hawaiian)
(Blue Hag (Celtic)	(Spider Woman (Native American)

In short, nearly every tradition depicts the Crone or Grandmother as sagacious, witty, and clever, which is very important because many also oversee death—one of the key issues with which humans wrangle. For example, a Biblical version of the Anatolian Grandmother-goddess is Hannahanna. In most of her legends, this goddess gives birth to the Lord of Death, and is seen as a death goddess who is also highly prophetic. So not only does the Crone oversee death, but she knows the exact time of all things and can look into our very souls; another thing that many humans find a bit uncomfortable!

Now, before you get the impression that building a relationship with such a being might be a bit disconcerting, also know that the Grandmother is warm and understanding. She has (as our youth put it) "been there and done that." There is very little that would surprise this ancient Lady, and consequently, she often knows exactly how to help us in times of need without the searing scorn or chastisement that the Mother sometimes bears.

Let's move on now to exploring her mythology and get a better feel for how various cultures envision the Crone.

Crone Mythology

Among the proto-Celtic people known as the Caledonii, we discover legends of an old blue woman called the Callieach. This mountain woman and bringer of ice was a giantess believed to protect the tribes from harm by nurturing them in the mountains. Sometimes called the Bear Goddess, Boar Goddess, or more simply, Ancient Woman, people sought her out for both her wisdom and the safety she afforded, especially in winter months when food might otherwise be scarce. In this, Callieach's story is different than some other Grandmothers' because she is awake and active when other goddesses sleep.

Another interesting twist to Callieach's mythology is that she is shown governing dreams, the subconscious, and the human unconscious, including those things we normally cannot see with mortal eyes or fully understand (such as the fey). This makes perfect sense when you consider the Crone's connection to the underworld as also potentially symbolizing the human inner worlds and the mysteries after which we seek. If you find this image of the Goddess interesting, stones are sacred to her (the earth's "bones") and her festival day is traditionally the 21st of November.

Second in our exploration of Goddess stories, we'll consider a folkloric cycle called the Crone's curse. In many regions, including Scandinavia and India, the Crone's mythology is intimately linked with the end of all things and her appearance is similarly doomsday-ish. Psychologists explain this phenomenon as simply the natural flip side of the birthing power of the Mother. What one deity creates, he or she (or another deity) can also destroy—it's part of the universal balance.

In particular, the Indian goddess we explored in the last chapter, Kali, is an excellent example of the Crone's curse. This fierce warrior goddess fights demons, yet gives her followers blessings. She is called Mother, and yet it is she who can easily destroy all of Creation because she hungers for blood. This blood-lust actually came about as an act of protection; Kali had slain a demon and if his blood hit the ground, it would have given birth to millions of evil beasts. Upon drinking the blood to keep such darkness from the world, Kali found ecstasy, and she wanted to dance the wild dance of death upon the demon to get more.

Another frightening image of Kali is that of her squatting over Shiva (her consort) during sex, while consuming his intestines. The powerful symbolism here of destruction and new birth is impossible to miss. In Kali and Shiva, the forces of life and death come together and dance, even as they do in each of our lives. But this dance is not without hope or goodness, as the cycle portrayed is eternal. Where one falls, one rises anew. Destruction makes way for creation.

Speaking of these forces, we must understand that the Crone also embodies a kind of universal justice. One goddess who helps reveal this is Lilith, whose myths appear in Sumerian, Babylonian, Persian, Hebrew, and Teutonic stories. In all these myths, Lilith rules over the night, often taking children's lives during birth and giving birth to demons. The question remains: *why?*

In one Hebrew myth, Lilith is likened to the moon, and she is resentful because her beauty is diminished by the sun (which represents God). In other words, her anger comes from being placed in an alienated place by the Father, the Yang of the universe. Another similar story of Lilith places her in the Garden of Eden, arguing with Adam as to why he should be the dominant person of the pair. She does not wish to lie under him, but be an equal with the freedom to choose. When she feels Adam may overpower her, she flees Eden and utters the ineffable name of God. For this she became the mother of demons, often shown with an owl companion and bearing a serpent's body. The implication here is that it was she who gave Eve the apple of knowledge!

It would seem that the stories of Lilith imply that one cannot be wholly free and still keep God happy. Thankfully, modern witches and women don't see her quite that way. Rather, Lilith represents a wholly liberated woman who is sexually indiscriminate, self-sufficient, and really has no need for the roles of mother or wife. The struggle for liberation, however, and living as she did, has very real balancing points. In particular the "dark" Crone's emotions are very full and compelling, bringing forth whatever is on one's mind! If you need anything to bear witness to this truth, observe a woman going through menopause.

Another Crone figure appears in the Scandinavian legend "Voluspa" (meaning Prophesy of the Seeress). This poem is perhaps the best source of information regarding the Norse pantheon as it recounts Creation, then continues until the very end of time. The poem itself appears in the *Elder Edda*, and was likely collected from local legends in the 12th century.

Voluspa is the Seeress speaking in the poem. She begins by talking of the giant Ymir who existed before all things, moves into the coming of the Fates (Norns), and talks of the slaying of Baldr (the god of light), which introduces all manner of evil into the world. Even when the gods beg Voluspa to stop, she does not. She is the Crone who knows the beginning and the ending, and at last her voice is being heard! In the first few stanzas she says:

Heidi men call me when their homes I visit,
A far seeing Volva, wise in talismans.
Caster of spells, cunning in magic.

To wicked women welcome always.
Arm rings and necklaces, Odhinn you gave me
To learn my lore, to learn my magic:
Wider and wider through all worlds I see.

Outside I sat by myself when you came,
Terror of the gods, and gazed in my eyes.
What do you ask of me? Why tempt me?
Odhinn, I know where your eye is concealed,
Hidden away in the well of Mimir:
Mimir each morning his mead drinks
From Valfather's pledge. Well would you know more?

"Well would you know more?" is the ultimate question of the Seeress Crone. How much do we *really* want to know of all things? How much should we know? These are very good questions. Voluspa's legacy, along with her name, which remains behind as the memory of this goddess, are now immortalized in the sacred poetry of the *Eddas*.

Activity: The Crone's Cauldron

As a holder of the deepest mysteries, the Crone is an obvious choice for those wishing to understand magick and the ancient art of divination. After all, she is already aware of life's beginning and end (and all moments in-between). She can see where mortal eyes cannot penetrate. The purpose of this activity is to call upon the Crone to help you develop your future-telling talents. Now, before you say, "I'm not psychic," remember that such gifts are natural, you just have to learn how to unlock them. The Crone is an excellent helpmate!

To begin, you'll need something that can function as a cauldron. I prefer a dark pot or bowl. Fill this item with water and set it on a table where you can sit or stand comfortably nearby and see the surface. Light a candle on that table to represent the Crone (brown or black are suitable hues). As you light the candle try an invocation such as:

Ancient Lady

She who came before, and She who will be at the end of time

Seeress, Witch, Wise Woman...

I call to you

Open my eyes to see with inner sight

Open my mind to the possibilities that lie just beyond

Here and Now

Open my spirit to your truths

I gaze into your cauldron of death and rebirth,

that swirls with time's mysteries

And ask you reveal to me that which I can know

Of the future, for myself or the world

I gaze and watch

And welcome your illumination

So mote it be!

If you've never tried scrying before, be patient with yourself. This isn't like trying to find the hidden picture. In fact, you need to let your eyes look just past the surface of the water and allow your vision to blur a bit. Try to breathe deeply and evenly and wait expectantly. You may see wisps of light or colors at first. This is an excellent beginning! Pay attention to the direction of movements or any symbols that form. As you get more proficient (or if you have a natural knack), you'll get pictures that you can make note of, then watch for those things to come to pass. You'll want to try this for about 10 minutes at first (it will seem like forever!) and slowly extend the amount of time you watch as you get better at it. When you're done, thank the Crone and blow out your candle, making notes of your experiences so you can confirm them.

The last Grandmother/Crone whose mythology we'll explore is that of Pele. Her story begins as a pilgrimage that illustrates the Crone's curse of bearing both creative and destructive energy. Pele followed a star in the northeast sky that was brighter than all else for what seemed to be forever. Then one day she awoke to the smell of something in the air. In the distance, a mountain poured forth hazy smoke and Pele knew she was home. She called the place Hawaii.

As she walked up the mountainside, she carried her magick staff along with an egg given to her by her mother. When she found a place where the earth had collapsed, she firmly put the staff therein, naming the crater Kilauea. The pit inside Kilauea was where Pele set up her residence. Little did Pele know that a fire god named Ailaau also wanted Kilauea for his home. In an effort to win this place, he and Pele tossed fireballs across the land. Ultimately, Ailaau fled and Pele ruled the islands.

Eventually, the egg Pele's mother gifted her hatched into a girl named Hi'iaka'i-ka-poli-o-Pele (Hi'iaka of the bosom of Pele).Several years later, Pele fell in love with an image in a dream. This man's name was Lohiàu and the dream indicated that he was a young prince who lived in Kauai. Pele sent her sister/daughter to bring back her love, but warned that if she did not do so in 40 days, there would be a terrible price to pay.

Upon reaching Kauai, Hi'iaka found Lohiàu dead. Using the knowledge of plants, she rubbed his body with herbs and chanted. The gods listened and brought Lohiàu back to life. In gratitude, Lohiàu agreed to return to the Big Island to meet Pele. Unfortunately, this trip took longer than 40 days, and Pele was certain the two had fallen in love. In a fit of sadness and anger, she used lava to turn Hi'iaka's friend to stone. To fight back, Hi'iaka took the young prince to the edge of the crater, knowing full well Pele could see them, and embraced Lohiàu. Again, Pele's anger struck out, killing Lohiàu in the flames.

At that moment, the two found their anger quelled and both were very sad (one having lost a friend, the other a lover). Pele wisely decided to bring Lohiàu back and let him choose whom he would love. He chose Hi'iaka. Pele, while sad, gave her aloha blessing and released them to sail back to Kauai. Pele remained on Hawaii where she rules the explosive fire that also feeds the land and makes it rich. It is said to this day that people report an old, wild woman walking the side of Kilauea, smoking a cigarette. One is never to take a piece of lava stone from this sacred place without permission, lest you be cursed by her anger. Those who receive permission, in their thoughtfulness, are granted good luck!

Attributes of the Elder Goddess

While humans often see the Crones function as destroyer as somewhat sinister, it is wholly natural. Remember that this being has already been through the other phases of womanhood, but now the wheel must turn once more to find balance. We could not appreciate light without darkness, sound without silence; and likewise, death gives life great meaning and appreciation. It is, in many ways, the ultimate form of recycling energy, and the Elder Goddess builds that bridge not simply between death and rebirth, but between *now* and *not now*, between the temporal and eternal.

In addition, one need not focus wholly on the dark side of the Crone, and in fact, so doing would cause you to miss much of import. There are the Grandmother attributes to consider here. For example, if we look at Sedna in Inuit tradition, we find a Crone who is the source of all nourishment, both for the body and the soul (that pretty well describes my grandmother's huckleberry muffins too!). Similarly, we can consider Cerridwen who meets out wisdom and inventiveness from her never-empty cauldron. In the words of the great Bard Taliesin:

Is not my chair protected by the cauldron of Cerridwen?
Therefore, let my tongue be free
In the sanctuary of the praise of the Goddess.

Another grandmother goddess comes to us from Hawaii. Her name is Papa. This ancient being was not simply a creatrix and guardian of the Spirit realms, but also the keeper of sacred mysteries. Through her we can come to understand our place in the universe with greater perspective.

It seems Papa is not alone in understanding what most humans perceive as a mystery. In Greece we find Hekate teaching humans the secrets of magick. She is, in fact, the patroness of many witches. Originally the daughter of Nyx, Hekate took her place in Olympian realms, finding herself even respected by Zeus, who gave her dominion over the heavens, the earth, and the underworld (somewhat personifying the "as above, so below" on an intimate level!). In addition, she received the power of granting or withholding from humans anything they asked.

Later stories mostly recognized Hekate as the Goddess of the Underworld and of death's mysteries. But as with the Grandmother, Hekate still possesses the attributes of the Maiden and Mother Goddess. She is the Queen of magick, ritual, and prophecy, but also rules over childbirth and regeneration. As an interesting aside, even in her role as the death goddess, she seems to be a gentle guide for those who leave the mortal plane unnaturally. Thus when one wished to call on her to aid a spirit, to gain a glimpse of the future, or to empower a spell, it was appropriate to go to crossroads and make an offering of a cake (the meeting of two worlds).

Next we come to Grandmother Moon, another very ancient figure in Native American mythology. After Grandmother Moon gave birth to her children and made sure they could take care of themselves, she journeyed to the sky. This way, her children could see her and know she had not forgotten them. When Father Sun is sleeping, Grandmother Moon comes into glory and watches her children through the night. From this position she helps her children with dreams and visions, both in attaining them and in understanding their sometimes elusive imagery.

Tradition says that Grandmother Moon oversees all aspects of the feminine energies. She can teach us intuition, introspection, and most importantly, transformation. She is also known by the name Nissa, being a guide on our paths, a leader to all women, and controlling the ocean's movements. As is said in an Iroquois thanksgiving address: "...with one mind, we send greetings and thanks to our grandmother moon. Now our minds are one."

Activity: Moon Meditation

Wait until the moon is starting to wane to try this meditation. If possible, go outside beneath the full moon's rays. Look upward and try to visualize the profile of the Grandmother superimposed on the lunar sphere. All the small lines become wrinkles from smiles and thoughts. Her eyes sparkle with wit, her mouth in a gentle smile. Once you have that image firmly in your mind, close your eyes and bask in Grandmother's light and breathe deeply.

Next, begin to draw that image ever closer to yourself. It will seem huge at first, but know that the distance between you and the stars is nothing but a thought. Reach out and cup the moon in your welcoming hands, gently and expectantly. Whisper a welcome to Grandmother Spirit in a way that feels right, then bring the image of the moon directly to your heart where it sinks in and becomes part of you.

In this magickal moment between time and space, you are one with the Grandmother and with all eternity! Look at the world and the universe with her knowing eyes. Look at yourself in a whole new, mature way.

Gather whatever insights you most need, then release the moon back to the sky and write of your experiences in a journal for future reference.

As you begin to see, Grandmother and Crone offer a wide variety of attributes to those who seek them. They can teach us quick speech; how to open our psychic self; how to use money, energy, and resources wisely; and how to apply the vital forces of nature with care and compassion. They also teach us, as Lilith, not to be a slave to emotion, nor repress those feelings that really matter to us. We can be intimately involved and still look at things with detachment.

There are many other wonderful things about the Crone, including her dependability. This lady is no stranger to hard work or service, and once a promise is made, it's kept! Call on the Grandmother to witness those promises and oaths that you want to honor, allowing her sense of commitment to guide your actions.

Finally, I would add that the Grandmother spirit is not "all work and no play." If anything, she understands the human need for down time and leisure far better than most. When the Crone comes to us in this capacity she says: *All that you wish to do cannot be done when your inner well is dry. Come to me ... come to Cerridwen, and be refreshed!*

The Grandmother Spirit for Men

The question has been posed: How do we go about building a relationship with the dark Grandmother who holds all the laws of life and death in the balance? At times she seems overly harsh, and her knowledge overwhelmingly precise. Typically, the best time to consider this aspect of the Goddess is during the times of transition, such as when you move, when you start a new job, when you break off a relationship, and so forth. Why? Because these junctures mark both an ending and a beginning—the very domain over which the Crone presides.

In these moments where the hinge of your life is moving, lay your changes before her, and seek balance and insight. The Crone's eternal lifetime of experience allows us to confront the normal fears that accompany change, embrace it, and release it. For men, in particular, she helps in coping with emotion, especially those you might otherwise suppress. She is your guide through any darkness.

I've chosen Grandmother Spider for this part of our exploration because she has been a guide and spiritual force in life's network. We see images of her everywhere in the world under various names including the Nornes, Urd, Verdandi, Skuld, and Lachesis. By any name, Grandmother Spider watches over the structure of time itself, monitoring the past, measuring the present, and moderating the future.

What's important to men here is that the Grandmother helps you work outside the box (outside the material plane). Typically, archetypal male energy is oriented toward logic and rationality. It's the main reason there have been apparently less men than women who practiced magick and psychism throughout the ages. Her primal energy releases some of the constraints that lie between your external construct and internal realities. In fact, she can also help you with encouraging spiritual dreams and understanding their meaning.

Activity: A Grandmother Spider Dream Charm

This is a very easy item to create, and it should be placed above or below your bed, or underneath your pillow when you want Grandmother to empower your dreams, help you remember them, and give you insight as to their meaning. Begin with a plain dream catcher. You can find these at a lot of New Age or Native American gift shops and online stores. Next, you'll want to decorate it in a manner that honors the Grandmother. You can utilize the symbolism provided in this chapter, or focus on *one* Grandmother Spirit and use her sacred symbols to adorn the item.

When you've completed the dream catcher, stand beneath a waning moon and bless it saying:

Grandmother Spider—Goddess of Time, not time,

From whom dreams may come

Send down your silver strand to bless this token

Wrap your protection into each cord so that night visions

Be good, and meaningful

I give my dreams into your care even as I

Hold them in my soul

Place the dream catcher as recommended on those nights when you want to have spiritually centered dreams (make sure you have a tape recorder or paper handy so you can record them). Also, sometimes it helps to burn some dream-evoking incense as you're lying down. Aromatics for this include jasmine, marigold, and rose.

Hopi legends tell us that Spider Woman connected east to west and north to south with her strands. So, because of her spider nature, Grandmother can help you with networking between individuals and in making deep connections. In particular, this seems useful in developing good communication skills geared toward acquaintances, friends, family, and groups. The reasoning center of the archetypal male can sometimes miss nuances in conversation (whereas this archetypal Crone picks up on them all!). When you feel like what you said is NOT what someone else heard, call on this goddess!

Finally, for men and women who are firekeepers in their respective Neo-Pagan communities, you might like to know that Grandmother Spider may make an excellent patroness for your efforts. Choctaw legend tells us how she found clay, made a special container, and spun a web to go to the East, where she found fire. Grandmother wisely put the fire in the clay pot and brought it back to all people. It was she who taught humans how to feed fire, how to keep it safely burning in a ring of stone, and how to keep those sacred flames from ever going out. Aho!

Symbols for the Crone

Most visual depictions of the Crone are pretty ugly and Halloween-ish. She is often wrongly illustrated as a wicked witch, complete with black cat and cone-shaped hat. What's interesting, however, is that image does have real power. It's obvious that people knew that the Crone was not a Lady with whom to trifle!

A cauldron is very common among the many symbols of the Crone (think Shakespeare with an attitude). In this case, the cauldron represents the womb from which all life originates, and where it must return. As the waters of the cauldron stir, matter breaks down and reforms. Here are more of the Crone's representations and sacred items:

☾ **Colors:** Dark brown (like rich soil), black, and midnight blue.

☾ **Moon phases:** Waning to dark; moon in Taurus (leisure), moon in Gemini (transformation), moon in Libra (revealing secrets and truths), moon in Capricorn (the hidden self or inner life), moon in Pisces (psychism).

☾ **Stones:** Smoky quartz, fossils, albite, feldspar, moonstone, amethyst (dreams), carnelian (communication), sugilite (spirituality), jade (wisdom).

☾ **Hours:** Sunset to dawn, in particular 9 p.m. (understanding universal law), and 11 p.m. (coping with changes).

☾ **Season:** Winter.

☾ **Plants:** Holly, mandrake, nightshade, most things that grow underground (root crops), mugwort.

☾ **Other items:** Withered items, dried or preserved foods, antiques, crossroads.

Let's put this together in an example:. Say you're facing the death of a loved one. It's either on the horizon or has just happened. The Crone is exceedingly helpful in getting us through such times and comforting us. To inspire that energy, you might wish to make a portable Crone charm that will saturate your aura like a balm of strength and healing. To construct a Crone charm, I'd take a 4" × 4" piece of natural dark-blue cloth (blue speaks of inner peace) and place a piece of holly and smoky quartz therein. Tie it with a dark cord that you knot three times (once for each face of the Goddess) and incant something such as:

Maiden lift my burden

Mother heal my pain

Crone make our lives whole again!

Repeat the incantation with each knot you tie, then carry it with you. When you find your heart and your family returning to normal, give the contents of your charm back to the earth with a thankful heart.

Celebrating the Crone

It might seem odd to consider celebrating the Crone because by so doing, we're celebrating death and endings. The truth is that many Western cultures are simply not prepared for the Crone's workings. We've glamorized death, or worse, made it all too sterile and impersonal. The Crone does not allow that to be so. She is the midwife between the worlds, and she does not let us wander alone or become lonely. The key here is looking at it slightly differently—rather than worrying over what you're loosing, think about welcoming a fresh beginning! Or as a poet friend of mine said, *"Mourn not the candle's passing, but celebrate how brightly it burned."*

Whether we are the one who dies or lives, the Grandmother takes us through the darkness to facilitate new life. The Harvester of Experience is also the one to whom we should be turning in our Eldership rites. At such times, she gives us the ability to see what we keep from ourselves, and to look at the face of aging with appreciation and respect rather than distain. Call upon the Grandmother to overcome those inner darknesses and unhealthy perceptions so we can be *real* to ourselves and others. And in fact, so doing is perhaps the best way to celebrate her. Another way to honor the Crone is by retreat. This ancient woman knows the power of solitude and silence. In these moments, Spirit can truly talk to you, and you have time to truly *listen*. There is so much noise in our lives—so much hurrying that we rarely get to pause and integrate. Getting away, communing with ourselves and Spirit, this is what begins to tap our human potential.

Activity: An Hour of Silence

Once a month, or whenever it's practicable, give yourself one hour of silence where you can be alone with your thoughts and the Crone. Turn off the phone, put up "do not disturb" signs—whatever it takes to ensure you have quiet. You'll find that it opens psychic pathways, releases stress, and gives you a much greater "ear" for the sounds of the universe that we often miss in daily living. It also is one step toward personal wholeness. Until you can be alone without feeling lonely, you cannot really come to know the strength and wisdom the Crone offers. Silence is part of spiritual completion. It is part of fulfillment.

If you're looking for a specific time to celebrate the Crone, most winter holidays are quite suitable, as they take place during her dark months. No matter what rituals or spells you intend to do, confront the Dark Mother willingly and without dread. Just as winter turns to spring, our life's wheel is ever turning and it is the Crone who brings us back to life once more.

God/Goddess
Final Word

God Final Word

Thou art God.

"So, why write this book?" a friend asked me. My style and the style of my writing companion in this project are so very different. My friend next asked, "What will happen if someone reads her half and thinks it is your writing? Worse yet, what happens if someone reads part of what you wrote and thinks it was her creation?" They would think she has developed a split personality.

So I would like to take a moment to answer these questions publicly. I accepted this challenge for just that reason: Because Patricia and I are obviously completely and totally different people. But guess what? We are also good friends. She has her opinions, I have my opinions, and yet we were able to put both of these views into one book without much risk of spontaneous combustion. Imagine what the world could accomplish if in its great diversity it could do the same. Sure, all Trish and I managed to do was write a book. But imagine if a few billion people came together in one such common goal.

Blessed be and live free,

A.J. Drew

In the glory of our Lord and Lady, so mote it be.

Goddess Final Word

—Patricia Telesco

In parting, I'd like to say it's impossible to focus on anything for 40-plus hours a week and not have it manifest in your life somehow. This exploration has proven no less so, and in fact, has become very special for me. Various aspects of the Goddess have emerged in my life and heart in more viable ways than ever before. I find their energies shining within and without. In addition, I've found my understanding of feminine energies has taken on whole new, unexpected, and wonderful dimensions. I pray this book inspires similar awareness in you about both the God and Goddess, and that spark of the Divine that resides in each of us. Blessed Be!

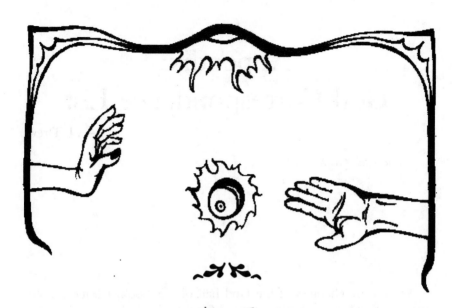

Appendix:
God and Goddess
Correspondence Lists

Appendix:
God Correspondence List

—A.J. Drew

Thou art God.

Within the chapters of the God half of this book, I listed the God forms applicable to each aspect of the God. In those chapters, the listings were for the purpose of illustrating the subject at hand. In so doing, only a tiny portion of the story of each god form was mentioned. I would like to say this section includes the rest of each archetype's story, but that is well beyond the scope of this, or any, book. You see, as with us, each deity is a living, growing thing that simply cannot be confined to a single book, much less a single paragraph.

However, it is too often that we think of our Lord as God of this or Lord of that. Too often do we hear that Vulcan is a god of war without also being told that he is god of the smith. So, presented here is an attempt to look at many of the gods mentioned in this book from a more rounded perspective. If you would like a lengthier list, I invite you to read *A Wiccan Bible*. But even there you will not find the whole of the story, for our Lord is alive and well, living not in books, but in the hearts of men.

Abderus (Greek): His name means "Son of battle." Although not exactly a great example of intelligence found in our lore, his story does warn of the cost of friendship. While watching the man-eating mares of Diomedes for his kith Heracles, he was himself eaten. In his honor, Heracles named the town Abdera. Interestingly enough, the inhabitants of that town were later considered to be less than intelligent.

Aengus the Younger (Celtic): Also known as Angus, Anghus, Aonghus, and Angus Og. He is the primary Irish god of love who appeared as a handsome young man with four birds flying about his head. The birds are sometimes said to be similar to the arrows of Cupid. Other times they are said to be his kisses flying through the air.

In a dream, Aengus the Younger fell desperately in love with a young maiden he had never met. He spoke of this dream to his mother, who searched in vain for a year and a day to find her. He then called on the Dagda, who did the same. Finally, the Dagda's aid and trusted friend took up the search and found her, but not alone. She was amidst more than 100 other maidens, and yet he spotted the woman from his dreams instantly. For the rest of the story, see the listing for **Oengus Mac Oc**.

Aeolus (Greek): Also known as Aeolos and Aiolos. The caretaker of the four winds: Eurus (East), Notus (South), Zephyrus (West), and Boreas (North). Such that those winds did not cause havoc when the gods did not desire such strife, Aeolus and the four winds were placed in a cave on one of the Lipara islands. Aeolus took a liking to Odysseus, so he gave Odysseus, a ship captain, a bag containing ill winds in the hopes that because those ill winds were contained in the bag, they would not plague Odysseus's sails. Unfortunately, while Odysseus slept, curiosity got the better of his crew. They opened the bag to have a look-see, thus releasing the ill winds that blew the ship far off course and provided us with many further tails found in the *Odyssey.*

Agni (Hindu): Although a god of fire himself, Agni is also the messenger of the Vedic gods. He is also the guardian and spirit of the hearth fire, accepting sacrifices therein. But he is neither confined to the hearth, nor to fire. He is the fire of the soul as well, and thus carried in every living thing. In this way, his role as messenger of the gods is also our connection to those gods. As we consume food, he is the fire that consumes that food as if it were a sacrifice made to the gods.

Airyaman (Persian): He is the personification of friendship and healing, and that is where most Pagan references seem to stop. He is also an early god of marriage, social ties, bonds, and oral agreements made in good faith. As a final gesture of friendship from the gods, when the end of time comes, Airyaman will retrieve the souls of many who had previously been damned.

Aizen-Myoo (Japanese): Understanding Aizen-Myoo requires that one understand the people who worshipped him. At the peek of his worship, those people were what one might call the working class of today's Western culture. He was widely praised by prostitutes, but at the time, prostitution was not looked down upon, as it often is today, as a lower class occupation. He was also praised by the artisans and musicians. His fierce appearance, having three eyes and the head of a lion woven into his hair, is perhaps commentary on his role as protector of the hearts and emotions of the working class. He is, after all, the chief god presiding over love to the social class that praised him.

Akba-atatdia (Native American): He was chiefly responsible for Creation in the lore of the Crow. His name loosely translates as "He who has made everything." He is one of the many god forms that have been lumped into the term "Great Spirit" by the many New Age Native American revivalists who seem intent on creating one universal tradition to represent the many diverse Native American traditions.

Ambat (Melanesian): A culture hero turned god, Ambat taught many arts; most notably the art of pottery and cultural rituals.

Amor (Roman): He was son of Venus whose attributes are so close to Cupid that most believe that Amor is another name for Cupid. His name is also the Latin word for *love*.

Apollo (Greek): Also known as Apollon. Most often cited as a god of medicine, Apollo is more specifically known in that area as the destroyer of plague. In that capacity, he is called Smintheus, which may come from the term *sminthos*, which loosely means "rodent killer" or "mouse destroyer." It is a widely known fact that plague is spread by parasites that ride in the fur of rodents (particularly rats). Where locusts were a common plague, he was called Parnopius (a word with connection to the root of the word for grasshopper).

He was also a talented musician. As such, he became the leader of the Muses. With this and the name Smintheus (mouse destroyer), one might see a link to the story of the Pied Piper.

He is the twin brother of Artemis (goddess of the hunt who is depicted with a bow). Apollo is also sometimes depicted with a bow and is said to be an excellent archer; however, his skill in that department is reserved for sport and never hunting. Where his sister presides over the hunting of wild animals, Apollo is the protector of domestic animals. This is perhaps good commentary on the discussion of kith and kin familiars.

Although it is an attribute that is often overlooked, Apollo is quite an inspiration of lust. In his time, he is said to have chased after the nymphs

Daphne, Cyrene, and many others. But his lust was not confined to nymphs; he chased after and bedded many mortal women as well. Most notably, he fathered a child with Hecuba (the wife of the King of Troy), as well as her daughter Cassandra.

Then there is his bedding of Coronis (daughter of the King of Lapiths) who conceived his son Asclepius. When Apollo discovered that Coronis had cheated on him, he sent his twin sister, Artemis, to kill her. Ah, didn't know Artemis was an assassin did you? After the deed was done and the body was on the pyre, Apollo reached into the flames, sliced open his lover's abdomen, and removed his son Asclepius. But that was the least of Apollo's acts of rage.

He once became so enraged by an insult to his mother that he killed all of the male children of the woman who had caused the insult. His sister, Artemis, joined him in this killing spree and took the lives of all the woman's daughters. On another occasion, the satyr Marsyas found a flute created by the goddess Athena. Such a beautiful noise it would make that he challenged Apollo to a competition to see who could make the more beautiful music. Apollo won, but he was a sore looser. After the contest, Apollo chased Marsyas into a cave where he killed him by gutting him alive. So much of Marsyas's blood flowed that it became the river know known by his name.

His lust was not confined to women alone. He fell in love with a man named Hyacinthus (a prince of Sparta who Apollo's father, Zeus, lusted after as well). Unfortunately for Hyacinthus, the god of the west winds (Zephyrus) had lusted after him at the same time as Apollo. As an act of jealousy, Zephyrus caused a discus that had been thrown by Apollo to travel off course and accidentally kill his male lover. In memory of the fallen love, Apollo caused the hyacinth flower to grow from the man's spilled blood.

Apollo's collection of male lovers also included a man named Cyparissus. To this young man, Apollo gave a gift of a deer that became the young man's companion. While practicing with the javelin, the young man accidentally killed his companion. With tears flowing from his eyes, he begged Apollo to forever mourn his dead companion. Apollo granted his request, transforming him into the cypress tree (a symbol of grief).

Apoyan Tachi (Pueblo Zuni): He was Creator and sky god. With his wife, he brought into manifestation all things that exist.

Asclepius (Greek): Also known as Asklepios and Aesculapius. The son of Apollo and Coronis who was ripped from his dead mother's womb by his father, Apollo, after she was murdered by Artemis at the request of Apollo. Asclepius was instructed in the art of healing by the centaur Chiron (also known as the Thessalian god of medicine). His symbol, a staff with a snake curling up the shaft, is still in use today as the symbol of our modern medicine, healing, and physicians.

The skills of Asclepius were so great that he was once called upon to raise the dead. Feeling that such an action was in defiance of the natural order of things, Zeus killed Asclepius with a lightning bolt. But that did not stop Asclepius from continuing his healing arts. After his death, he has been said to visit the sick in their dreams, and there he assists them in the healing process.

Not only is Asclepius skilled in the art of healing medicine and surgery, he is also reported to have the knowledge of love potions. He is often called upon in that endeavor.

Basa-Jaun (Basque): Also known as Basajaun. He is "Lord of the woods" to the Basque. Protector of domesticated animals and responsible for teaching humanity the art of farming, animal husbandry, the forging of metal, and other matters of negotiating with nature.

Buzyges (Greek): The Greek folk hero who greatly improved the art of farming by instructing the Greek people in using animals to pull the plough to till the soil.

Chronos (Greek): The Grandfather of time who is the personification of time itself. Some references indicate he is equated to the Roman Saturn. He is said to have existed prior to Zeus or any of the elder gods. Interestingly enough, he is often cited as a god of sowing, which leads me to think that perhaps his lore is associated with the term "A stitch in time saves nine." Chronos should not to be confused with Cronus, which is sometimes spelled Kronos or Cronos.

Consus (Roman): Traditionally referenced as the Roman god of stored food, Consus was the god who protected underground stores of grain. However, while we do not tend to store food in such hidden places today, he has become the god who protects hidden meeting places, covert exchanges, and advice given in secret.

Cuchulainn (Celtic): Also known as Cú Chulainn, Cuchulain, and Setanta. Celtic folk hero turned god, Cuchulainn's story speaks of duty. He was born Setanta, son of Sualtam, but changed his name after killing the guard dog of Culann. Due to his actions, he felt that duty bound him to take the place of that dog, and thus assumed the name Cuchulainn, or

"The Hound of Culann." So honorable and respectful of duty was this man that he was adopted in spirit by Lugh.

Before his death at the hands of Queen Maeve's forces, he was quite the lustful youth. His list of lovers is long, including both mortal women and even the Faery Queen Fand. Lore has it that the Queen called on him for assistance in an ongoing conflict. Cuchulainn accepted, but only under the condition that she become his wife. She agreed to meet him. Upon doing so, the two fell deeply in love and decided to wed. To prevent that marriage, her father, who felt such a union would cause disaster for the Faery Folk, used magick to cause each to forget the other.

Cupid (Roman): The son of Venus whose name comes from the Latin _cupido_, which means "desire." Although his modern representation is often of "cute love," as is his Greek counterpart Eros, he is god of the type of love that involves deeply felt sexual desire, passion, and lust.

Another note on the modern view of Cupid. Historically, he was most often depicted as an attractive, winged, and naked young man. He was not often depicted as an infant, but he was shown with his mother, Venus. The confusion comes about because he was sometimes depicted as being accompanied by winged infants (the Amoretti).

See also **Eros** for a further discussion of the transformation of this lusty god into the modern-day depiction.

Damon (Greek): Culture hero who demonstrated perfect love and perfect trust for his friend Pythias, who had been condemned to death by Dionysius the Elder. Pythias was allowed to leave in order to put his affairs in order before his execution, but only if someone stayed in his place and accepted the punishment of death if Pythias did not return. Damon did just that. Upon the return of Pythias, both were released because Dionysius felt it wrong to destroy such a friendship with death.

Although this story is told time and time again, the lore is oftentime reversed, with Damon being the one consigned to die. Either way, the story is one of the strongest examples of friendship and trust that can be found, as either of the two men could have evaded death, so it does not matter how the story is told. One by not stepping forward and the other by not returning. The name Damon is sometimes cited as the source of the name Damien.

Dionysus (Greek): Also known as Dionysos. Most often cited as the Greek god of intoxication, wine, and patron of the performing arts, he is also the god of spiritual intoxication and the patron of ritual. It is almost as if when we look at Dionysus, we see two gods at the same time. One involved with fertility, agriculture, and the intoxication that relieves the pain of the world in which we must live. The other is involved with matters of spirit and the intoxication of the soul, which relieves the pain of the world in which the spirit and heart reside. From a philosophical viewpoint, one might call him a drunken Buddha.

Orphaned by the death of his mother, Semele, while he was still in her womb, he was resurrected by his father, Zeus (who had been tricked by Hera into killing Semele). He was then given to the nymphs by his father to be raised. Similar to his friend Pan, he grew into a lusty youth who pursued the nymphs on many occasions.

Domovoi (Russian): Also known as Domovoy and St. Paraskeva.* A household spirit called either the "Grandfather" or "Master" of every house. Although he is most often depicted as a small elderly man, he is a shapeshifter and often adopts both the physical and spiritual attributes of the folk who share their house with him. Thus, he becomes a kind spirit in the homes of the kind and a mean spirit in the homes of the mean. Sometimes he inhabits courtyards, backyards, gazebos, and other places where people spend time.

Be warned that he does not like people who do not maintain their homes. Remember, there is a Domovoi for every house and every place where people meet. So it is your responsibility to maintain your household to keep in the blessings of your Domovoi, lest you raise his tendency to become a very mischievous spirit in an unkempt home. Now, where did those car keys go?

(*On the Russian conversion to Christianity, the church replaced Domovoi with St. Paraskeva.)

Dyaus Pita (Hindu): Vedic Sky Father whose Earth Mother wife is Prthivi. United they are called Dyavaprthivi (the sum total of all that is). They were initially separated by Varuna in a story that brings to mind the separation of Ying and Yang by Pan-gu. Thus, the story of Dyaus Pita (yang) and Prthivi (yin) is yet another example of ancient lore that serves as the foundation for the Wiccan concept of deity.

Elli (Norse): Also known as Elle. Elli and the strongest of the Norse gods agreed one day to have a wrestling match. Although Thor was much greater in strength and size than Elli, he soon tired and was defeated because Elli is the personification of that which no one can defeat—old age.

Enki (Sumerian): The Babylonians called him Ea. Both Babylonians and Sumerians called him the Creator. But he was more than a creator god, for not only did he take part in the creation of the world, he also instructed humanity in the art of mastering not only the visible natural world, but the occult (hidden) world as well.

He invented culture (called "me") and taught humanity how to farm and how to negotiate with nature. But he also held the secrets to such powerful medicine that it would make a man immortal, raise the dead, and bring all forms of magick into manifestation.

Eros (Greek): Although considered one of the oldest of gods, being a cohort with Chaos, Eros is depicted as a beautiful young man who inspires sexual desire in both men and women. Sometimes cited as the Roman god of love, when he is called by this name it is usually in reference to sexual desire and raw lust. When he is called Amor (also the Latin word for love) he is generally seen more in his role as god of love.

Some references record his lineage as being born of Nyx (night) by Erebus (darkness). Others state it was Aphrodite (goddess of love) by Ares (god of war). But in some traditions he is said to be a constant, manifest and yet unborn, who was the very inspiration for the union of our Sky Father as Uranus and Earth Mother as Gaia.

He is depicted as a naked, winged youth with a bow and arrows with which he inspires both love and lust. Oftentimes he is shown with the goddess Psyche (soul) in his arms. This is perhaps commentary on the touching of the soul by passion.

Faunus (Roman): Roman god of unbridled nature and the fertility found therein. Although he is often equated to the Greek Pan, Faunus was depicted in mostly human form prior to that association, after which he received hooves and horns similar to those of Pan.

In his role as protector of livestock, he is called Lupercus, which means something in the order of "the one who staves off the wolf." As such, although very few modern-day Wiccans have herds and flocks to protect, he continues to be a favored god form to call on for assistance in protecting domesticated animals.

Funzi (African): Also known as Mfuzi. Shortly after the Fjort people received fire from a water spirit, Funzi appeared to instruct them in the use of that fire. In addition to its use to warm the home at night and the preparation of food, Funzi instructed in the use of fire to work metal into tools and implements. He was also responsible for teaching them how to use these functional crafts in negotiations with nature.

Gama (Japanese): Also known as Gama-Sennin. He is the god of good health and long life. He is most often depicted as a kind old man riding a stag with an armful of scrolls, representing the wisdom and teaching of the ages. However, he is also said to be able to change his skin and hair at will, becoming a young man any time he so pleased. He is strongly associated with Japanese medicine and makes a fine figure as patron of the modern-day pharmacist.

Ganymede (Greek): He was the cupbearer to the gods of Mount Olympus in more than one sense. He was also one of Zeus's male lovers. So beautiful was this young man that he was desired by gods and goddesses alike. He was kidnapped by the goddess Eos (dawn) when she took fancy to him, but he was either retaken by Zeus, or maybe Eos cut a deal to return him. As with most things, it depends on who is telling the story.

Gucumatz (Mayan): He was a serpent god who instructed on the art of community building. He is the inventor of social law and taught humanity how to farm and negotiate with nature so that they would not find it necessary to steal from their neighbors.

Hephaestus (Greek): Also known as Hephaistos. Patron to all craftsmen and especially so to blacksmiths, metalworkers, potters, and anyone who works with fire. But Hephaestus is much more than a fire or volcano god. He is more than patron of craftspeople. He is an inspiration for anyone who has ever been tread upon. Born with a disfiguring limp, he is sometimes called the lame god. So disgusted was his own mother (Hera) by his disfigurement, she cast him down from Mount Olympus (heaven).

Determined to seek revenge, he created a most beautiful throne and had it presented to Hera. She was thrilled, but when she sat in it she discovered it had been a trick. The chair imprisoned her and although the other gods and goddesses begged him to release her, he refused. Well, he refused until Dionysus got him snookered and returned the drunken Hephaestus to Mount Olympus. By some accounts, he then released Hera after being promised a night in the arms of Aphrodite, by others it was a marriage. Either way, I think Hephaestus received the better end of the bargain. For his part in the release of Hera, Dionysus (who was not always on the best of terms with the gods of the Mount) was allowed to join *Team Mount Olympus.*

Hippomenes (Greek): An example of a young man who understands the sport that love can often involve. Having fallen in love with the virgin

Atalanta, he discovered that she would not welcome a man to her bed unless that man had bested her in sport. Knowing he could not possibly outrun her, he decided to outwit her. Not feeling much up to that challenge either, he turned to Aphrodite (goddess of love) for assistance. Aphrodite gave him three golden apples and the instructions that would win both the race and the hand of Atalanta. He put all of his energy into the very first part of the race. Atalanta set her own pace, believing he would tire and she would defeat him. But once Hippomenes achieved the lead, he began dropping the golden apples one at a time. Each time he dropped an apple, Atalanta slowed to pick it up and Hippomenes won the race.

This is an important story because it says something about love magick. As a result of the trickery involving the golden apples, Hippomenes and Atalanta became wed and were indeed very happy. A similar golden apple and trickery were responsible for putting two other lovers together and that affair led to the Trojan War.

Ilmarinen (Finnish): He was a smith god who forged the sky, sun, and moon. He is responsible for giving fire to humanity and instructing them in the working of metals. He was so skilled at his craft that he forged his own wife of hard metals in such a way that she was soft and remained forever warm to his touch. In his role as sky god, he was friend to sailors and anyone who relied on favorable winds.

Iolaus (Greek): His friendship with Heracles was legendary. Not only did he help Heracles defeat the Hydra, he was there to lead his good friend's funeral and to light his pyre.

Jurojin (Japanese): The Shinto god of good health and long life. Although most often cited as a Japanese god, Jurojin originally migrated into Japan from China. He is depicted as a happy, friendly old man with a staff that has a scroll wrapped around it. Although he comes to you smiling and polite, the names and times of death of everyone who is now living is written on that scroll. His appearance is not always welcomed, especially not when he moves to introduce himself just after reading from that scroll.

He is most often accompanied by a turtle or tortoise. However, he is sometimes depicted with a stag, crane, or another creature with longevity. He is often equated to Fukurokuju (god of wisdom). Other times he and Fukurokuju are said to inhabit the same body. Thus, we see a clear connection between wisdom and old age.

Kaakwha (Native American): Also known as Hawenniyo. The Old Man or Grandfather Sky God of the Seneca. He is the personification of the eternal sun. His lodge is on the other side of the earth, where he goes to retire every night.

Kama (Hindu): He is the Hindu god of love in much the same way as Cupid and Eros. In modern lore, he is a constant reminder that our sometimes narrow view that modern movement is based on European standards, are really universal constants. In this case, those universal constants are love, lust, and desire.

Kamado-gami (Japanese): This is not a single deity, but a reference to the watchful spirits of the home and hearth.

Kutkinnaku (Siberian): He is the raven god of the Koryak. He is sometimes cited as a benevolent spirit rather than a god form. Kutkinnaku is a teacher god who taught humanity the art of creating fire, negotiating with nature, and the shamanic use of the drum to alter consciousness during ritual.

Laran (Etruscan): He is often shown either skyclad except for his helm or with nothing but a loincloth and a helm. Laran is a youthful Etruscan god of war. As with many gods of war, Laran is associated with fire and the sun. However, it is important to note that among his attributes is reference to his responsibility of keeping the peace.

Maponos (Celtic): His name means "Divine Youth." Although Celtic in origin, most of the information available about Maponos comes from Roman sources. In a time when the Roman army relied heavily on foreign conscripts, or pseudo-volunteers, Maponos was a favored god form among the ranks of many Roman hired soldiers. In those ranks, he was sometimes equated with the Greek/Roman Apollo. However, keep in mind that many Celtic gods were equated to Apollo.

Marunogere (Melanesian): Most often cited as the Melanesian god who taught the Papuans how to create the long house, our modern lore seems to jump right over the fact that he was also the god responsible for creating women. His lore is a prime example of how it was not the advent of Christianity alone that led to a patriarchy.

Mentor (Greek): Mentor was a trusted friend to Odysseus who watched over his household and son (Telemachus) as Odysseus was off to fight in what has come to be called the Trojan War. During that time, the goddess Athena took the form of Mentor several times and gave Telemachus divine council in the guise of the council of a mortal friend. Since that time, the word *mentor* has been used to refer to a person who gives advice on a more personal level than what the word *teacher* would imply.

Minga Bengale (African): He was the hunting god of the Shongon people. While I cannot be sure when his lore began, it was obviously influenced by the modern world, as his primary attribute is the inventor of the net for capturing animals. He did so because his people did not have the hunting advantage of the shotgun. I believe the lore about his discovery of and teaching about nets probably predates the existence of modern firearms and that the lore about why he created it was added later.

Mithra (Persian/Ancient Iranian): Also known as Mitra. I have yet to find it, but somewhere in Neo-Pagan lore someone must have published a book that stated Mithra was the Zoroastrianism name for Satan. I say this not because it is true, but because although most academic references are devoid of this little bit of bunk, conversations with many seemingly enlightened Neo-Pagan folk include it. The truth is that Mithra was not a god form in Zoroastrianism. He was a god form in the earlier Iranian religions. There he was associated with friendship and oral contracts.

When Zarathustra, the founder of Zoroastrianism, started teaching a religion in which there was one good god (Ahura Mazda) and one evil one (Angra Mainyu), most other god forms (Mithra included) were demoted to the role of servant/messenger of Ahura Mazda.

While it is true that some of the more uneducated folk involved in the establishment of the current Pagan community spread propaganda stating that Christianity was the start of the dualistic system of Good (God) versus Evil (Satan), if we hope to shed that misinformation, we should not do so by perpetuating our own propaganda. The seemingly uniquely Christian concept of Good (God) versus Evil (Satan) was alive and well long before Christianity, and present in Zoroastrianism where the structure was the same—Good (Ahura Mazda) versus Evil (Angra Mainyu).

Mu Gong (Chinese): Also known as Mu Kung. After he received influence from Taoism, he became the personification of the principle of Yang. Xi Wang-mu, his wife, is the personification of the principle of Yin. Together, they are an ideal example of the Wiccan principle of the Creator as a marriage. Apart, they are precisely what is meant by the Wiccan concept of Lord and Lady. Together, they created all that is. Apart, they created nothing. But without that ability to separate, their union could not have taken place. Hence the term, "Separated for the sake of Union," which is a central concept to my view of the Wiccan religion.

Musubi-no-Kami (Japanese): Unlike Eros, Cupid, and other gods of love from Pagan lore, Musubi-no-Kami was also the god of matrimony and the unions formed in love. He primarily appeared to young women, popping out of a cherry tree to surprise them with the appearance of a beautiful male youth. His promise was that the young woman would meet an idyllic young man who would become her own.

Nabu (Sumerian/Babylonian): Often cited as the son of Marduk, Nabu was a god of the written word and the recording of history. Under a statue in front of a temple of Nabu, which has been dated to about 800 B.C.E., an inscription has been translated to read "Trust in Nabu, do not trust in any other god." I believe this reference intends to imply not that one should believe the written word, but the truth as recorded by Nabu concerning history. It is perhaps an early observation that those who do not remember history will repeat it. I incorporate this into my belief that the Wiccan Book of Shadows should record all portions of a person's life, not just ritual. It should be a personal journal, which is handed down to one's children so that they have the advantage of our trials and errors.

Narcissus (Greek and Roman): If you look up the term self-centered, you should see the name Narcissus. His story was recorded differently by the Greeks and the Romans. An early Greek tale states that he was pursued by another man, Ameinias. In the later Roman version, he was pursued by nymph after nymph, woman after woman, and he rejected them all. While it is fine to reject undesired attention, the story of Narcissus is centered on the theme that he rejected love because he was entirely too busy being in love with himself. *Oh, look at me. Am I not great?* He did not see the beauty and greatness in other people, so he rejected them right up until the day he caught a reflection in a body of water of the most beautiful thing he had ever seen. He stopped and gazed at the beauty looking back at him. Because it never moved, he was trapped in that gaze for eternity. He was, of course, looking at his own reflection. This story is an ancient way of saying *Get over yourself.*

Nereus (Greek): Patron of those who travel by water, Nereus is the wise grandfather of the sea. In particular, he is said to bring blessings to those who travel the Aegean Sea, where he and his 50 daughters are said to live.

Nisse (Scandinavian): Also known as Gardvord. He is most often depicted as the classic image of a pudgy elf or dwarf. He is short and often shown wearing a floppy, pointed hat as he toils away while keeping lists of the daily challenges of maintaining a household and farm.

As with most household spirits, he is temperamental. To remain in his favor, one must give respect not only to the household, but to him as well. Interestingly enough, one of the most often cited ways of keeping him pleased is to leave a plate or bowl of food out for him on the nights of Yule. In later times, the practice evolved into leaving a bowl of porridge on Christmas Eve. A further evolution might be seen in the modern-day tradition of leaving cookies and milk for Santa Claus. While this might be wild speculation, it is interesting to note that the Nisse comes from the same lore that gives us Odin, who is often cited as the origin of the current image of Santa Claus. Aha! What was that folklore about Santa and his little helpers? So that's how he gets to all those houses on a single night, there is a Nisse helping in each house .

Nuada (Celtic): Also known as Nudd and Ludd. Nuada has been compared to the Roman god Neptune. While this is primarily due to his connection to the ocean, Nuada is more of a general, but high-ranking god figure to the Irish Celts and some of the other diverse Celtic people. There, his role on Earth is commented on mostly as a god king and as a god of war. Having lost one of his hands in combat, it was replaced by one fabricated of silver by Bres. He was also the owner of a sword that easily cleaved people in half. It was said that with this sword, Nuada was invincible.

With the sword that makes him invincible and his ascending to the throne, it is easy to draw a parallel between Nuada and the legend of King Arthur.

Odin (Norse): Also known as Woden, Wodan, and Wotan. Odin is the chief god of the Aesir pantheon. He is a wonderful example of how the gods cannot be reduced to a list of attributes. Odin was god of both war and poetry. God of destruction and creation. God of life and god of death. If one were to assign a single attribute, the best choice would be god of wisdom. For it is his great wisdom that determines when it is time to write poetry and when it is time to make war, when it is time to create and when it is time to destroy, when it is time to live and when it is time to die. In fact, the wearing of the *valknutr*, also known as *valknot* (his symbol), expresses that very thought. It screams, *Odin here I am. Take me if you please.*

He is traditionally called Alfadir, which translates to All Father. Perhaps this is commentary on his role in the rank structure of the Aesir pantheon (father of the gods), but it is also a likely reference to his involvement in creating the human race from the ash and elm trees. The Norse

Creation story is that after the Great Flood, Odin carved the first man and woman from the ash and elm trees. The story is also told that they were carved from a floating log of ash and elm that were discovered by Odin as the floods receded.

This Norse Creation story is likely a way to tell the story of the historic flood that allowed humanity to migrate into Europe as discussed in A Wiccan Bible.

Oengus Mac Oc (Celtic/Irish): Also known as Aengus. Son of the Dagda, his name means "son of the young" or "son of the youthful." His story is one that not only assures that love prevails, it also warns the same thing. For what is sometimes the prelude to this story, see **Aengus the Younger**.

After falling in love with a woman from his dreams, he set about searching for her in the waking world. After a long search, he found her, but she was destined to be transformed into a swan on Samhain. Forsaking his natural form, he changed himself into a swan to join her. They flew off together.

Most lore states that Oengus Mac Oc and Aengus the Younger are the same god form. A few references list them separately. I believe this is yet another example of how the Celts were not the unified people that today's books on the subject present them to have been.

Ogma (Celtic/Irish): The son of the Dogda and Danu who reportedly created the Ogham alphabet. See also **Ogmios**.

Ogmios (Celtic/French): Also known as Ogmios Sun-Face. Where *Ogma* is the specifically Irish Celtic term for this god form, *Ogmios* or *Ogmios Sun-Faced* is the more general Celtic and, in particular, French Celtic term. He is the god of scholars and historians, and also god of the formalities of exchange, the stately and proper god. Because of their similarities, but different names, he and Ogma serve as another example of how the Celts were not a unified people with the same gods. Although they had similar lore, if you want to state that Ogma and Ogmios are the same god form, then you must also toss in Odin and any other inventors of language. Thus yielding the perception that the prominent god forms in Pagan lore represent the same human archetype. Guess what? That, too, is true. The names themselves denoting a cultural view of a portion of the masculine half of the Creator rather than a single dictated view of the Creator for all cultures.

Old Man Coyote (Native American): Old Man Coyote is a matured trickster/coyote god. As the younger incarnation of Coyote, he does indeed yank a few chains. But in so doing, he aspires to teach the lessons learned with age to the youth of the world. He is sometimes called Grandfather Coyote and serves, with the younger Coyote, as an excellent example of maturation without the loss of youthfulness.

Orpheus (Greek): Upon the death of his wife, he sung to death himself, asking that if his love not be returned from Death to him that he be taken by Death himself so they would be united once again .

> O deities of the under-world, to whom all we who live must come, hear my words, for they are true. I come not to spy out the secrets of Tartarus, nor to try my strength against the three-headed dog with snaky hair that guards the entrance. I come to seek my wife, whose opening years the poisonous viper's fang has brought to an untimely end. Love has led me here, Love, a god all-powerful with us who dwell on the earth and, if old traditions say true, not less so here. I implore you by these abodes full of terror; these realms of silence and uncreated things unite again the thread of Eurydice's life. We all are des-tined to you, and sooner or later must pass to your domain. She too, when she shall have filled her term of life, will rightly be yours. But till then grant her to me, I beseech you. If you deny me, I cannot return alone; you shall triumph in the death of us both.

—From *Bulfinch's Mythology: The Age of Fable*, Chapter XXIV

Upon hearing his plea, Death did grant her leave from the under-world under one condition: Orpheus's wife would follow him from the underworld, but should he doubt that she followed for one instant, she would be pulled back into its darkness. Just before he left the caverns, he felt doubt and looked back only to hear her scream a final farewell as she sank into the darkness.

Despite his wife being dead, he forsook all other women. He was so committed to never touching another, that even when women were raised to the peek of excitement by the rites of Bacchus, he continued to refuse their affections. After several attempts, those women became frustrated with him. One took a javelin in frustration and flung it at him, but his song was so great that upon hearing it, the javelin fell harmless. Next, they threw rocks at him, but upon hearing his song, the rocks fell, harmless. Indeed, his song brought joy to all who heard it; even weapons flung in anger could cause no harm. The women screamed so loud that their anger drowned out his sorrow, and then the rocks could, and did, strike him. His song stopped and the women tore him to pieces with their rage.

In his death, he was again united with his beloved wife. He received exactly what his heart desired and we, humanity, receive the message that sometimes we are more deaf to the songs of love than are inanimate objects and that sometimes rage can overpower love.

Pan (Greek): The randy son of Hermes, head of the Satyrs, and good friend of Dionysus. Although today he is commonly thought of as a friendly god form who plays music and dances in the woods, he was not always seen as the best influence on humanity. For this and many of his other antics, he was not much liked by the other gods. He is also the embodiment of unchecked male sexual power. He is said to have chased nymph and shepherd boy alike, making no distinction as to where he aimed his desire. His name is perhaps commentary on this attribute as it means "all inclusive" or "including everything" and has thus given rise to the term *panfidelity* to indicate the openness to sexually expressed love in its many forms.

Pan-gu (Chinese): Also known as P'an-ku. The primordial giant whose role in Creation is akin to the power of the nameless one. He was the primordial existence before the yin (darkness) and yang (light) was separated. Living in their union (a united cosmic egg), he grew in size so much that he shattered that egg, and then pushed the two halves apart. The top half (yang) he drove upwards. The bottom half (yin) he drove downwards, thus creating heaven (yang) and earth (yin).

Central to the understanding of this story from a Wiccan perspective is that the cosmic egg was not born of woman because neither woman nor man existed prior to the existence of the egg. The egg simply existed much the same way the matter for the Big Bang simply existed, without known origin. And that within that egg did grow something that we have yet to explain the driving force behind both union and separation (Pan-gu). In essence, Pan-gu is the fifth element. He is that which causes the other four elements to manifest in form and shape as the result of both separation and union.

This is the greatest mystery of them all. What is the universe prior to its existence if not the universe after its existence? What is that egg prior to the union of yin and yang if that egg is the union of yin and yang? The best statement to understand what is expressed in the story of Pan-gu is that the sum total of the universe equals zero, but that zero does not indicate *nothing* because it too can be quantified and expressed.

0 = |-1| + 1 = 2 therefore 0 = 2; however, 0 = 0 as well.

Penates (Roman): Also known as Di Penates. Called the "inner ones," the Penates early lore is that they were the guardians of goods stored in the household or of the storage room. However, they quickly became the guardians of the entire household. They are praised by offerings from the evening meal given unto the fires of the hearth. Today, simple offerings made outside the back step or away from the garden will do if a fireplace is not at hand.

Sulpa'e (Sumerian): The Sumerian personification of the planet Jupiter, who is often described as a god of war or of military training and action. He is, however, closely connected to nature, fertility, and is patron to undomesticated creatures in all orders.

Takami-Musubi (Japanese): A Shinto Creator from who all things came. He is the driving force to create; however, he did have a wife named Amaterasu (also known as Ama Terasu) with whom he now rules the world. I say now because there was a time when she was her brother's consort and lover. For some odd reason, people just love to get Takami-Musubi confused with Susanowa (Amaterasu's brother and storm god). While running around with Susanowa, she was frightened by his bad boy conduct; but instead of returning to her husband, she hid in shame of having run around with such a thug. Finally, she was tricked from her hiding place and returned to her place in the heavens with her husband, Takami-Musubi.

It is interesting to note that this story is more often told with only the presence of Amaterasu and Susanowa, as if to say the male involved in the story was decisively evil. But it was Takami-Musubi (male) who was betrayed, and yet he remained constant, welcoming Amaterasu back and not demanding shame for her actions.

When we examine this tale as it was written, we see a very important story: You can leave the bar with the bad boy on his Harley Davidson, but your relationship will be short-lived and storm-filled.

Tecciztecatl (Aztec): Also known as Tecuciztecal. Tecciztecatl is a grandfather image of god who reminds us that not all gods were sun gods and not all goddesses were moon goddesses. He is one of the many male personifications of the moon. Depicted as an old man, sometimes with a long beard, he is sometimes considered time itself. With him and many other moon gods who were said to be the grandfathers of time by cultures who had developed a lunar calendar, we see a connection between the moon and time from a strictly utilitarian vantage point. The moon was a method of keeping track of time.

Thoth (Egyptian): Also known as Djeheuty, Tehuti, Tahuti, and Zehuti. Ah, another lunar god to challenge the myth that all gods are associated with the sun and goddesses with the moon. Thoth is not actually an Egyptian name. When he was referenced in Egypt, the most common name was Djeheuty. But they also called him Tehuti, Tahuti, and Zehuti. Or maybe these names have arisen due to the problems associated with translating hieroglyphs into English. Either way, it was the ancient Greeks who decided his name is "Thoth."

He is the Egyptian deity whose advice was always well respected and sought. However, that advice was more scientific and factual in nature than wisdom. Perhaps we could say that it was knowledge-based rather than wisdom-based. Despite mixed references to his lineage, Thoth is firmly seated in the household of Isis and Osiris. He is a firm supporter of Horus (child of Isis and Osiris). In the battle between Horus and Set for the throne, Thoth did not waver from his dedication.

Although he is the mediator of both gods and humanity, he is also a god of truth. This is why he stood behind Horus and against Set, who had killed the father of Horus. This is also why he is depicted in the judgment day that so many Pagans seem insistent on writing out of our modern lore. On that day, Thoth is the one to question the deceased just prior to the weighing of their heart. If this measure and the answers to the questions proved that the deceased was of good nature and report, that soul would be granted a wonderful afterlife. If not, they were consigned to be consumed until nothing remained.

Uranus (Greek): Also known as Ouranos. He is the Greek sky god. He is sometimes considered the son of Gaia (the earth), but he is always considered her husband. Their children include the 12 Titans, as well as many others. Uranus is also said to be the father of Aphrodite. The reference to her being "foam born" is the most often cited, but lore states that the foam from which she was born was created by the semen spewing from his severed testicles when they were cast into the sea. As Gaia is not only his wife, but also the earth, it is easy to see how one can state that Gaia's womb is the ocean, and thus come to the conclusion that Aphrodite's mother is Gaia and her father is Uranus.

It is interesting to note that modern medicine reveals that testosterone is the driving force behind sexual desire in both men and women.

When we consider the birth of Aphrodite (desire itself) having taken place by the foam created from the very organs that are associated with testosterone, we see ancient Pagan lore mixing with modern science so harmoniously that it gives support to the idea that our great lore was divinely inspired.

The story of his castration changes from one tale to another. In one, the central theme is that Gaia had tired of giving birth to so many children as a result of her husband's lust, so she begged her children for help in keeping her from becoming pregnant yet again. Only one would help: Cronus castrated his own father with a sickle. This brought about the separation of Earth and Sky. Cronus became the chief god, but was later overthrown by Zeus.

Vulcan (Roman): Vulcan is the Roman god of fire who perfectly personifies fire. Not only is he the god of destructive fire, but also of the fire of the smith. Thus he is creation and destruction all rolled up into one god form. He is identified with the less destructive Greek Hephaestus.

Wadd (Pre-Islamic): Another God form who shatters the modern concept of lunar deities being female. But his stereotype of shattering lore does not stop there. His symbol is the snake, which Neo-Pagans seem insistent on ascribing to Goddess as well. Ah, but wait, he is also a god of love and friendship, something that seems to be presented more often as Goddess attributes.

In the glory of our Lord and Lady, so mote it be.

Appendix:
Goddess Correspondence List
—Patricia Telesco

The Moon! Artemis! The great goddess of the splendid past of men!
—D.H. Lawrence

Throughout this book I've discussed a great many goddesses, one of whom may appeal to you spiritually. Perhaps you'd like to call upon her for aid in a spell or ritual, or perhaps you'd like to build a relationship with her as a personal Matron. In either case, it is both respectful and wise to get to know more about that deity. Find out about the culture from which she came. Discover her myths. Uncover her *"herstory,"* and as you do, you're bound to have a greater appreciation and understanding of that goddess than you did before. In turn, it will help make your magickal interactions with that being far more positive and effective.

This appendix is provided as a brief starting point in that exploratory journey. Here you'll find the goddesses discussed in the book in alphabetical order. Use this as a quick reference and a brief glimpse into the goddesses whose qualities and attributes appeal to you. From here, you can then research the region from which she hails and gather more personalized information that will help you honor her (or them) daily.

Amaterasu (Japanese): The great sun goddess whose name means "Shining Heaven." She is the supreme Goddess in Shinto tradition and oversees the forces of nature

Amicitia (Roman): She is a goddess of friendship. Honor her with wine, beer, or any other items shared between friends.

Amma (Norse): A Grandmother goddess who gave birth to the race of Freemen. Patroness of traders and skilled craftspeople who may also be venerated with handcrafts.

Amphictyonis (Greek): Goddess of friendship between nations. Her sacred beverage is wine.

Anne (Syrian): Goddess whose name means Graceful One. Great Grandmother Goddess of earth and fertility. She is considered the Mother of Mary, and was Christianized as a saint.

Aphrodite (Greek): Foam-born goddess of sensual love. Equated with the Mediterranean Astarte. Her sacred items include copper, turquoise, rose, and sandalwood. Her animals are the dove and swan. Her tarot card is the Empress.

Arete (Greek): She is the goddess of virtue. She was sometimes offered mead. Her color is white.

Artemis (Greek): She is the goddess of the moon and nature, mistress of magick, and the sister of Apollo. Artemis protects women, children, and travelers. Sacred items include all wild animals, quartz, moonstone, hazel, almond, the bow, and the arrow. In the tarot, she can represent the High Priestess.

Aspelenie (Lithuanian): She is a hearth goddess represented as a serpent (which is sacred to her along with all yellow-gold colored items).

Athena/Athene (Greek): Great warrior goddess who also ruled over the mind, peace, and creativity. She was the patroness to spinners and other artisans. Her sacred items include the plow, flute, shield, spear, ruby, onyx, turquoise, coconut, and geranium. Her sacred animals include the peacock and the owl. In the tarot, she may be represented by the Star.

Baba Yaga (Slavonic): She is old woman autumn. Legend says she lived in the last sheath of harvested grain (the person bound by it would be certain to get pregnant). Also the goddess of birth and death to whom grain is a suitable offering.

Bast (Egyptian): The playful cat-faced goddess to whom dance is a fantastic offering. Thought to be Ra's wife, Bast's sacred symbol is the cat, and most things that cats like (cream, cat nip, etc.) are all pleasing to her.

Befana (Italian folk witch): An old woman that appears outside homes on January 5 to witness the passing of winter's darkness. She came down chimneys bearing gifts much like a female Santa Claus.

Bellona (Roman): She was Crone battle goddess, ruler of Death, wife of Mars. Call on her at Samhain for best results. Her sacred items include crows, the staff, apples, and bloodstone. Her card in the tarot is the Tower.

Benzautin (Japanese): The goddess of luck, joy, talent, and romance, and a protectress of endangered men. As the Queen of the Sea, you can honor her with salt water or fish.

Blue Hag: *See* **Cailleach**.

Brid/Brigit (Celtic): Her name means "fiery arrow." As the goddess of inspiration and fertility, she is often considered to bear three faces. Her festival is February 1, her season is spring, and you can honor her by lighting candles.

Butterfly Maiden (Hopi): A goddess of fertility and dreams whose symbol is the rainbow. New blossoms are a good gift for her.

Cailleach/Cailleach Bera (Celtic): A very ancient Crone goddess that controlled the seasons and the weather. This "Bringer of the Ice Mountains" is the great blue Old Woman of the highlands. Her sacred animals are the boar and bear, and she can be honored with anything blue, snow, or ice. Her festival day is November 21.

Callisto (Greek): A moon goddess depicted sometimes as a female bear. The whole universe revolves around her. In addition to bears, willows are sacred to her. She was later linked with Artemis.

Cerridwen/Kerridwen (Celtic): A goddess of harvest, nature, the muse, wisdom, and the moon. A cauldron is the perfect symbol for her. Other sacred items include corn, fish, and a hawk's feather.

Cybele (Greek): A goddess of caverns, and an earth goddess who later merged with Rhea. Sacred items include lions, scourge, myrrh, and pearls. Celebrate her with sacred dancing.

Demeter (Greek): An earth goddess who is bountiful. Her sacred items include cat's-eye, sunflowers, the color green, wine, cakes, mead, and fabric.

Drvaspa (Persian): An ancient goddess who protects cattle, children, and friendship. The 14th day of the month is dedicated to her, and rightly spoken words are considered a suitable offering (such as poetry).

Edda (Scandinavian): The great grandmother, and the term *eddas* ("tales of great grandmother") is the word used to describe the great stories in Scandinavian mythology. The dwarf-ish Edda was the mother of humankind.

Erzulie (Haitian): Goddess of love, beauty, sweetness, and sensuality whose roots begin in Africa. She can be represented by water gathered at a stream, lake, or waterfall.

Esotre (Saxon): Goddess of fertility after whom Easter is named. Her sacred objects include the egg, and her animal is the hare or rabbit. Known as Ostara in Germany.

Freya/Frigg (Teutonic): The most beloved goddess of this pantheon, she is wife and sister to Odin, who protected marriage. Jewelry is a suitable offering. Other sacred symbols include all silver (lunar) items, pearls, roses, sandalwood, and rich perfumes or incense.

Gaia (Greek): Mother Earth, the first being born from Chaos, often invoked in oath-taking. All things of nature are under her care. Offerings of first fruits are appropriate.

Gauri (Hindu): An aspect of Parvati who represents fertility and abundance. Balsam and rice are both sacred items to her.

Ghar Jenti (Assamese): Goddess of good luck, specifically within the sacred space of home. Lights of any type are a good means of representing her because her name means "light in the house."

Grandmother Moon (Native American): The mother of all and guardian of the people, especially by night. Mugwort and moonstone are sacred to her.

Grandmother Spider (Native American): She is the inventress of the alphabet, and Crone under whose dominion wisdom, dreams, and mysteries reside. Represent her with dream catchers, webs, and labyrinths.

Hanna (Asia Minor/Hittite): Grandmother and Queen of heaven; oldest of all, who rules all deities; goddess of wisdom. Her animal is a bee. In the Bible she is the Anatolian grandmother who gave birth to the Lord of Death and who blessed women with the gift of prophesy.

Hathay (South Indian): A Grandmother/Crone figure who communicates in dreams.

Hathor (Egyptian): The ancient sky goddess sometimes described as the wife or mother of Horus. Hathor presides over love, happiness, and sacred dance and song. She also inspires the best of the yin energies in her followers. Bronze mirrors make an excellent offering, and her sacred items include a cow and the sistrum.

Hel (Scandinavian): She is goddess of the underworld, known also as the "one who hides." Wolves are sacred to her, and her color is black.

Hera (Greek): She is goddess of marriage and embodiment of the good partner, similar to Juno in Roman tradition. Represent her with budding flowers. Her sacred animals include the cuckoo and Her fruit is the pomegranate.

Hestia (Greek): The equivalent of Vesta, Hestia was the first born of heaven and she is the goddess of the hearth who protects family unity. One way of honoring her is to recite the names of your female relatives in succession.

Hlodyn (Germanic): A Mother figure who protected both hearth and home.

Holda (Anglo Saxon): A goddess associated with winter (thus a Crone), Holda was considered gracious and loyal. Water drawn from wells or melted snow may represent her.

Hsi Wang Mu (Chinese): The highest goddess and queen of the west (where the ancestors reside), she is the ultimate female energy. The peach is her sacred fruit.

Inanna (Sumerian): Queen of heaven and a great Mother goddess type. Ishtar was likely assimilated into this persona. Her sacred items include grains and wine. She can be honored with woven items, and represented by divinatory systems.

Ishtar (Assyro-Bablyonian): A Mother goddess under whose care were matters of love and war, marriage and child bearing, and divination efforts. Honor her during the full moon.

Isis (Egyptian): The most complete goddess in all of history, Isis bears 10,000 names. In effect, she is the ultimate female principle in action. Wine, beer, and grains were among the traditional offerings given for her.

Kali (Hindu): Black Mother who both creates and destroys. The inventor of the Sanskrit alphabet and protectress of abused women. Honor her on Wednesdays.

Kamui fuchi (Ainu): A hearth goddess best worshipped at dawn by allowing streams of light from the new day to touch your stove or fireplace.

Kikimora (Russian): A household guardian and goddess who only seemed to appear when danger was imminent. Honor her with spinning yarn.

Kore (Greek): The maiden aspect of Persephone. This goddess embodies renewed energy and a youthful earth that is fresh, vital, and blossoming. Honor her in early spring with bundles of buds.

Kwan Yin (Chinese): She is the beloved goddess of mercy, healing, fertility, magick, and protectress of children. Lotus and lions are sacred to her.

Lakshmi (Hindu): The goddess of luck, providence, and true beauty. Jewels, coins, rare items, and cows are sacred to her.

Lilith (Hebrew): Demonized first wife of Adam who refused to submit, but wished for equality in her relationships. Her animal attributes include the wolf, owl, and jackal.

Mati Syra Zemlya (Slavonic): Moist Mother Earth, a goddess who empowered and protected her people. Honor and represent her with rich soil.

Minerva (Roman): She was the wife of Jupiter. Minerva rules over industry, trade, and educational pursuits. Best honored during the Spring Equinox.

Mir: An angel presiding over the month of September and the 16th day of the month. Mir watches over friendship and love. Note that depending on the source, Mir is sometimes depicted as male.

Morrigan (Celtic): Her name means "Great Queen." She has a three-fold nature. A Crone, she is the patroness of witches. She was one of the triple forms of Badb. Her symbol is the the raven or crow.

Mut (Egyptian): Great Mother who is very protective of her young. Symbolized by a vulture.

Nanosuelta (Gaulish): Goddess of plenty to whom the raven was sacred. Her symbol is a cornucopia.

Ninhursag (Sumerian): Earth goddess who invented agriculture. Her symbol is the cow. Both water and milk make suitable libations.

Nokomis (Algonquin): A Grandmother goddess who nourishes all things. She is creator of food and is often symbolized by corn.

Norns (Teutonic): The goddesses of fate for both gods and men. Their names are Urd (the past), Verdandi (present), and Skuld (future). Typically honored on New Year's.

Oshun (Nigerian): Water goddess and wife of Shango, the sign of Capricorn is a suitable representation for her.

Papa (Polynesian): Mother Earth and creatrix of all things. All forms of damp heat are sacred to her, and rainwater poured to the earth's soils makes an excellent offering.

Parvati (Hindu): Wife of Shiva and good companion, she empowers all things. Her domain is one of love and wise counsel. Lotus is a good incense to use in working with her.

Pecunia (Italian): Goddess who presides over all forms of commerce and money. She can be represented with a silver or gold coin upon the altar, and honored by placing the first money you make in a special spot to celebrate her gift of prosperity.

Pele (Hawaiian): Wizened old woman of the volcano who created land by her eruptions. Offerings of hair, flowers, sugarcane, and berries are most welcomed by her.

Persephone (Greek): An underworld and corn goddess to whom the narcissus and pomegranate are sacred.

Philia (Greek): Goddess of friendship who gave her love and trust to Aphrodite.

Radha (Indian): Incarnation of the beloved Lakshmi and consort to Vishnu, she presides over sexual love with spiritual implications. Honor her on the altar with jewelry and flowers. Her rituals should be performed skyclad.

Renpet (Egyptian): Maiden Goddess of cycles and the year. She is also called the Mistress of Eternity. Celebrate her in spring with young plants on your altar.

Sarasvati (Hindu): Goddess of communication, sagacity, intelligence, and creativity. Flowers, garlands, palm leaves, drums, and lotus are all sacred to her.

Sedna (Inuit): The Mother and Crone aspect of the triple goddess. Common symbols for Sedna include water, an eye, and fish. Sedna embodies the attributes of thankfulness, providence, nature, and abundance.

Sekhmet (Egyptian): Protectress of women, marriages, and children. She is a fierce warrior goddess. Lions are her sacred animals, her color is gold, and her festival day is January 7.

Shakti (Tantric): The active feminine principle of the universe. Represent her energy with light.

Siduri (Sumerian): Maiden aspect with prophetic powers. Wine and dance are both suitable gifts for this being.

Sif (Scandinavia): Grain goddess with golden hair and mate to Thor. She presides over hospitality and friendship. Offer her snippets of your hair.

Spider Woman (Native American): Goddess of wisdom, dreams, connections, and communication. Use a web to represent her in the sacred space.

Tiamat (Assyro-Babylonian): Mother Goddess of the sea. Symbolized by a dragon or serpent. Honor her with salt water.

Uma (Hindu): The maiden aspect of Parvati.

Ushas (Hindu): Goddess of dawn to whom horses and cows are sacred. This goddess bears blessings with her beams of light.

Vesta (Roman): Goddess of fire, both for the home and temple. She is best represented by the fire of a hearth or candlelight.

Voluspa (Scandinavian): Goddess of history and prophecy, she is best honored with poetry and bardic efforts.

Wah kah nee (Chinook): Maiden goddess who can communicate with spirits and protect people from harsh weather. Represent her with an ice cube.

Yuki Onne (Japanese): Snow maiden who frowns on those who break their oaths.

Zorya (Slavonic): Goddess who protects warriors. A libation of fresh water (from a live source) is suitable for her.

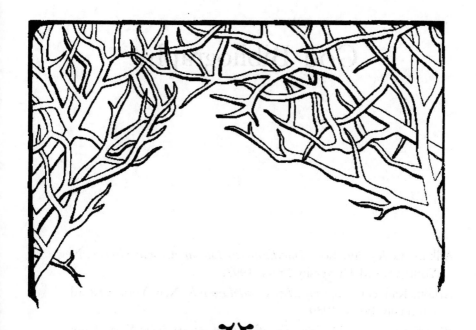

Bibliography

God Bibliography

Adkins, Lesley and Roy. *Handbook to Life in Ancient Greece.* New York: Oxford University Press, 1997.

Arnott, Kathleen. *African Myths and Legends.* New York: Oxford University Press, 1989.

Blanchard-Lemee, M. *Mosaics of Roman Africa.* New York: George Braziller, 1996.

Bocking, Brian. *A Popular Dictionary of Shinto.* United Kingdom: Curzon Press, 1996.

Bulfinch, Thomas. *Bulfinch's Greek and Roman Mythology: The Age of Fable.* New York: Dover, 2000.

Bullock, M. *Daily Life in Ancient Egypt.* New York: McGraw Hill, 1964.

Cook, Stanburrough. "Ibn Fadlan's Account of Scandinavian Merchants on the Volga in 922." *Journal of English and Germanic Philosophy* 22 (1923): 54–63.

Cotterell, Arthur. *Dictionary of World Mythology.* New York: Oxford University Press, 1979.

Cotterell, Arthur and Rachel Storm. London: Harper Collins, 1992.

Dallapiccola, Anna. *Dictionary of Hindu Lore and Legend.* London: Thames & Hudson, 2002.

Danielou, Alain. *The Myths and Gods of India.* Rochester, Vt.: Inner Traditions, 1991.

Davidson, Hilda. *Scandinavian Mythology.* New York: Peter Bedrick Books, 1986.

———. *The Road to Hel.* Westport, Conn.: Greenwood Publishing Group, 1968.

———. *Myths and Symbols in Pagan Europe: Early Scandinavian and Celtic Religions.* New York: Syracuse University Press, 1989.

———. *The Viking Road to Byzantium.* Lanham, Md.: Rowman & Littlefield, 1976.

Dimmitt, Cornelia (editor). *Classic Hindu Mythology.* Philadelphia: Temple University Press, 1978.

Ellis, Peter. *A Brief History of the Druids.* New York: Carroll & Graf, 2002.

Fincher-Schreiber. *Encyclopedia of Eastern Philosophy and Religion.* Boston: Shambhala Publications, 1984.

Knappert, Jan. *Pacific Mythology.* London: Harper Collins, 1992.

Mathews, Caitlin and John. *Encyclopedia of Celtic Wisdom.* Rockport: Element, 1994.

Poinsias, Mac Cana. *Celtic Mythology.* New York: Peter Bedrick Books, 1983.

Spence, Lewis. *Myths of the North American Indians.* New York: Dover, 1992.

Taube, Karl. *Aztec and Maya Myths.* Austin: University of Texas Press, 1994.

———. *The Gods and Symbols of Ancient Mexico and the Maya.* London: Thames & Hudson, 1993.

Goddess Bibliography

Aldington, Richard (translator). *New Larousse Encyclopedia of Mythology.* Middlesex, England: Hamlyn Publishing, 1973.

Ann, Martha and Dorothy Myers Imel. *Goddesses in World Mythology.* New York: Oxford University Press, 1995.

Bonheim, Jalaja (editor). *Goddess.* New York: Stewart, Tabori and Chang, 1997.

Bruce-Mitford, Miranda. *Illustrated Book of Signs & Symbols.* New York: DK Publishing, 1996.

Budge, E.A. Wallis. *Amulets & Superstitions.* Oxford, England: Oxford University Press, 1930.

Cavendish, Richard. *A History of Magic.* New York: Taplinger Publishing, 1979.

Cooper, J.C. *Symbolic & Mythological Animals.* London, England: Aqarian Press, 1992.

Davison, Michael Worth (editor). *Everyday Life Through the Ages.* Pleasantville, N.Y.: Reader's Digest Association Ltd., 1992.

Doty, William G. (editor). *World Mythology.* Hammersmith, London: Barnes & Nobel Books, 2002.

Farrar, Janet and Stewart. *The Witches' Goddess.* Custer, Wash.: Phoenix Publishing, 1987.

Gordon, Stuart. *Encyclopedia of Myths and Legends.* London, England: Headline Book Publishing, 1993.

Hall, Manly P. *Secret Teachings of All Ages.* Los Angeles, Calif.: Philosophical Reserach Soceity, 1977.

Ions, Veronica. *The History of Mythology.* China: Octopus Publishing Group, 1997.

Jordan, Michael. *Encyclopedia of Gods.* New York: Facts on File, Inc. 1993.

Kunz, George Frederick. *Curious Lore of Precious Stones.* New York: Dover Publications, 1971.

Leach, Maria (editor). *Standard Dictionary of Folklore, Mythology, and Legend.* New York: Harper & Row, 1984.

Leach, Marjorie. *Guide to the Gods.* Santa Barbara, Calif.: ABC-Clio, 1992.

Lurker, Manfred. *Dictionary of Gods & Goddesses, Devils & Demons.* New York: Routledge & Kegan Paul Ltd., 1995.

Monaghan, Patricia: *The Book of Goddesses & Heroines.* St. Paul, Minn.: Llewellyn Publications, 1993.

Motz, Lotte. *Faces of the Goddess.* New York: Oxford University Press, 1997.

Sargent, Denny: *Global Ritualism.* St. Paul, Minn.: Llewellyn Publications, 1994.

Spence, Lewis. *The Encyclopedia of the Occult.* London, England: Bracken Books, 1988.

Walker, Barbara. *The Woman's Dictionary of Symbols & Sacred Objects.* San Francisco Calif.: Harper & Row, 1988.

About the Authors

A.J. Drew

A.J. Drew is the author of *Wicca for Men, Wicca Spellcraft for Men,* and *Wicca for Couples.* He is the owner of one of the largest Pagan shops in the Midwest (Salem West), and the Webmaster of an interactive Pagan search engine/Internet database *(www.neopagan.com).* He is best known as the host of the Real Witches Ball, an annual event that draws thousands to Columbus, Ohio.

A.J.'s entire life centers on the modern Pagan movement. He works in a Neo-Pagan environment and lives in a Neo-Pagan household. Due to his strong ties to this ever-growing movement, he is commonly asked to assist local officials in their understanding of this community and the people within it. This assistance has taken the form of providing workshops and other educational forums for Law Enforcement and Children Services agents. He has spoken often on local affiliates of ABC, CBS, and NBC television and has conducted lectures at the local university.

A.J. considers himself Pagan in the classic sense of the word, which is "common folk." He follows the Creation 92s Covenant tradition of Wicca. This is a tradition that forms families and households rather than secret orders and covens. It is A.J.'s ambition to see the Pagan community obtain its rightful position as "yet another spiritual option available to all who seek."

Patricia Telesco

Trish Telesco is the mother of three, wife, chief human to five pets, and a full-time professional author with numerous books on the market. These include the best-selling *Goddess in my Pocket, How to be a Wicked Witch, Kitchen Witch's Cookbook, Little Book of Love Magic, Your Book of Shadows, Spinning Spells: Weaving Wonders,* and other diverse titles, each of which represents a different area of spiritual interest for her and her readers.

Trish considers herself a down-to-earth Kitchen Witch whose love of folklore and worldwide customs flavor every spell and ritual. While her actual Wiccan education was originally self-trained and self-initiated, she later received initiation into the Strega tradition of Italy, which gives form and fullness to the folk magic Trish practices. Her strongest beliefs lie in following personal vision, being tolerant of other traditions, making life an act of worship, and being creative so that magick grows with you.

Trish travels once a month to give lectures and workshops around the country. She (or her writings) has appeared on several television segments including *Sightings* on multicultural divination systems, *National Geographic Todday—Solstice Celebrations,* and one for the *Debra Duncan Show* on modern Wicca. Besides this, Trish maintains a strong, visible presence in metaphysical journals including *Circle Network News,* and on the Internet through popular sites such as *www.witchvox.com* (festival focus), her interactive home page located at *www.loresinger.com,* and the Yahoo! Club *www.groupsyahoo.com/groupsfolkmagicwithtrishtelesco,* and various appearances on Internet chat and bbs boards.

Her hobbies include gardening, herbalism, brewing, singing, handcrafts, antique restoration, and landscaping. Her current project is helping support various Neo-Pagan causes including land fund for religious retreats.

A.J. and Patricia have known each other for several years now, having met through the Witches Ball. Their mutual respect, love of magickal traditions, and strong beliefs in building a community that "plays nicely together" in this sandbox called Earth has brought them together to write this book.